"Coward," he taunted softly.

"I'm not. I have nothing to fear from you."

"Who's talking about me? You're afraid of yourself," O'Rourke commented dryly, stalking her as she retreated. "Surely you're interested in the outcome of this experiment?"

"No, I'm not."

"And you pride yourself on being a modern woman," he chided. "Where's your sense of adventure? A mere man is calling your bluff. Doesn't that inspire you? Where's all your big talk now, Katie?" He backed her right into the wall, his hands moving swiftly to capture her shoulders. "Put your convictions where your...mouth is."

His eyes lingered on her slightly parted lips.

Kate felt the familiar liquid heat rising from the pit of her stomach to spread through every limb, undermining her resolve, weakening her, until she was mastered, albeit willingly, conquered and claimed....

Dear Reader,

Welcome to the Silhouette **Special Edition** experience! With your search for consistently satisfying reading in mind, every month the authors and editors of Silhouette **Special Edition** aim to offer you a stimulating blend of deep emotions and high romance.

The name Silhouette **Special Edition** and the distinctive arch on the cover represent a commitment—a commitment to bring you six sensitive, substantial novels each month. In the pages of a Silhouette **Special Edition**, compelling true-to-life characters face riveting emotional issues—and come out winners. All the authors in the series strive for depth, vividness and warmth in writing these stories of living and loving in today's world.

The result, we hope, is romance you can believe in. Deeply emotional, richly romantic, infinitely rewarding—that's the Silhouette **Special Edition** experience. Come share it with us—six times a month!

From all the authors and editors of Silhouette **Special Edition**,

Best wishes,

Leslie Kazanjian,
Senior Editor

JESSICA ST. JAMES
A Country Christmas

Silhouette Special Edition

Published by Silhouette Books New York

America's Publisher of Contemporary Romance

This book is dedicated to our families,
who have been so generous in allowing us to indulge
our obsession with the British Isles.

SILHOUETTE BOOKS
300 East 42nd St., New York, N.Y. 10017

Copyright © 1990 by Lynda Varner and Charlotte Hoy

ISBN: 0-373-09631-3

First Silhouette Books printing November 1990

Printed in the U.S.A.

Books by Jessica St. James

Silhouette Special Edition

The Perfect Lover #561
Showdown at Sin Creek #603
A Country Christmas #631

JESSICA ST. JAMES

is the pen name for a Kansas-based writing team. The two women write contemporary and historical romances and often set their novels in England and Scotland, where they have enjoyed doing hands-on research. In addition to writing and travel, the authors share a love of books and cats.

ENGLAND

Cross
Coombe

Bath

London

Cross Coombe village

Chapter One

As soon as the taxi entered the sweeping tree-lined driveway to the elegant old hotel, Kate knew her decision to come had been a mistake.

Oh, it was beautiful, every bit as lovely as the brochures had promised—a venerable fourteenth-century manor house in the English countryside, surrounded by acres of garden and parkland, green even in December. But she realized she'd envisioned seeing it for the first time with O'Rourke at her side. Somehow, arriving by herself only emphasized the *aloneness* of her life these days.

The taxi glided to a halt before an ivy-hung portico, and while Kate paid the driver, struggling with the unfamiliar British pounds, a uniformed doorman came down the front steps to greet her.

"Welcome to Cross Coombe Manor, madam. May I assist you with your luggage?"

A second doorman beamed at her and, with a courtly bow, opened the heavy wooden doors hung with cedar wreaths and red velvet streamers. As she stepped into an oak-paneled entrance hall, a rush of warm air filled with a mixture of fragrances met her. Open log fires gave off a faintly smoky smell; burning candles contributed a waxy scent; and from somewhere came the spiciness of cloves and cinnamon. And over and above these was the tanginess of freshly cut cedar. Cross Coombe Manor contained all the essences of Christmas.

"Mrs. Callahan?" The clipped British accent of the young woman standing behind the hotel desk broke her reverie. "We've been expecting you. You're the last of the guests to arrive."

"Oh?"

"Yes, indeed. Some of the others are already getting acquainted in the residents' lounge." With a smile, she indicated a room to the left of a wide staircase. "You may wish to stop in after you've seen your room. Now, if you'll just sign the register..."

As Kate followed a bellboy up the curving stairway, she got a quick glimpse of the lounge. It was a large high-ceilinged room with a fireplace and tall leaded-glass windows. An undecorated pine tree stood in front of the windows, waiting, she knew, for the decorating party that would take place later in the evening. At the sight of several guests sitting in the room, Kate's depression deepened.

Couples, she thought gloomily. *Of course! I should have known. Everyone here will be with a husband or wife... or lover.*

Kate's attention focused upon a young couple sitting on a couch in one corner, oblivious to the rest of the world. As she watched, the boy laughed and leaned forward to kiss the pretty blond girl. With a faint gasp of dismay, Kate wrenched her eyes away, confining her gaze to the faded Persian carpet passing beneath her feet.

Damn you, O'Rourke Callahan, she chanted silently with each step. *Damn you, damn you, damn you!*

"You've been given the Highwayman's Chamber, Mrs. Callahan." The bellboy had stopped to unlock the heavy oaken door with a brass key, which he then presented to her.

"It's one of our finest," he added proudly. "I'm quite sure you'll be comfortable here. Even though 'tis said to be haunted by the ghosts of the highwayman and his lady-love."

The boy winked broadly, then moved toward a monstrous armoire where he put her suitcases. He made a ceremony of adjusting the shutters at the long windows and lighting the logs in the fireplace.

Kate walked into the room and stood looking about her. She realized that should it prove to be haunted, it would probably only be by the spirit of O'Rourke Callahan. He should have been there with her. She observed the bottle of champagne on a bedside table and raised an inquisitive eyebrow.

"To ward off the chill of a winter afternoon," the bellboy explained with a cheeky grin. "Now, is there anything else I can get you?"

"No, thanks. I'll be fine." Kate fumbled in her purse for a tip so generous it made the boy's smile complete the stretch from ear to ear.

When he had gone, she dropped her purse into a chair and shrugged out of her caramel-colored wool coat. Pulling off the fashion boots she wore, she began a somber exploration of the room.

It was magnificent, better even than she had imagined. The main walls were covered with antique wood paneling, the high ceiling crisscrossed with heavy beams. Older, undoubtedly original walls of rough-cut stone were amazingly medieval in appearance.

As she walked about, her stockinged feet sank deep into thick dark crimson carpet. The color was repeated in the velvet draperies at the leaded windows and in the roses scattered across the upholstery of the two overstuffed chairs placed before the open fire. Cedar boughs and pots of brilliant poinsettias filled the mantel and the wide windowsills, and a basket of pinecones and greenery sat near the hearth.

The bed was straight out of romantic fantasy. It was a Jacobean tester bed with crimson hangings and a quilted patchwork coverlet of crimson, ivory and forest-green velvet. How O'Rourke would have loved that bed!

Chagrined at the direction her thoughts were taking, Kate hurried across the room to admire a tufted fainting couch placed along a wall that eventually curved into a turret. The small round tower room contained a writing desk, narrow bookcases and two arched windows with views of the picturesque village that adjoined the hotel grounds.

A private bathroom boasted stone walls, exposed timbers, thick carpeting and stained glass. In addition to a bathtub that was at least nine feet long, there was a modern shower stall and a vanity complete with makeup lights and hair dryer. She emerged from the bathroom thinking everything about the bedchamber was perfect....

Then a sudden glimpse of her own reflection in the cheval mirror outside the bathroom door gave her pause. If it was so perfect, why, she wondered, did she look so unhappy?

She stepped closer to the mirror and took a second, harder look. She appeared tired, but surely that was to be expected after an exhausting trans-Atlantic flight and the lengthy taxi ride from Bristol. Still, there was something else—a sort of shadowed wariness in her deep-set navy-blue eyes, a certain vulnerability to her wide mouth. Her face with the prominent bone structure that had long been the envy of her friends, seemed even more fine-drawn than usual. Thick chestnut hair, too contrary for its own good, had started the day pinned neatly atop her head, but now it straggled willfully over her temples and down the nape of her neck. Even at that, instead of merely looking messy, it only enhanced the waiflike image in the mirror.

Kate swallowed deeply. She hadn't been aware she looked like that. Here all this time, she had thought she was projecting her best imitation of a strong modern woman by being brisk, aloof and efficient. In total control. She had believed herself successful in hiding the pain with which she had been learning to live.

No, she told herself firmly, turning away from the mirror, I didn't look like this back in Kansas City. It's jet lag and lack of sleep, that's all.

She crossed the room to lift the bottle of chilled champagne from its silver urn. A drink was what she needed, she decided. Something to perk her up and put a little color into her cheeks.

Since O'Rourke's departure, she had been forced to learn a certain independence, and though she was still somewhat clumsy uncorking the occasional bottle of wine, this time the resulting *pop* was vaguely satisfactory, and the champagne that frothed into her glass was delicious. She tipped the bottle and poured some into a second glass. Setting the bottle aside, she raised a wineglass in each hand.

"Merry Christmas, Kate," she declared, taking a sip from first one glass, then the other. "Here's to you and the best damned new year of your life!"

Setting the glasses aside, she went to the armoire, where she searched through her suitcases until she found what she was hunting for. Returning to the high bed, she sat Indian-style and opened a folded brochure. She studied the glossy color photographs of Cross Coombe Manor Hotel.

"Spend Christmas in the country," she read softly. "Enjoy a traditional British holiday in delightful surroundings...." With a sigh, she reached for the champagne again. How long had she and O'Rourke planned this trip to England? It was to have been a special Christmas for them.

They had met last New Year's Eve for the first time... well, at least for the first time in their present lives. Their coming together had been so swift and incendiary that Kate had been fancifully inclined to believe they had known and loved each other in previous lifetimes. A belief proven embarrassingly groundless by the equal suddenness of their parting and subsequent divorce. They had been married six months when, at a candlelit dinner to celebrate their half-year anniversary, O'Rourke had produced two plane tickets and the very brochure she now held.

"I want our first Christmas together to be something special," he'd said in that deep, sexy voice with its slight Irish lilt. "I've been booked in this hotel on business trips, and it's fabulous. If you like it, we'll stay on to celebrate our anniversary."

Christmas all alone with O'Rourke in a romantic country manor halfway around the world—what a marvelous dream it had been. And then, as quickly as it began, their marriage was over. The problem that had separated them had surfaced with complete unexpectedness—and, as far as Kate was concerned, had proven totally without solution.

Restlessly she tossed the brochure aside. Why had she thought she could make this trip alone? What idiocy had convinced her a change of scene was what she needed? That it would do her good to get away from friends and family, and from the memories and regrets that plagued her?

Why hadn't she foreseen how it would be? As a single, she would be the odd woman out in every gathering. She'd be reduced to huddling in corners with ancient dowagers—weren't there always ancient dowagers in these English country hotels? She pictured herself seated at a table for one in a vast, echoing dining room. She'd better hope there was a bookshop in the village, because something told her she was going to be doing a great deal of reading for the next week!

She drained the champagne in her glass and briefly considered pouring another, but fortunately her common sense kicked in and she sprang off the bed, a determined look in her eyes.

She would not hole up in this room getting drunk and feeling sorry for herself. She had come a long way for this vacation, and she was going to enjoy it, no matter what. To hell with thoughts of O'Rourke Callahan and his lying Irish eyes.

What she needed was a vigorous walk in the fresh cold air. It would clear the cobwebs in her head and combat the fatigue brought on by jet travel. Then, when she returned to the hotel, she'd have a hot bath and choose something sensational from the new wardrobe she'd brought with her. Tonight was the Welcoming Champagne Party for which the brochure denoted "Black Tie," and Kate thought she just might attempt to knock some of the gentlemen guests onto their very proper British ears.

O'Rourke had once told her the village of Cross Coombe was the prettiest he had ever seen, and though that was high praise, it still had not prepared Kate for the reality. She'd picked up a local map at the hotel desk, glancing over it as she walked down a lane that wound from the manor lawn into a back street of a village that had been in existence since the wool-weaving days of the Middle Ages. Her first look at the heart of the village assured her very little had changed since that time.

To her right was the Church of Saint Matthew with its sturdy Gothic tower and moss-covered graveyard; to her left was the ancient market cross that gave the village its name. Ahead, gently curving away over the river was the main street lined with rows of neat cottages, all built of mellow butter-colored Cotswold stone, topped with slate roofs and hung with the tracery of winter-dead vines.

As she strolled along, Kate had to search for signs of the twentieth century. There were no cars in the streets, for one thing...and for another, no television antennae. Even the electric lines and garbage cans had been artfully hidden, she noticed. Cross Coombe looked like the set for a Walt Disney movie! A footnote on her map informed her that the townspeople took pride in maintaining a storybook village and enforced strict rules for those who lived there. Tourism was big business in Cross Coombe, but even that fact could not destroy the magic it held for Kate. She was fascinated—and thoroughly enchanted.

Many of the cottages bordering the narrow cobblestone street were private residences, offering tantalizing glimpses into the lives of the people who dwelt there. Every cottage had a wide-silled front window; some were filled with plants or Christmas greenery, some with books or porcelain figurines; Kate's favorite contained a huge tortoiseshell cat curled up on a woolly shawl, languidly watching the world pass by. Every residence had a gaily decorated Christmas tree, some had swags of cedar or holly above their doorways. Discreet colored lights in the windows of the few shops twinkled brightly in the gathering gloom of the winter afternoon.

At the end of the street, near a row of charming weavers' cottages, a triple-arched stone bridge crossed the shallow, icy clear Rush River. Kate stood on the bridge, hands buried deep in her coat pockets, and looked at the village from the opposite end. It would be impossible to find an unflattering angle, she decided, making a mental note to bring her camera on the next walk.

Her breath was smoky in the chill air as she watched the other people who were out and about. A postman on a rickety bicycle rang his bell in greeting as he wheeled by her. Two ladies with heavily laden baskets left a shop, laughing merrily, and a gentleman walking his dog tipped his hat as he passed them. In one of the weavers' cottages, she saw a woman arranging a nativity scene in her front window. When she looked up and saw Kate, she waved a friendly hello.

Filled with an unwilling envy, Kate returned the wave and started back in the direction of the market cross. She wished she could be as busy and cheerfully purposeful as the inhabitants of this quiet little place.

Halfway along the street, she paused to look into the window of the Black Sheep Gift Shop. Admiring the woolen scarves, hand-carved chess sets and colorful jewelry displayed, she reflected that this was the first year she hadn't had any last-minute Christmas shopping to do. She had purchased all her gifts early and wrapped and deposited them at her mother's house.

She felt a twinge of guilt as she thought of her mother. They had not parted on the best of terms....

Kate remembered the day her mother had told her she was thinking of remarrying. Remarrying? Kate hadn't even known she'd been dating anyone. Grimly she supposed she had been too wrapped up in her own problems to be aware of what was going on in her mother's life. But to find out that she wanted to marry again, after all these years was somehow unbearable. How could she ever hope to replace the dearest man in the world?

Knowing it had been selfish and rude, Kate had avoided meeting Charlie, her mother's boyfriend. Childishly she clung to the belief that if she never saw him, the threat he posed could not be real. Lord, the discussions—no, make that arguments—she'd had with her mother and older sister Beth about it. She knew she was being horrid and unfair, but how could they just forget Dad that way? As if he'd never existed, never been the center of their lives.

Kate's father had been a detective with the Kansas City police force. Stern, incorruptible and highly dedicated while on the job, he had somehow managed to be calm and indulgent at home. He'd been blessed with a gentle sense of humor that could heal any hurt, or right any wrong. Kate had adored him. They all had. Life in their small suburban home had revolved around him.

Then, when Kate was fifteen, he was shot to death by a thief robbing a convenience store. By sheer accident, he had walked in on a robbery in progress, and the young hoodlum had panicked, firing carelessly as he ran from the store. Later, when he'd been apprehended, it was determined the robber had netted exactly twenty-two dollars in the holdup.

Kate would never forget that day as long as she lived, nor could she ever again summon pity or forgiveness for the criminal element of the city. Her father had loved to tease her about her tendency to be a "bleeding-heart liberal," an idealist who saw all miscreants as underprivileged and misguided. But now that her family had been so cruelly deprived of someone precious and irreplaceable, her sympathy for wrongdoers had ended. Fired with an unrelenting determination, she had gone on to law school, graduating with enough honors to win a position with a prestigious legal firm, where she had swiftly earned a reputation as the most hard-nosed female attorney in the state. She had no patience with lawbreakers or with the excuses society tried to make for them. A thief was a thief and should be behind bars. There was no longer any leniency in her soul.

She realized such an implacable attitude had spelled doom for her marriage right from the start. After her father, there had never been another man of any importance in her life until she met O'Rourke Callahan. Now she knew that she had made herself see something in O'Rourke that simply wasn't there and, in so doing, had overlooked character flaws she should have noticed from the first. When the truth about O'Rourke had suddenly surfaced, the failure of their marriage and the divorce that followed were inevitable.

Though the circumstances were completely different, O'Rourke was just as lost to her as her father. Leaving O'Rourke had broken her heart and seemed to bring back all the pain associated with her father's death. So when her mother had made her announcement, new grief and resentment had stirred to life.

Beth, busy with her husband and children, had not reacted the same way Kate had. Her approval of the situation became apparent when she insisted Charlie be included in their holiday celebrations so the family could get to know him. Desperate for a way to keep from meeting the man who would usurp her father's place, Kate had felt an overwhelming sense of relief the day she discovered the plane tickets in the back of a dresser drawer. She had forgotten all about them, but they were the solution to her problem.

At first she had considered trying to find someone to use O'Rourke's ticket, but all her friends preferred to be at home with their families for Christmas. Finally she decided it would be best to be alone anyway—she had some serious thinking to do. She'd shoved the extra ticket back into the drawer, then found an opportunity to announce her intentions. Guiltily she realized she must have become a terrible shrew, for not one of her family tried to talk her out of going. In fact, they seemed so relieved she knew they had foreseen her ruining the holidays for all of them.

In a brief, bitter moment, she wondered what they were doing now. Back home it would be midmorning, and with only three days left before Christmas, her mother would probably be busy in the kitchen. She'd be baking her famous date ball cookies as usual. The only difference was, this year she'd be baking them for *Charlie*.

Kate deliberately jutted her chin out and squared her shoulders. Enough negative thoughts! She was in England now—what went on in Kansas City mustn't concern her.

With a burst of energy, she started off down the street, but had only taken a few steps when she was stricken with sudden dizziness. Her knees nearly buckled as everything grew dark, and, knowing she was about to faint, she clutched at the stone wall beside her.

A firm hand gripped her elbow, and a concerned masculine voice spoke. "I say, are you all right?"

Kate looked into a pair of worried brown eyes, groping for the support the man offered. His other arm went about her waist as he assumed the burden of her weight.

"I think I am trying very hard to faint," she said with a slightly alcoholic giggle.

He looked a little startled. Then a suspicious smile curved his firm mouth.

"Oh! You think I'm drunk, don't you? But I only had one glass of champagne—really." Kate clapped her free hand over her mouth.

He nodded understandingly. "Am I safe in assuming that one glass followed a long air flight?"

"Yes . . . how'd you know?"

"The very American accent. No doubt jet lag gave that one glass the effect of three. And no doubt you failed to eat a proper lunch."

"I hadn't thought of it, but . . . you're right." She straightened, tentatively removing her hand from the sleeve of his expensively tailored coat. "Thank heavens I'm not sick. Tired and hungry I can handle."

"And I would be delighted to assist. Where are you going?"

"Back to the Manor Hotel. I've got a room there." She smiled. "Complimentary champagne and all."

"Then you must allow me to accompany you. I'm booked for the holiday week also. I've just been out to post some letters. My name is Jared Harwood, by the way."

"Hi, I'm Kate . . . Kathryn Callahan."

They fell into step, though Kate's knees were wobbly enough that Jared insisted on taking her arm for safety's sake. By the time they arrived back at the hotel, she was glad he had. Her first priority was going to have to be a nap before dinner.

Jared suggested he accompany her right to the door of her room, and when, on reaching the first landing, she again felt weak and dizzy, he gallantly swept her into his arms for the next flight of stairs.

Her face close to his, Kate realized he was a very striking man. Tall and broad shouldered, he had dark blond hair and brown eyes with a multitude of laugh lines at the corners.

"I'm feeling much better," she stated, searching in her purse for the door key. "You can put me down now."

"Nonsense. I'm enjoying the unexpected chance to play Sir Galahad. A chap can't do that every day."

"No, I suppose not."

The door opened easily, swinging inward, and Jared crossed the threshold with Kate held against his chest, her arm around his neck. The door shut behind them with a loud click.

"What the hell is going on here?"

The angry voice came from the shadowy depths of the tester bed. The dark-haired man who had been lounging there leaped to his feet and advanced menacingly.

"Get your hands off my wife!"

Kate's mouth dropped open in shock as she stared into the furious eyes of her ex-husband, O'Rourke Callahan.

"What are *you* doing in *my* room?" she demanded.

"*Our* room," he corrected. Then the grim lines of his face relaxed, and he favored her with a slow, devilish smile. "Merry Christmas, Katie," he said softly.

Chapter Two

Merry Christmas. Kate must have heard the phrase hundreds of times in her life, but never before had it filled her with so many conflicting emotions. She felt resentment and anger, even embarrassment that their meeting must occur in front of a stranger. But there was also the tiniest spark of elation at seeing O'Rourke again. Elation...and fear. Of course, at this moment, she wasn't yet able to determine if that fear was of O'Rourke or of her own reaction to his unexpected presence.

The devilish smile was becoming a bit strained. "I don't like to repeat myself," O'Rourke drawled, "but would you mind turning loose of my wife?"

Jared Harwood, still surprised by the latest turn of events, dropped the arm beneath Kate's knees and let her feet fall to the floor. Because his other arm was still around her waist, she remained draped against the length of his body, her arm curled about his neck. This fact was definitely neither overlooked nor appreciated by the man facing them. A low growl issued from his throat, causing Kate to hurriedly extricate herself from Jared's unintentional embrace.

"What are you doing here?" she demanded.

"I was waiting for you," he stated evenly. "I should have known you wouldn't be alone." He nodded his head toward the two wineglasses on the bedside table. "Started celebrating a little ahead of the season, didn't you?"

"We didn't . . ."

He stepped closer to Harwood. "Tell me, what did you have in mind? Thinking of giving Kate her Christmas present early?"

"O'Rourke Callahan!" she exclaimed. "How dare you? Jared doesn't have to stand here and listen to you make crazy accusations."

"No, he doesn't," O'Rourke agreed easily. "He can leave at any time."

Kate's breath escaped her lungs with a wrathful wheeze. "Why are you being so horrible?"

"Because you're my wife, and I'm not exactly fond of you playing bride and groom with another man."

"Now see here," Jared protested. "I think you have made a mistake. I was only assisting your . . . wife to her room because she felt faint."

O'Rourke's grin was nasty. "Come now, Kate," he chided. "You could have done better than that in the old days."

"Better than what?"

"Fainting—that's a pretty lame excuse."

"For your information, I'm under no obligation whatsoever to give you an excuse of any kind! Now, will you please get out of here?"

"I'm not going anywhere."

"Oh, we'll see about that," she promised.

"Yes, we will. In the meantime, tell your friend to run along. Playtime's over."

Jared's chin went up and his hands curled into fists. With an exasperated sigh, Kate pushed between the two glowering men, keeping her back turned to O'Rourke. "I must apologize, Jared. I'm really sorry you had to put up with this . . . this rudeness."

At her emphasis on the word *rudeness*, Jared seemed to recover his British aplomb and visibly relaxed. "It's of no consequence, Kathryn," he politely assured her. "Actually, I can understand how your husband got the wrong idea."

"But he's not—"

"Angry any longer," O'Rourke finished for her. "Just anxious to be alone with my wife."

Kate whirled on him. "Will you stop calling me that?" she cried. "I am not your wife!"

"A mere technicality."

"You consider a divorce a mere technicality?"

"Let's discuss this later, shall we? In privacy." O'Rourke glanced pointedly at Jared Harwood, causing Kate to wince at his tactlessness.

"Jared, I'm sorry. . . ."

"Not to worry. I'll just go along to my own room now, and perhaps I will see you at dinner."

She walked him to the door, uncomfortably aware that O'Rourke was watching every move.

"Will you be all right?" Jared asked in a low, concerned voice. "Do you want me to call the manager or something?"

"No. I'll be okay. O'Rourke is only trying to irritate me, but I intend to have him removed from this room as soon as possible. He shouldn't prove to be a problem."

"I'm in the Lord of the Manor Suite, if you should need me," he informed her. "Promise you won't hesitate to call?"

"I promise. But really, there'll be no need."

He cast a quick glance at O'Rourke and looked doubtful. "I hope you're right. The man seems somewhat dangerous to me."

"He's not, I assure you. I've dealt with him before. I'll be fine."

"Very well. Then I'll see you downstairs, shall I?"

"Yes, of course. Thanks for your help."

Kate shut the door and reluctantly turned to face the man to whom she had once been married.

Jared Harwood had been right. O'Rourke was dangerous. She might not be physically afraid of him, but she knew he was a definite threat to her emotional well-being. She had struggled for peace of mind, hoping to insulate herself against the pain of his betrayal. Now he was back and, she feared, could strip away layer after layer of that hard-won insulation with just a smile or a touch.

O Lord, she thought in sudden dismay, I cannot allow him to get close enough to touch me.

What if nothing had changed? What if she still turned to liquid heat beneath the caress of those hard, lean hands? She let her eyes linger on the hands in question...realizing it was not the hands or their skill that were in question, but her response to them.

O'Rourke had moved to the fireplace, and now he stood facing her, one hand resting on the mantel, the other at his hip, his thumb hooked carelessly into the front pocket of the jeans he wore. Against the slightly faded denim, his skin looked tan. The fine black hairs on the back of his hand were plainly visible, and his fingers were long, blunted at the tip, with short, square nails. She had always thought O'Rourke had beautiful hands.

"The way you're staring at me makes me think you've read the book on body language, too," he said lazily. "And that you're interested. Experts say that when a man stands with his thumb in his pocket, fingers pointing downward, he's actually advertising his—"

"Don't say it!" she warned. "I know very well what it means, and let me set you straight...if you'll pardon the pun...I am not now nor have I ever been, particularly interested in anything you have to advertise."

"You still can't tell a lie without getting those little pink spots on your cheeks." His voice grew husky. "Oh, Katie, it's so damned good to see you."

To her horror, he strode toward her. She backed away, one hand out as though to ward him off. He chuckled, advancing until the tips of her fingers barely brushed the softness of the blue cashmere sweater he wore.

"Stop..." she managed to say, her words fading into nothingness as she gave in to the compulsion to really look at him.

He was as handsome as she had remembered, and certainly more vibrant and alive than in the dreams she had continued to have even months after their separation.

She was tallish for a woman, but he seemed to tower over her—something that had made her feel deliciously feminine in the past. Now it only increased the trepidation she was already feeling, making her tremble nervously.

She couldn't keep her eyes off his hair; she deemed it a major victory that she could refrain from raising her hand to touch it. It was thick and black, a soft, clean black with a tendency to curl. As always, it tumbled casually down onto his broad forehead, enhancing his brashly charming good looks.

"What are you thinking, Kate?"

When he spoke quietly like that, his deep voice fell into a natural cadence, a faintly blurred shaping of words, that could only have resulted from birth in the Emerald Isle. And, as Kate remembered very well, when he spoke in such a tone, it was best to be wary. As her sister Beth had once said, "O'Rourke doesn't sound as if he merely kissed the Blarney stone...he sounds as if he made mad, passionate love to it!"

He leaned perceptibly closer, causing her fingertips to press into the cashmere. Startled, she met his gaze, and it was as if the champagne she had drunk were hitting bottom all over again. His eyes were that incredible shade of hyacinth blue common among those people known as the "Black Irish." That color framed by thick, sooty eyelashes made such a devastating combination that Kate, in the past, had spent an inordinate amount of time trying to find a way to adequately describe them. As usual, she got no further than "Paul Newman blue" or "sapphire blue" or even the more mundane "sky blue" before giving in to a desire to lose herself within their depths. She fought against that desire now, wrenching her gaze from his and moving it downward to his mouth. That was another terrible mistake.

Seeming to sense her confusion, O'Rourke gave a pleased smile, and there, right before her eyes, that damned elusive dimple of his appeared. Kate's heart went into a painful little death spiral. He knew all too well the effect that stupid dimple had on her—it was a low-down trick he played in those moments when he really wanted to impress her. The dimple was deep and, oddly enough, singular. It slid into place just to the right side of his mouth, looking both incongruous and irresistible.

"Katie? Will you let me kiss you hello?"

"No!" To her shame, she dropped her hand and fled.

Halfway across the room, reason reasserted itself and, knowing how much he would enjoy seeing her panic, she made herself stop and calmly remove her coat, throwing it onto the bed. With shaking fingers, she attempted to tidy her hair. "Whew," she breathed in what she hoped was a nonchalant voice, "that's better. It was getting awfully hot in here."

Hot? Oh, hell, she groaned silently, why did I choose that of all words? She wished she could have bitten off her tongue instead of uttering the suggestive inanity. She had to get a grip on herself.

O'Rourke's unbridled laughter sounded behind her, and, stung, she spun about to face him. For a long moment, their eyes clung, and she was rooted to the spot, breathing rapidly.

O'Rourke's smile slowly died as he made a deliberate, unhurried survey of the wife he had not seen in six months.

Nothing had changed about her, except her attitude toward him. Even poised for flight, her eyes wide and distrustful, she was still the prettiest woman he had ever known.

Kate was an elegant beauty, with patrician features and warm coloring. Her dark hair, which was too thick and heavy for the upswept style she usually attempted, poufed softly about her oval face, giving her a look reminiscent of the old-fashioned Gibson girls. Her indigo eyes were flattered by perfectly arched brows and long lashes.

At this moment, the nostrils of her straight nose were flared as though she feared him, and her soft rose-colored lips were tight with disapproval. Even so, O'Rourke had no trouble remembering the way her mouth looked when relaxed and smiling, or moistly parted in invitation. Kate always had the most kissable mouth....

She was as slender as ever, with shoulders that might have been a shade too wide on a shorter woman. Her figure had the same fine-boned look as her face, giving her the appearance of a model. Not, he acknowledged, the stick-thin, anemic type of model, but the more softly rounded, feminine type. Kate could wear absolutely any style of clothing and look great.

"You're looking wonderful, Kate," he said, breaking the silence between them. "I like those clothes."

She was dressed in a tan sweater and calf-length tan-cream-and-brown plaid skirt. The wide crinkled-leather belt at her waist matched the boots she wore. She glanced down at her skirt as though she had forgotten what it looked like. When she raised her eyes, he could see she had regained her determination and would not let him sidetrack her from the issue at hand.

"Why did you come here?" she asked bluntly.

"To spend Christmas with you."

"Isn't it a little late for that?"

"Christmas is still three days away."

"Don't be obtuse. You know what I mean."

"Yes, I know what you mean, Kate. And no, it isn't too late. It can't ever be too late for us. We belong together."

"The hell we do!"

Kate was relieved to find that searing anger still burned within her. For a while she had been afraid it had disappeared, leaving her vulnerable to the kind of hurt this man was capable of inflicting. She straightened her shoulders and unleashed the rage she felt inside.

"There may have been a time I was foolish enough to think we belonged together, but that was before I found out the truth about you."

"Are you so certain you really know the truth?"

"Does anyone ever know the whole truth about a man like you? Probably not. But at least I know enough to realize I don't ever want to have anything more to do with you."

His face darkened in anger. "Well, that's too damned bad, because I've come to get you back."

"Get me back?" Her laugh was harsh and derisive. "You don't stand a chance!"

"Oh, don't I?"

"No."

"Your cheeks are turning pink, darlin'."

"Probably because you send my blood pressure sky-high."

"I always could do that, couldn't I? And in so many delightful ways..."

"Listen to yourself," she snorted. "You sound more than a trifle overconfident."

"Why wouldn't I be?" he queried. "You act awfully *married* for a divorcée. You're still wearing your wedding ring, I notice, and when I checked in, the desk clerk told me *Mrs. Callahan* had already arrived. Who could blame me for thinking you might not be as fond of the single state as you claim?"

"I'm only wearing this ring because it's too tight," she snapped. "You told me it was a family heirloom, and I didn't want the jeweler to cut it off. As for my name...well, it seemed more sensible to keep using my married name. After all, living in a big city, a woman doesn't want to advertise she's alone."

"And that's another thing," O'Rourke continued, taking a few steps toward her. "You are alone, aren't you,

Kate? There haven't been any other men in your life since you threw me out."

"Since you left, don't you mean?"

"There haven't been, have there?"

"How do you presume to know that?"

"You didn't think I was simply going to disappear and leave you up for grabs, did you?"

"What a genteel way to express it," she fumed.

"Well, did you?"

"I had hoped you'd be gentleman enough to do that very thing."

"Sorry to disappoint you, but I had no intention of letting anyone else step into my place. I've kept tabs on you these past few months, and you can be damned sure that if I'd heard anyone was coming around too often, I'd have put a stop to it."

"You arrogant bas—!"

"Ah, ah, Katie," he cautioned, grinning. "A lady doesn't use language like that."

"That's just the problem. I never could be a lady around you!"

He rolled his eyes heavenward. "And don't I just know it?"

"That does it," she stormed. "Trying to talk to you is a waste of time. I'm asking you, once and for all, to please go away."

"Not on your life."

"Then you leave me no choice but to appeal to the hotel manager."

"Well," he smirked with an exaggerated imitation of Groucho Marx, "you certainly appeal to me!"

She glared at him as she stalked past on the way to the door.

"There might have been a time I'd have thought that was clever and disarming, but not anymore."

O'Rourke followed her. "How about my John Wayne routine? Would you rather see that?"

Kate's breath came in short angry gusts as she flounced down the stairs. "I'd rather see your backside..."

"That can certainly be arranged...."

"Going out the front door of this hotel," she finished.

He laughed, and the rich, mellow sound of it floated down the second flight of stairs, causing the desk clerk to look up with a smile.

"Isn't Christmas wonderful?" she chirped. "Everyone is always so happy."

"I want this man out of my room," blurted Kate without preliminaries. "Now!"

The woman looked shocked, her big brown eyes flashing from one to the other of them. "I don't understand. Isn't he your husband?"

"No!" Kate denied.

"Of course I am," O'Rourke proclaimed.

"Not anymore." Kate whirled on him. "You forfeited the right to call yourself my husband when you..."

O'Rourke managed a graceful shrug, turning the full force of his charmingly rueful grin on the young woman behind the desk. "I'm afraid we've had a...silly little tiff...."

"Tiff?" Kate choked.

"You know how it can be," O'Rourke hurried on. "Jet lag always makes Kate so testy."

"Testy?" she fairly shrieked.

"Dear, you're repeating everything I say. Don't you think you're just tired and overwrought?"

"I want this man moved to another room," Kate demanded, ignoring O'Rourke. "As far from mine as possible."

"Well," the girl began uncertainly, "that is a problem. There are no other rooms available."

"What? In a hotel this size? I'm afraid I don't believe that."

"Nevertheless, it's true. Here's our booking schedule— see for yourself."

She turned the room chart around so Kate could study it.

"All the rooms in the main part of the hotel are occupied for the holiday weekend."

"What about all these?" Kate questioned, tapping the chart impatiently.

"That entire wing is shut off for the winter. The furniture is dust covered ... there's no heat."

"I'm sure Mr. Callahan wouldn't mind," Kate said sweetly.

"Oh, but I would," O'Rourke put in. "No heat? Brr! You know it takes a lot to keep me warm in bed."

Kate's face burned, but she steadfastly refused to let him rattle her. "Well, what about it? Can't you give him one of those rooms?"

"I'm sorry, madam, but it's out of the question. Our manager, Mr. Smythe, has left strict orders, you see, and he won't be back in until tomorrow."

"Then what are we going to do? I came here for a restful week in the country, and those plans certainly didn't include sharing a room with a perfect stranger."

"Thanks, Katie, but I'm hardly perfect. Damned close, maybe..."

"Will you move him or not?" She fixed the desk clerk with a steely gaze.

"I'm ... I'm terribly sorry, Mrs. Callahan, but there is really nothing I can do."

"Very well." Kate heaved an aggrieved sigh and turned away, starting back upstairs. Behind her she could hear the murmur of voices and knew O'Rourke was using his considerable charisma to smooth matters over—at her expense, no doubt.

At the landing, she began a half run, flinging herself down the hall and into her room, slamming and locking the door behind her. She leaned against it for a long moment, trying to catch her breath and control the weakness in her knees.

Across the room, the bed beckoned invitingly. She truly needed a rest, a chance to gather her scattered thoughts and plan some sort of strategy against O'Rourke. Something told her he wasn't going to go away.

She had just removed her boots and slipped beneath the coverlet when she heard a scrabbling at the keyhole and the door swung open. O'Rourke stood on the threshold, holding up a brass key.

"They gave me my own key when I checked in," he said lightly, closing the door.

"How convenient."

"Look, Kate, let's be adult about this. We might as well accept the fact we're going to be sharing this room for the next few days. Why not try to get along?"

"Is that by your definition or mine?"

He crossed the room to stand beside the bed, looking at her. Kate felt compelled to draw the coverlet up to her chin.

"What do you mean?" he asked.

"I mean that I will attempt to tolerate you, if that is the only choice I have. But I refuse to *get along*…at least in the way I suspect you mean."

"Fair enough. I realize that tolerance is something you don't often deal in."

"Keep goading me, O'Rourke, and I won't even grant you that much."

He held up his hands in surrender. "All right, I'll be good," he promised.

"You'd better be. Now, I think we should set up some ground rules."

"Such as?"

"For one thing, I'll expect you to keep to yourself. In fact, I'd prefer that you spend as much time as possible away from this room. And when you're in it, stay away from me. We'll take turns with the bathroom. I'm willing to let you have equal time there, but under no circumstances are you to come near this bed. Do you understand?"

"But, Katie darlin', where am I to sleep?"

She pointed. "There's a fainting couch against that wall. It should be fairly comfortable."

"It looks too short to me. Why can't you take it and let me have the bed?"

"Because I was here first."

"I'll tell you what. You think about it...I mean, you seem willing to share the bathroom. Maybe after a little consideration, you'll decide it can't hurt to share the bed, too. Especially when it's as big as this one."

"They'll never make a bed big enough for the two of us!" she stated firmly.

"Interesting concept," he murmured.

Kate sat up. "Listen, O'Rourke, I'm only agreeing to try this because I have no other choice. But the first time you step out of line, I'll do whatever it takes to get you thrown out of this hotel. Now, go away and let me take a nap."

With those words, she reached up and pulled the bed curtains shut, enclosing herself in darkened privacy. Feeling safe from his probing gaze, she fell back upon the pillows and closed her eyes.

She had lied, of course. She did have a choice. She could walk out of the hotel and go back to Bristol, or even London. But, she told herself earnestly, she wasn't about to let O'Rourke spoil this country Christmas vacation for her.

Nearly twenty minutes had passed before Kate became curious about O'Rourke's silence. Cautiously she parted the curtains and peered out. He had settled himself in one of the chairs in front of the fire, his feet resting on an upholstered ottoman, his dark head nodding as he slept.

As much as she hated to admit it, the sight of him did funny things to her heart. The scene was so domestic and familiar...and somehow comforting. She corrected that thought. O'Rourke's nearness might once have been comforting, but that was before she discovered how flawed he really was. A master at concealing his deceitfulness and dishonesty, it had taken a catastrophe to reveal his true colors. Lord, she'd never forget that day....

Kate fell back onto the pillows and flung an arm over her eyes. My God, how ironic!

She was Kate Callahan, staunch champion of the rights of innocents—and she just happened to have married a handsome and charming rogue who turned out to be an international jewel thief.

Chapter Three

Kate came awake slowly, feeling much better after her nap. She yawned and stretched, discovering that muscles knotted by tension earlier had relaxed. She opened the curtains and slid out of bed, surprised but relieved to find the room empty.

She switched on the bedside lamp and glanced at the clock. She only had forty-five minutes to get ready for the first of the events scheduled for the weekend. Thank goodness, O'Rourke must have decided to honor her wish for privacy by going downstairs early.

She quickly went through her suitcases, hanging her clothing in the closet, perturbed that she had forgotten to do so earlier. Fortunately, the dress she planned to wear that evening was a synthetic, virtually wrinkle free. Now, more than ever, she intended to make a striking impression. It could only aid her cause for O'Rourke to see her with other men and know she wasn't pining away for him.

Grabbing her robe and a case containing toiletries, she went into the bathroom and indulged herself in a leisurely shower. She was just rinsing the shampoo from her hair when she heard someone moving about in the outer room. Turning off the water, she could hear cheerful whistling and knew O'Rourke had returned.

With frantic haste, she dried off and slipped into her bathrobe, wrapping a towel around her wet hair. Then she opened the bathroom door and poked her turbaned head around the edge.

O'Rourke, who was hanging up a freshly pressed tuxedo, flashed her a brilliant smile. "'Bout through in there, Kate? I want to take a shower."

"It's all yours," she said stiffly, avoiding his gaze as she crossed the room.

As soon as he had disappeared into the bathroom and she could hear the hum of his electric razor, she began rummaging through drawers for her underthings. Sitting on the edge of the bed, she pulled on a pair of sheer panty hose and then stepped into a scarlet lace teddy. Because she wanted to do her makeup before putting on her dress, she slipped back into the robe.

"Oh, damn," she whispered, realizing she had left her makeup kit in the bathroom. She glanced at the clock. It was getting late. She couldn't waste time sitting around waiting for O'Rourke to get out of the shower.

She heard the water running and decided to nip in to get her things. She could have the cosmetic bag and be safely out of the room before O'Rourke suspected what was going on.

Kate eased into the bathroom and, seeing that the door to the shower stall was closed, kept her eyes straight ahead. She didn't want even so much as a glimpse of O'Rourke through the frosted glass. Her fingers closed over the flowered bag containing her makeup just as his voice came from behind her.

"Forget something?"

Guiltily she clutched the bag to her chest and turned to face him. When she did, she could not prevent a small scream.

He was standing in front of the old-fashioned pedestal lavatory, stark naked. In one hand was a bar of soap.

"Goddamn it, O'Rourke!" she cried. "What do you think you're doing?"

"Getting ready to take a shower." He smiled. "But if you have something else in mind . . . ?"

Kate could feel a wave of heat sweeping through her body, starting at the soles of her feet and working its rapid way upward. In an instant her face began to burn. She tried fixing her gaze on a point just to the left of his bare shoulder, but her usual self-discipline had flown out the window and she couldn't help sneaking glimpses of him. He seemed all too aware of her fascination and, crossing his arms over his chest, struck an obliging pose.

Kate drew a shaky breath. "What kind of idiot turns on the shower before he gets into it?"

"The kind who doesn't want a faceful of cold water," he replied easily.

"The water wouldn't have been cold," she protested faintly, her eyes ranging along the width of his chest, her imagination busy with thoughts of stroking the swirling hair that grew there. "I'd just taken a shower, and there was plenty of hot water."

"I guess it was habit, darlin'. After all, most of life is governed by habit, wouldn't you say?"

"Mmm?"

O'Rourke took a step toward her, and with an effort she forced her eyes away from his tightly muscled waist and up to his face. She immediately interpreted the look she saw there as smug. Knowing she could never fake nonchalance at this point, she fell back on indignation.

"For heaven's sake, at least have the decency to put on some clothes!"

He came a step closer, almost as if stalking her. "Why? I'm going to take a shower. And, in case you'd forgotten, it is *my* turn in the bathroom. I know you said we'd share, but I didn't realize this is what you meant."

Kate began moving toward the door. "I forgot my make-up bag." She waved it in the air. "I thought I might be late if I waited for you to finish your shower. Next time, believe me, I'll opt for being late."

He chuckled and with a sudden, graceful move arrived at the bathroom door just as she would have slipped through it. One of his hands came down on her shoulder, and she could feel the heat of it right through the velour robe she wore. Slowly and deliberately he began to stroke his hand back and forth along the ridge of her shoulder, as though enjoying the sensuous feel of the fabric beneath his fingers.

"Please don't," Kate whispered, her mind a tangle of emotions. Unable to withstand the effect he had upon her, she closed her eyes, leaning weakly against the wall. She wanted to run, but her legs felt incapable of motion.

"Katie." The husky way he spoke her name sent tiny threads of electricity spiraling over her scalp. She could feel his warm breath grazing her cheek.

"Don't," she repeated. "Please. I . . . I'm not ready for this."

"Will you ever be?" he asked softly. "Are you ever going to let me kiss you again?"

Unwillingly her dark blue eyes opened, and she made herself answer honestly. "I don't know."

"I've been patient too long already," he warned lightly.

Instead of the show of anger they both expected from her, she experienced a pang of regret that matters between them could never again be simple and uncomplicated.

"You remember that I'm not a patient man, don't you?" he urged.

"I remember." She swallowed deeply, trying to ward off some of the more persistent memories of his impetuousness. Despite herself, a tremulous smile hovered about her mouth. O'Rourke's hand slipped from her shoulder and down her arm, his strong fingers curling around her wrist.

"Katie, if your reaction to my question was meant to soften me up, it's having quite the opposite effect."

Her unsuspecting gaze followed his rueful glance downward. She wished she hadn't looked!

"Oh!" she gasped. "Oh!"

He laughed, and blessed anger filtered through her once more. She jerked her wrist from his hold.

"I've got to go," she snapped haughtily. "Jared is waiting for me."

As she swept from the bathroom, O'Rourke stuck his head around the door and said, "So am I. But not for long, darlin'. Not for long."

Thirty minutes later, Kate sat in the lounge, sipping champagne and chatting with Jared Harwood. She had sought him out so that she could attempt to explain the bizarre situation existing between herself and her former husband. Jared nodded sagely and made no comment.

Lord and Lady Harwood, Jared's parents, were acting as host and hostess for the holiday weekend, and with much harrumphing and bumbling about, the mustachioed Lord Harwood announced that each guest must introduce himself and give a few pertinent details about his life.

"After all," he said, "we're going to be spending this holiday season together, so we shall want to get to know each other."

"Why don't you start by introducing us, dear?" his wife suggested. The woman looked exactly like her son Jared; the masculine version, however, was infinitely more appealing than the broad, nearly six-feet-tall woman in a bright paisley dinner dress. Her mannish face had been powdered and painted, with great attention having been devoted to the application of vivid magenta lipstick that outlined her full lips. Her dark golden hair, the color not as authentic as it might once have been, had been tortured into long corkscrew curls, fastened atop her head with a scattering of diamond hairpins. Diamonds flashed in her long-lobed ears, around her stout neck and on several large-knuckled fingers.

Her husband, a full head shorter than she, was the stereotypical British gentleman. Resplendent in dinner jacket and black tie, his silver hair and mustache added to his courtly old-world look. He had an enormous nose, faintly crimson in appearance, and a toothy smile. Kate was amused to notice that he even sported the requisite monocle, dangling from a chain fastened to his vest.

"Ahem . . . well, I'm Lord Cornelius Harwood of Harwood in Kent. This lovely lady is my wife, Carolyne. We were delighted to be asked to host Christmas at Cross Coombe Manor. Harrumph, such a pleasure meeting so many fine people."

"Quite," agreed Carolyne Harwood.

Kate became engrossed in the introductions, listening with real interest as the thirty-odd people standing about the room revealed insight into their diverse lives. Most of those present were British, but there were three couples from the States and two from Australia. The young man and woman Kate had seen earlier were newlyweds from Ontario, Canada.

When it was his turn, Jared, sitting beside her on the couch, made a modest introduction. "I'm Lord and Lady Harwood's eldest son, Jared. I'm engaged in the management of my father's estates in the south of England. My greatest passion is my hobby of breeding horses, which I find stimulating though exhausting."

Kate nearly choked on her champagne, but a surreptitious glance around the room showed her that no one else seemed to notice Jared's unwitting double entendre.

"Perhaps he would find it less exhausting if he'd purchase a stallion," O'Rourke murmured directly into her ear. Startled, she looked over her shoulder at him, half afraid someone else might have heard his whispered remark and half pleased that, just as in the early days of their relationship, their minds still operated on the same oblique level. She hadn't known he'd come downstairs yet and wondered how long he had been standing there behind her.

"It would seem I have arrived at an appropriate moment to introduce myself," he continued, straightening to speak to the room at large. "My name is O'Rourke Callahan and I am currently employed in...in a family business. This beautiful woman is my wife, Kate..." he paused to drop possessive hands on her shoulders "...and she is a highly qualified attorney back in Kansas City. We are about to celebrate our first anniversary, I might tell you, and we have no children...yet." His emphasis on the last word garnered several amused chuckles. "Do you have anything to add, Kate?"

"Not a thing," she said sweetly, thinking, at least nothing I'd dare say aloud! She stiffened beneath his hands, angry that he was able to call her bluff in such a way. He knew her well enough to know she wouldn't create a scene in front of strangers. Still, she could hardly allow him to persist in the charade they were man and wife.

Of course, she counseled herself, it would be awkward trying to explain why we are sharing a room if we aren't, in fact, married.

She wasn't certain enough of British protocol to guess whether such a situation would be socially acceptable or not. With an inward sigh, Kate decided she was simply too straitlaced to flaunt convention. She would let O'Rourke have his fun, but only when they were in the company of the other hotel guests. When they were alone, she would make it perfectly clear she had no intention of behaving in a wifely manner.

Just as the last of the guests, a rather plain librarian from York, had introduced herself and her mother, with whom she was traveling, the dinner gong sounded and the Harwoods led the way into the dining room.

Tonight the entire company was seated at a long, narrow table, but at some of the other meals, His Lordship assured them, they would be placed at smaller, individual tables.

"Don't want to overdo this group thing, y'know," he declared with a snort of laughter. "After all, we have to put up with each other for several days."

Both O'Rourke and Jared hurried to hold Kate's chair and, after she had slipped into her place, both reached for the neighboring chair.

"Sorry, old man, but it seems my name is on this place card," Jared said politely. "I believe you've been seated across the table."

Irritation flicked over O'Rourke's face, but he nodded calmly and, patting Kate's shoulder as he passed, went around to the opposite side.

"I wonder how that was arranged," Kate murmured, unfolding a snowy linen napkin.

"Easily enough. I slipped in earlier and switched the place cards." Jared's deep laughter combined with hers, though hers faded rather quickly when she happened to glance up and see O'Rourke glaring at them.

Kate found herself thinking he was unbelievably good-looking, even with a scowl on his face. His hair, still damp from the shower, was the same unrelieved black as the tuxedo he wore. He was an elegant study in black and white, the only color about him the blazing blue of his eyes. Eyes that plainly expressed his disapproval of her rapport with Jared.

Kate defiantly tipped her chin and glared right back at him.

O'Rourke was somewhat surprised by the strength of his desire to do violence to the very correct Englishman cornering the market on Kate's attention. Even at that, he had to admit a grudging admiration for the man's ingenuity. He knew without a doubt that somehow Jared had finagled the seat beside Kate away from him. O'Rourke would let it pass this time, but not again. From now on, he would have to see to it that he remained one step ahead of Harwood every moment. His intention of winning Kate back had increased a hundredfold since seeing her again, and no one was going to deter him.

With a crooked grin, he realized that it was probably a good thing he was seated across the table from her. The way she looked tonight made it very difficult to honor the

promise he had made to himself not to rush her. His palms
and fingertips actually tingled with the need to touch her.

She was wearing a stunning contradiction of a gown—its
simple classic lines bespoke *lady*; its clinging scarlet fabric
cried *wanton!* O'Rourke would have loved it had they been
dining in the privacy of their room. As it was, he gritted his
teeth and entertained thoughts of tossing the damned thing
into a roaring fire the first chance he got.

The dress had a high neck, long sleeves and a softly
draped skirt that brushed Kate's ankles. But the material
was so thin it left nothing to the imagination. O'Rourke's
eyes lingered on her breasts, jealous of the way the gown
molded itself to them. She wore a single gold chain with a
star-burst pendent that rested in a perfect position to draw
attention to the shadowy nipples beneath the flimsy fabric.
O'Rourke's jaw tightened, and he stirred restlessly in his
chair. As if sensing his discomfiture, Kate looked straight
into his eyes.

She was almost agonizingly beautiful, he realized—one of
those rare women who had been a lovely child and would
remain lovely even into old age. The fine, clean lines of her
face were enhanced by a very feminine hairstyle, one
O'Rourke had never seen her wear. She had fluffed her thick
hair with a blow dryer, then fastened one side back with a
gold clip, letting the other cascade forward over her shoulder. A thin gold hoop graced the shapely ear bared by the
style; the earring bounced gently against her slender neck as
she returned to animated conversation with Jared.

Kate was in the middle of a reply to Jared's question
about her career when she felt something nudge her ankle.
Suspiciously she glanced across the narrow table at
O'Rourke. The picture of innocence, he was chatting with
one of the gentlemen from Australia, half-turned in his
chair to face the man. He was paying absolutely no attention to Kate.

"I'm sorry, Jared," she said. "What were you asking?"

Suddenly she felt a stockinged foot slide upward along her
calf, hooking itself behind her knee to give it three short

tugs. In the old days, that had been O'Rourke's secret way of saying, *I love you!*

She attempted to pull away from him, but his foot curled upward, refusing to let her go easily, and she was aware of the caressing rub of his toes from her knee to her ankle. Unreasonably riled by his daring, she kicked out with one high-heeled pump, catching him on the shin.

"Oh!" O'Rourke exclaimed from across the way. "I mean, how very fascinating!" He couldn't control a grimace of pain. "I'd...love to hear more about ostrich farming...."

Kate caught his eye, smiled demurely and raised her wineglass, turning her full attention back to Jared, who, she suspected, recognized the interplay that had gone on between them.

Dinner progressed without further incident, and when it was finished, the entire company moved into the lounge for coffee and the continuation of the evening's planned festivities.

Lord Harwood backed up to the fire and made an announcement.

"Er...harrumph...we...that is, Carolyne and I thought it would be jolly good fun if we had a gift... harrumph...exchange on Christmas morning. Nothing elaborate, y'know—shall we set a limit of ten pounds?"

There were no objections, so a saucy mobcapped waitress in Victorian dress passed among them, letting each guest draw a name from the porcelain potpourri bowl she carried. Kate was pleased when the scrap of paper she drew had the name Norene Phillips on it. Miss Phillips was the librarian from York and would be more fun to buy for than a man might have been. Kate found herself looking forward to shopping for the gift in Cross Coombe village.

O'Rourke, the last to draw, broke into such a broad smile as he read his slip of paper that she had a sinking feeling she knew whose name he had gotten.

She didn't have time to worry over it, however, because the Harwoods were busily organizing the decorating of the Christmas tree and the lounge was quickly being transformed into a hive of activity. Kate accepted a second cup of coffee from the maid and found a quiet corner where she could watch the men get things under way by placing the electric candles on the tree. To her amusement, O'Rourke joined in with all the enthusiasm of a ten-year-old boy.

For a moment, she wondered how things between them would have worked out had he been a different kind of man. But he wasn't different—he was the same O'Rourke he had always been. Charming, charismatic... and thoroughly dishonest.

Seeking a distraction from her thoughts, Kate let her gaze sweep the room. How odd it seemed to be part of a group of amiable strangers, all dressed in formal clothing, decorating a stately pine to the strains of medieval Christmas music filtering through discreetly concealed stereo speakers. The noisy chatter of the guests proved that the spirit of Christmas could foster friendship and goodwill where it might not necessarily have flourished otherwise. At any other time of year, Kate suspected, these same people would tend to be much more aloof and guarded.

She saw Jared approaching and good-naturedly allowed him to pull her to her feet and present her with a handful of candy canes. "For the tree," he explained. "Or to eat, whichever."

"I love peppermint." She laughed. "But I promise to save some for the tree."

"Fair enough. Come on, let's join the others."

Kate hung three candy canes in quick succession, then stepped back to give someone else access to the tree. Idly she stuck one of the peppermint sticks into her mouth, enjoying its pungent taste. Her eyes followed Jared as he placed glass ornaments on some of the higher branches.

"Fascinating fellow, Harwood." O'Rourke's mocking voice broke into her thoughts. "But don't get any bright ideas, Katie. He's not for you."

She removed the candy from her mouth. "And just how do you know that?"

"Elementary." He grinned. "You already have one man. What do you need with another?"

"I believe you must be mistaken. There is no man in my life."

He took the candy cane from her. "That may have been true a week ago, darlin'...but it doesn't apply anymore. *I'm* back in your life now."

She watched in fascination as he rolled the peppermint onto his own tongue, closing his mouth about it and drawing it slowly through his lips. Kate swallowed hard, unexpectedly filled with disturbing memories of the things that mouth had once done to her own. She was treading on dangerous ground again!

"What? Wasting an opportunity like this, mate? And with your own wife?"

O'Rourke's Australian dinner companion was pointing upward at the ball of mistletoe hanging from the chandelier beneath which Kate and O'Rourke were standing.

"Well, I'll be damned," O'Rourke said softly. "Would you look at that?"

"Don't you dare—" Kate's whispered warning was effectively muffled as he pulled her into his arms and brought his mouth down on hers in a firm and uncompromising kiss.

Aware that everyone in the room was probably watching them, Kate had no choice but to accept O'Rourke's kiss. But just at the point when she thought it prudent to pull away and end their contact, he tightened his hold and his mouth began to express something close to desperation. Kate suddenly found herself drowning in sensation; it was all she could do to survive the moment.

O'Rourke's hands spread a sheet of flame along her spine as they moved in slow, massaging circles up and down her thinly clad back. His lips coaxed hers, forcing them to gentle and warm beneath his touch. His deliciously minty breath mingled with hers as he drew back slightly to let his tongue tease the corners of her mouth. Almost playfully he allowed his teeth to lightly graze her lower lip. Then, with a muffled groan, he deepened the kiss again and took her with him.

Some awareness of the total silence of the room inched its way into Kate's shattered mind, and she moved restlessly within his arms. Abruptly O'Rourke lifted his head and drew a deep, ragged breath, giving her a chance to break his hold and step away. To her utter embarrassment, the rest of the guests broke into spontaneous applause and a gabble of ribald comments which, strangely enough, sounded congratulatory. Kate was too stunned to make sense of any of it, but O'Rourke received their approbation with his usual aplomb. An imperceptible tightening of his jaw was the only clue that he might have been as affected as she.

Moving rapidly in an effort to conceal the blush staining her cheeks, Kate hurried back to the tree, but her fingers were shaking so badly it took three tries before she managed to hang a single candy cane.

At the first opportunity, she made her excuses to the Harwoods and, murmuring a few good-nights to the other guests, started upstairs. O'Rourke caught up with her on the first-floor landing.

"Kate?" He looked concerned. "Where are you going?"

"It has been an extremely long day," she replied. "I'm going to bed."

The dimple came and went in his cheek. "Need any help?"

"No, thank you."

"Sure? I'm pretty good with buttons." He reached out to touch the two small buttons at the neck of her dress. "Remember the game we used to play? Doctor...*lawyer*..." he intoned.

Kate backed away from his touch. "I'm through with games."

"Are you?"

"Yes. I don't want to play anymore."

"But why?"

She put out a finger to touch the first of the four buttons on his vest.

"Doctor . . . lawyer . . . beggar . . . *thief*." She raised huge shadowed eyes to his face. "You're a thief, O'Rourke, and that's what you'll always be. Please, just go away and leave me alone."

His face grew stern as she turned and fled up the stairs. In a few seconds he could hear the slamming of the door to their room.

Once again, she had shut him out.

Chapter Four

Kate locked herself in the bathroom and, leaning against the lavatory, concentrated on taking long, deep breaths. It was several minutes before the accelerated beating of her heart slowed to normal. She looked into the mirror, startled by the reflection that stared back at her.

She saw a grown woman with a child's fear in her eyes. Again she was stunned that the image she projected was so different from the one she wished the world to see.

What had happened? She'd gone downstairs looking her best and feeling confident, certain she could get her emotions under control and salvage something of her pride. But nothing had gone according to plan....

She had come to England to begin a new chapter in her life, and suddenly she was as good as right back where she started. Old hurts and memories plagued her, undermining her determination to forget the past.

Why did O'Rourke have to show up now? And why was his presence so threatening in so many ways?

Kate stripped off her evening dress and underclothing, then stepped into severely tailored pajamas. Removing the clip, she brushed her hair and left it down, swirling around her shoulders. After gathering her clothing, she unlocked the door and went back into the bedroom.

She hung the scarlet dress in the closet and, for the first time in months, observed her clothing and O'Rourke's hanging side by side. It was a symbol of what he wanted, and what she could never again accept.

Preoccupied with thoughts of the past, Kate wandered across the room to stand at the window overlooking the village. The tiny strings of colored lights along the fronts of houses and shops danced and swayed in the wind. She could see a lighted pub sign swinging, and though she couldn't make out the words from that distance, she seemed to remember it was the White Stag.

Life with O'Rourke had been something special, she suddenly found herself thinking. They'd been well matched, with much in common from the very beginning. They liked the same books, the same movies, the same foods. Their minds worked alike, causing them to agree on what was serious and to otherwise see life for the humorous proposition it tended to be. They had mapped out a wonderful future that involved extensive foreign travel before they settled down in a rambling farmhouse in the country to raise a family. They hadn't come to terms on the size of that family just yet. Kate thought two children would be sensible; O'Rourke leaned toward four... or more. Depending, he used to say, on how well they handled parenthood.

Falling for O'Rourke and marrying him in such an indecently short time had been the first really improvident thing Kate had done in her well-organized life. Not that anyone had tried to stop her. Her family had fallen for him every bit as hard as she had, and she supposed it intrigued them to see her in over her head for once.

Maybe, she mused, the planets had been out of control for those few months, casting strange, disturbing influences on her life. She had temporarily lost every ounce of caution and reserve she'd ever had. Now, looking back, it seemed impossible that someone like her could have married a man who was so vague about his past.

She knew nothing of O'Rourke's family... only that, according to his terse statements, they were extremely rich and owned several private businesses in Europe. His own background was shadowy but definitely diverse, as she had learned by the bits and pieces he had revealed from time to time. He'd been born in County Galway, Ireland, he told her, but she had never learned anything of his childhood or schooling. He spoke of London or Copenhagen with the same familiarity as he did Kansas City or New York. She'd heard him discuss North Sea oil rigs, Dutch art museums and corn farming in Nebraska all within the space of an hour. The mystery fascinated her, and in her newfound contentment, there seemed no need to demand a full accounting from him. She had actually anticipated learning all the details of his past throughout the years that stretched ahead of them.

They'd had six months of the most intense happiness she had ever known. After the wedding, she had begun making plans for lightening her work schedule even though O'Rourke had never asked her to do so. He was proud of her ability and reputation, and made no demands on her career. In fact, many times in the middle of a heated legal battle, she had looked up to find him there in the back of the courtroom, observing her. Even across the crowded room, with little more than a discreet wink, he could convey the message that he fully expected her to win the case, but he was on her side no matter what. Since he had come into her life, the desire to avenge her father's death, which had been so strong for so many years, had subsided and she experienced a new inner peace. Because she did, she felt no compunction about making a start toward easing herself away from her work; she reasoned that when they traveled, she'd have to do so anyway.

O'Rourke was busy with his own business affairs, which he told her were conducted in an office located uptown, though she'd never seen it. He put in long hours from time to time, but never consistently. When he was involved with work, he didn't seem to want to talk about it, and Kate was willing to overlook what later could only be described as his secretiveness. At the time, she surmised he was not especially happy being employed by relatives, and suspecting his reasons were personal, she tried not to press him for information.

Even the erratic nature of his job seemed to work out all right, for it allowed him the freedom to take unexpected weekend trips or surprise her with candlelit dinners at midnight and impromptu carriage rides through the park on free afternoons.

It had been at one of those midnight suppers that he had presented her with the plane tickets to England.

"It'll be a special Christmas for us," he'd said, "and our first experience with foreign travel as an old married couple. I really want you to see Britain, Katie—it's a wonderful place."

Less than two weeks later the dream had been shattered, opening Kate's eyes to brutal reality. O'Rourke was a liar, and their life together a part of the lie.

They'd been having breakfast on the deck that morning—it was the weekend, so they were having croissants and coffee and sharing the Sunday newspaper. One minute she'd been sitting on the sun-dappled deck, laughing at something he had said, and the next she'd been watching in horror as five plainclothes policemen had swarmed into their apartment, flashing their badges and a warrant for O'Rourke's arrest.

The police had been scrupulously correct in their actions—after all, she was a well-known lawyer. They had insisted she accompany them as they made a thorough search of the house, and because they had, she was a witness to their discovery. In a bedroom drawer, not even very cleverly hidden, was a stack of faked credit cards and a pouch containing several pieces of jewelry, which later proved to be stolen and very much in demand by certain insurance companies.

Her first reaction had been denial. She hadn't wanted to believe O'Rourke was capable of crime, but one look at his stricken face convinced her there was no mistake. Even confronted with irrefutable evidence, he hadn't looked so much guilty as surprised by the untimely intervention of the law.

Some of the plainclothes cops had known Kate since the days her father had been on the force, and it was obvious they had not relished their task. Kindly they offered to let her ride with O'Rourke to the station, but she couldn't make herself go. She was so crushed by what she saw as his betrayal of her trust—a trust she had never before given so easily—that he became linked in her mind with the young hood who had shot her father. In some inexplicable way, O'Rourke suddenly symbolized every thief, con man or gangster she'd ever faced in court. He had, in an unbelievably short span of time, become the enemy.

Kate had only seen him once after that. The day following his arrest, she had started divorce proceedings and, ever ethical, wanted him to know what she intended. She'd visited him in the city jail, staying just long enough to inform him of her plans.

He'd asked her to believe in him a little while longer, to give him time to prove he wasn't what the police thought him to be. But the memory of her slain father had strengthened her resolve, and she had turned her back, refusing to listen to another word he had to say. Sometimes, in the dreams that had plagued her ever since, she still heard his last, anguished shout—*"Katie, please listen to me! For God's sake, don't you think you owe me that much, at least?"*

Maybe she did, but it was a debt she had not been able to bring herself to honor. She had made it clear to family and friends that she wanted no news of O'Rourke. She avoided the papers and television for months. Daily she engaged in a humiliating struggle to hold her head high and proceed with her job, as though she didn't realize that rumors and speculation followed her everywhere. Eventually the story was phased out by fresh scandals, and her life returned to a semblance of normalcy.

At some point after the divorce, she had overheard the district attorney telling one of the lawyers in her firm that charges against O'Rourke had been dismissed due to lack of evidence. She guessed that somehow he had used his family's considerable influence to his advantage, but as far as she was concerned, the evidence she had seen with her own eyes was proof enough of his guilt.

Over the months, she made no effort to find out where he was, nor had he contacted her. Naturally she had assumed he'd gone to some other part of the world to take up his life. But now he was claiming he had stayed close to her all the time. She wondered...

The bedroom door opened and closed softly. "Kate? Are you all right?"

She turned warily. "I'm fine. Just tired."

She could not ignore the heat that leaped into O'Rourke's eyes at the sight of her in pajamas. She sensed that it stirred in him recollections of their married life as, she had to admit, sharing this room did to her.

There was danger in the unexpected intimacy of the moment. Fighting against the pull of the past, she made herself move. She crossed the room and briskly began pulling back the bedcovers.

As she folded the velvet coverlet at the foot of the bed, he came up behind her.

"I never did understand how a woman could wear men's pajamas and look so damned sexy," he murmured, running a knuckle lightly from the nape of her neck all the way down her backbone. Kate shrugged away from his touch.

"Good night, O'Rourke," she said pointedly, closing the curtains along one side of the bed and moving around to the other.

"I'm not a thief, you know," he said quietly, hand dropping back to his side.

"Oh?" She put a world of sarcasm and doubt into the single syllable.

"You never stayed around long enough to find out the truth. They dropped the charges, Kate. You were the only one who condemned me without a fair hearing."

"Those credit cards and the stolen jewelry were all the hearing I needed."

"Surely you've heard, counselor," he chided, "that a man is supposed to be innocent until proven guilty."

Kate was plumping the pillows; now she paused, turning to face him, one of the pillows clasped in her arms.

"I don't want to talk about it anymore, O'Rourke."

"We've got to talk about it. Hell, I've followed you halfway around the world to talk about it. I didn't push matters before, Kate, because I was trying to give you time to get past the first shock. I wanted you to learn to trust me again."

"I'll never trust you again," she stated firmly. "And I don't want to talk to you."

He looked grim. "Want to or not, you're going to have to. That's what I came here for, and I won't be put off forever."

She thrust the pillow into his arms. "Here, you can use this. There are extra blankets in the chest at the foot of the bed."

She would have turned away, but he flung the pillow aside and took her arms instead.

"Don't be like this, damn it," he said, giving her a small shake. "I can explain everything if you'll give me ten minutes of your time."

"No!" she cried, wrenching her arms free. "I don't have *any* time for you . . . not now, not tomorrow . . . not ever!" Unsure of what else to do, she started toward the bathroom.

"Stop running away."

"I'm not running away!"

"Then where are you going?"

"None of your business . . ."

"I'll make it my business," he threatened, and before she could prevent it, he had swung her up into his arms. She struggled fiercely, one fist pounding at his shoulder.

"Katie..." he warned, his blood rushing heatedly through his veins as her silk-clad body writhed against him.

"I don't feel like putting up with your stupid horseplay," she retorted wrathfully.

His face was only inches from hers. At the sight of the righteous anger within her clear eyes, he grinned and the elusive dimple slid magically into place. The deep jade green of her pajamas turned her skin ivory and brought out the copper highlights in her dark hair. He was suddenly convinced he'd never seen her look more desirable.

"How about a little foreplay, then?"

He dared the remark, knowing it was a definite possibility that she might try to slap him silly. Neither of them was prepared for the quick, hot tears that sprang into her eyes.

Kate realized she was an emotional wreck. It took every ounce of strength she possessed to keep from burying her face in O'Rourke's broad shoulder and crying her heart out. What was wrong with her?

He drew a deep breath. "I didn't mean to make you cry, Katie," he whispered, bending his head so that his lips rested against her temple. "Believe me...I've never meant to hurt you."

He lowered her onto the huge bed, drawing the bedcovers up to her chin. "We'll talk tomorrow, all right?"

Feeling weak and foolish, she nodded. "All right..."

"Good night, darlin'."

He pulled the curtains shut and, with a resigned sigh, began making up his own bed on the fainting couch. O'Rourke eyed the couch with certain misgivings. It was a charming antique, to be sure, but how in the hell was he supposed to get any sleep on it? It was no longer than any ordinary sofa, and one end curved gracefully upward, leaving only an area about four feet long for him to stretch out on. He tested it with one hand and groaned at the lack of resiliency in the tufted upholstery. Lord, it felt like granite.

He flung down the blanket and pillow he carried and stalked away to the closet, stripping off his jacket and unbuttoning his vest as he went.

Months ago when he'd made the reservations at Cross Coombe Manor, he'd specifically asked for the Highwayman's Chamber because he'd remembered the magnificent old tester bed. Since then, at the oddest moments, he'd often found himself delightfully distracted with visions of the hours he and Kate would while away within its curtained depths. Even after the divorce, those thoughts had sustained him. And now he was here and so was Kate…and he was sleeping on the damned couch!

He dropped into a chair in front of the fire to pull off his shoes and socks, a wry smile playing about his lips as he recalled stroking Kate's leg with his foot underneath the dining room table. He chuckled softly thinking of her indignant retaliation. He stood and dropped his trousers, searching for the bruise he was certain existed on his shin.

One of the most fascinating things about Kate was the way her cool, ladylike exterior hid the fiery hellcat that lurked just beneath the surface. God, but he loved to provoke that part of her nature! He reveled in being able to make her lose her ordinary control and simply *react*. Of course, her reactions had never been calm or predictable, but, he thought with a grin, they were definitely gratifying.

Though he usually slept nude, O'Rourke had packed a pair of pajamas for the sake of propriety. Until he was on a little better footing with Kate, he decided he'd better wear them. After all, the sight of his nakedness earlier in the evening hadn't done much to win her over—instead, it had sent her scurrying in the opposite direction.

As he came out of the closet, dressed in a pair of low-slung black pajama pants, he saw a pair of Kate's panty hose draped over one of the chairs. It was such a domestic sight that it gave him an odd feeling of poignancy—as if nothing had changed between them. Noticing a splash of color on the carpet behind the same chair, he bent and scooped up a scrap of silk. Unfolding it, he found himself staring at a one-piece red lace ... undergarment. The subtly spicy scent of Kate's perfume clung to the teddy and with a jolt hit him like an unexpected fist to the stomach. He knew the dainty tidbit had been the only thing she'd had on tonight beneath that provocative dress.

His black brows drew together in a fierce frown. What had happened to her? The old Kate would never have dressed so brazenly...at least, not in public. Come to think of it, her behavior had been pretty out of character ever since she'd arrived at Cross Coombe. Back home he'd had no indication she had so much as given another man the time of the day. But here she had picked up Jared Harwood within an hour after checking into the hotel.

He glared down at the red lace. It could only mean one thing: she was tired of being alone. His imagination went wild. No wonder she had made the trip to England! Not wanting to tarnish her respectable image at home, she had traveled overseas to sow her wild oats. Well, damn it, he'd sure as hell have something to say about that!

With a burst of temper he cranked open a leaded window and threw the teddy out into the night. Then he strode across the room and grabbed two handfuls of the velvet curtain that enclosed the bed. He experienced a powerful urge to rip the curtain open, yank Kate out of her warm bed and make her explain what her motives had truly been in taking this trip.

Then another urge thrust its way into his overwrought mind, suggesting that he simply climb into the big bed with her, overcoming her protests with fervent kisses and caressing hands. The temptation was so powerful that he had actually placed one knee on the edge of the mattress before sanity returned to him. Still clutching the curtains, he closed his eyes and dropped his head. If he tried something like that, she'd never give him another chance. He had to go slowly, no matter what his frustrated hormones advised. Getting Kate back was too important for him to take crazy risks.

He realized he could hear her rhythmic breathing on the other side of the curtains and was thankful he hadn't awakened her. Releasing the fistfuls of velvet, he backed away from the bed. Suddenly he remembered tossing her underwear out the window.

Good Lord, what was I thinking of? he raged silently, hurrying to the window. Oh, for Pete's sake!

The lacy teddy had caught on the wrought iron sign that hung over the front of the hotel, and now it was waving in the floodlighted breeze like a red banner!

"Hellfire and damnation," he swore under his breath. Well, he had no choice but to go after it. Kate would never forgive him if the entire hotel awoke to the sight of her lingerie gracing the sign below their windows.

He knew the slate roof was going to be cold, so he rummaged through his suitcase for a pair of moccasins. Then, shrugging into his pajama top, he moved a pot of poinsettias aside and hoisted himself onto the windowsill.

The roof was slippery with frost, so he was forced to move slowly, shivering in the sharp night air. With each step he took, he cursed himself anew for his stupid, irrational jealousy. He was behaving as if thirty-three were his IQ instead of his age! He earnestly swore that if he rescued the teddy and made it back to safety, he would never again act rashly. He'd be as prim and proper as ... as Jared Harwood.

Holding tight to the guy wire that supported the hotel sign, O'Rourke leaned forward over the gutter and stretched his hand out to retrieve the teddy. Just as he had it firmly in his grasp, a voice from below rang out in the still night.

"No need to ask if you're enjoying your holiday, eh?"

Stunned, he looked down to see the night security guard, swathed in a greatcoat and beaming suggestively. O'Rourke forced a feeble smile in return.

"Yeah, I'm having a jolly good time," he muttered.

"Need any help with that?"

O'Rourke glanced at the incriminating piece of silk. "No, everything's under control now. Thanks anyway."

The guard chuckled. "Lord, but I envy you young chaps! G'night."

"Good night."

O'Rourke crawled back into the room, eager for the warmth of the fire. Just as his feet touched the carpeted floor, he looked up and saw Kate standing beside the bed, watching him.

Hiding the crumpled teddy behind him, he moved toward the fainting couch where he casually dropped it into the folds of the blanket. "Now, Kate," he said softly, "I can explain this. It isn't what it looks like...."

She stared straight ahead, refusing to even acknowledge his presence.

He sighed. "Don't you ever get tired of being mad at me?" he asked in quiet desperation.

She took a few steps forward, her hands coming up in front of her as if she were blind. Beneath his puzzled gaze, she groped her way toward the stone wall behind the bed.

"What the hell?" he murmured to himself. If he didn't know better, he'd swear Kate was walking in her sleep.

She began running frantic fingers over the rough stones, mumbling incoherently.

"By damn," he whispered. "You are sleepwalking, aren't you, Kate, my girl?"

Quietly he closed the distance between them. She half turned and he could see the fright in her eyes.

"Hurry!" she rasped. "You've got to hurry, love. They'll come for you at any moment."

"Katie..."

"Oh, where is it?" she moaned. "Where?"

Moving slowly so he wouldn't frighten her more, O'Rourke reached out to capture the hand she was pressing to the stone. It felt so cold that he held it to his chest to warm it. Kate turned and, with a tremulous sigh, slipped her free arm around his waist and nestled against him. It seemed impossible that two chilled bodies could generate such immediate heat, but he didn't waste time pondering the matter.

For the first time in five months, Kate had come to him without reservations, actually letting him hold her. This was a sweetly compliant Kate. A Kate who still fit every curve of his hands and arms as if she had been created for his embrace alone. He breathed in the fragrance of her hair and enjoyed the softness of her slender body. When, after a few minutes, she stirred, he reluctantly let her go.

"I was so afraid for you," she whispered, looking up into his face. Her eyes, wide and glazed with sleep, told him she was still ensnared by whatever force of night held her.

Gently he led her back to bed and tucked her beneath the covers once more. She raised trusting arms and drew his dark head down, touching his mouth with an infinitely tender kiss.

"Go, my love," she breathed. "Go quickly...."

Her eyes blinked shut, and she drifted back into sleep with such ease it was difficult to believe she had ever left the bed.

O'Rourke cranked the window shut and replaced the poinsettias. What, he wondered, had all that been about?

Still wondering, he switched off the lamp and, seizing a blanket, stretched out on the fainting couch.

Kate awoke early the next morning. Hearing O'Rourke's faint snores, she pushed the bed curtains aside and peered out.

To her surprise he was lying facedown on the carpet, the pillow squashed beneath his head and shoulders. A blanket straggled over the edge of the rumpled fainting couch, barely covering half his body. His legs were sprawled wide, his pajamas bunched around one bent knee, revealing a well-muscled calf. One arm was curled beneath him, the other flung outward. She noticed a scrap of something red clutched in his hand, but the light was too dim to discern what it was.

She sighed. If only he was as innocent as he looked when he was sleeping. If only she could ever really trust him again...

Her sleep had been plagued with strange dreams, but there was one that seemed more realistic than the rest. In it she had seen O'Rourke crawling back into the room through an open window, looking like a cat burglar caught in the act.

Why couldn't she shake off the dread that it hadn't been a dream at all?

Chapter Five

Kate slipped quietly into the bathroom to dress. She hoped to make an escape from the room before O'Rourke awoke. Today she wanted to be as free as possible from the confusion his presence caused.

She tucked the shirttail of a blue-and-rust plaid blouse into the waistband of her rust corduroy slacks and pulled a cream-colored fisherman's knit sweater over her head. Working quickly, she French-braided her hair, leaving the single plait to hang down her back.

She tiptoed across the room, stopping to get her purse and coat from the closet. At the door to the hall, she paused with her hand on the knob and sneaked a last look at O'Rourke. He was still asleep, lying on the carpet which, she realized guiltily, was probably softer than the couch. For an instant, she wondered if she should cover him with the blanket, but reason told her that if he was cold, he would rouse enough to do it himself. No need to start fussing over him at this late date.

Tossing her coat onto an already loaded hall rack in the downstairs entryway, she went into the small dining room and headed straight for a table in the far corner, half-hidden by potted palms. Though she smilingly returned the other guests' friendly greetings as she passed through the room, the isolation of a table in the back appealed to her. Just as she reached it, however, she saw that it was occupied by the librarian from York and would have turned away had not the woman tendered a shy smile.

"Good morning, Mrs. Callahan."

"Good morning, Norene. And call me Kate."

"You remembered my name," Norene exclaimed, pleased. Obviously it was something that did not happen often. "Would...would you care to join me?" As soon as the words were out of her mouth, she blushed painfully. "Oh, silly me...of course you'll be wanting to sit with your husband."

"Not at all," Kate said with fervor, dropping into a chair next to the other woman. "I mean, he's going to sleep in today. I wanted to get an early start so I could do some shopping in the village."

"Exactly what I had in mind."

"Where is your mother this morning?" Kate asked idly, looking over the breakfast menu.

"She's sleeping, also. She never rises earlier than eleven. She likes to watch the late shows on the telly, you see."

Looking up, Kate found herself studying Norene. At first glance she seemed the stereotypical librarian, but Kate suspected there was more to her than that. At this moment, her hazel eyes were alight with pleasure, and a faint rose tinge touched each cheekbone. It couldn't be any more evident that the few extra hours her mother slept each morning were the only free time the poor thing had. Kate observed her with new interest.

Norene Phillips was probably in her late twenties or early thirties—with her simple hairdo and no makeup, it was difficult to tell. Her brown chin-length hair was shiny but lank and straight, her face totally devoid of cosmetics. The bone structure was good, Kate decided, and her figure wouldn't be half bad if she wore suitable clothing. This morning she was wearing a straight mud-colored wool skirt with a sweater set in a dishwater-gray hue that did nothing to flatter her paleness.

"I have an idea," Kate said brightly. "Let's go shopping together. Would you mind?"

"Mind? Heavens no! But . . . what about Mr. Callahan? Won't he . . . ?"

"He's sleeping late, remember? And I'm sure he'll have things of his own to do."

"Then I'd love to go with you. It's really very kind of you to ask."

"Nonsense. I want to look for some gifts to take home to my family, and I'd appreciate someone else's advice."

Just then the waitress came to take their orders, and, with abandon, they both decided on the full English breakfast.

"I'm looking forward to the theater tonight," Norene said, sipping her orange juice. "Of course, we Britons do enjoy our pantomimes. It wouldn't be Christmas without them."

"Well, I've never seen one," Kate stated, "so it will be a new experience for me."

They were halfway through the meal when Kate, poking at a grilled sausage with her fork, heard Norene emit a small fearful squeak.

"Oh! Mr. Callahan . . ." She jumped to her feet as O'Rourke slid into an empty chair.

"Please sit down, Miss Phillips," he said calmly. "I don't bite." He flashed a quick smile in Kate's direction. "At least not indiscriminately."

Kate glared at him, and Norene sank back into her chair, looking miserable. Kate realized the librarian must be terrified of men, especially big, virile-looking ones like O'Rourke.

"I believe I've finished," Norene murmured, crumpling her napkin. "I'll just leave the two of you alone. . . ."

"No," Kate said quickly. "There's no reason for you to run away. Why, you haven't even touched your eggs."

"Don't feel you need to go on my account," put in O'Rourke. "I'd like to have breakfast with two such lovely ladies."

Norene's blush tinted her skin brick red, and she hastily seized her knife and fork to begin sawing frantically at a rasher of bacon. Kate frowned at O'Rourke over the woman's head.

"I...uh...thought I left you sleeping soundly," she commented.

"You did. But the bed got so dam...darned cold without you that I woke up." His dimple flashed briefly as he boldly lied. "You know how it is."

"Yes, I do," she uttered faintly.

Seeming to sense some off note in the verbal exchange, Norene glanced up, looking from one to the other of them. Kate avoided her gaze, stirring sugar into a cup of tea.

"Did you sleep well, darlin'?" O'Rourke purred, reaching for the teapot to pour himself a cup.

He had to control a smile when she rolled her eyes heavenward in disgust. She'd make him pay for the fun he was having at her expense, he reckoned, wondering what form her retaliation would take. With Kate, you never knew!

"Yes, I slept very well." Kate stabbed a second sausage.

"I suppose it's this country air," O'Rourke mused, "and all that vigorous exercise." Casually he faced Norene and added, "My wife and I had been apart some months before our arrival here at the hotel. We were...uh...very glad to see each other again."

The librarian nearly choked on a bite of toast, and as Kate patted her on the back, she gave O'Rourke a blistering look. He smiled placidly and turned to give his order to the waitress.

"There you are, Kathryn. I've been looking for you." Jared Harwood, dapper in tweed, stepped up to the table. "Good morning, everyone."

"Hello, Jared. Have you met Norene Phillips?" Kate asked.

Jared politely extended his hand, leaving Norene no choice but to give him hers.

"How do you do, Miss Phillips?"

Norene's reply was so faint as to be inaudible. Jared dropped her hand and turned back to Kate. Norene busied herself spooning jam onto another square of toast, while O'Rourke looked first at Jared, then back at Norene with sudden calculation.

"Have you plans for the day?" Jared was asking Kate.

"Norene and I are going shopping this morning," she replied. "Why?"

"I wondered if perhaps you and I could have luncheon at the White Stag?"

"Well, I'm not sure that..." Kate began, nervously twisting the gold wedding band up and down on her finger. She was hoping to remind Jared that, as far as Norene knew, she was a married woman...a married woman having breakfast with her husband at that very moment.

"Great idea," O'Rourke interrupted. "Why don't the four of us meet there at one o'clock? What do you say, ladies?"

"Oh, I couldn't," gasped Norene. "My mother..."

"I'll explain matters to your dear mother," O'Rourke assured her. "I'm certain she'll understand. The lunch plans all right with you, Kate?"

Neatly trapped again, she thought.

"I suppose so," she answered somewhat ungraciously.

"Good, it's settled then. See you at one o'clock, Harwood."

Jared's jaw clenched slightly, but he merely nodded. "Right. One it is."

"Norene, we really ought to be going," Kate said grimly as soon as Jared had left the table.

"I wish you would finish your breakfast, Kate," commented O'Rourke with elaborate concern. "You seem to have lost a great deal of weight lately."

"Don't be silly," she snapped, rising to her feet. "What makes you say a thing like that?"

"Why . . . your wedding ring. Just a few months ago you couldn't get it off at all, and now it slides up and down your finger so easily I'm afraid you'll lose it."

There was no mistaking the look of guilt that passed over her face. An expression of ire quickly followed.

"Then perhaps you'd like to take care of it for me," she said through clenched teeth. She pulled the ring from her finger and dropped it into his half-empty cup of tea.

Norene's fork clattered onto her plate.

Kate smiled sweetly at O'Rourke. "And maybe, if we're all terribly lucky, you'll choke on the damned thing."

Norene hissed in shock and then, as Kate walked away, realized she was being left alone with O'Rourke. She jumped to her feet and nearly ran from the dining room.

Kate was waiting for her in the entryway, forehead pressed against the cold glass of the front window.

"I should never have said that to him," she fretted. "I don't know what's the matter with me lately." She smiled apologetically. "Breakfast must have seemed pretty strange to you. I'm sorry."

Norene looked puzzled. "I just don't understand why Mr. Harwood would invite a married woman to lunch—and right in front of her husband! Doesn't he know who Mr. Callahan is?" Her eyes grew wide. "And that business about the ring . . . ?"

Kate laughed a little unsteadily and shrugged into her coat. "Come on, Norene. I think there are a few things I'd better explain to you as we walk to the village."

Kate was well pleased. The shopping had been an un-qualified success, and Norene, once she had stopped wor-rying about her prolonged absence from her mother, proved to be an amusing companion.

Kate discovered the young woman was as intelligent and sensible as she looked, but also that she had a wonderful sense of humor and a whimsical quality to her personality.

Kate hoped that, if only for the few days of this holiday, she could help Norene step out of her mother's shadow and see that it was possible to have a life of her own.

The quaint tucked-away shops of Cross Coombe were delightful and, they found, crammed with treasure. Kate bought hand-knitted sweaters for her mother and sister, as well as herself. Seeing Norene contemplating the purchase of a slate-gray cardigan, she suggested a pullover in a pretty dusty rose.

"It's a super-looking sweater," Norene said wistfully, "but I can't wear pinks... even though I love them. My mother told me that ages ago. You see, my own color sense has always been so awful that she insists on choosing my clothing."

I'll just bet she does, Kate thought indignantly. When Norene wandered into another part of the shop, she bought the sweater and stuffed it into the bottom of her shopping bag.

Kate found a carved pipe and tins of tobacco for her brother-in-law, books and games for her niece and nephews. There were framed watercolors and pottery cats and soft woolen scarves too lovely to resist. And, she was convinced, the most remarkable find of the day was the beautiful hand-carved figure of a highwayman, fashioned, the shopkeeper informed her, after the real highwayman who had once resided right there in Cross Coombe. Kate didn't quite know why, but the intricate details of the outlaw's face cut into the polished wood fascinated her. She could no more have walked out of the shop without the statue than she could have sprouted wings and flown.

In the last shop they visited, she felt she had won a major victory when she persuaded Norene to splurge on a pair of small gold hoop earrings. She had seen her admiring them and said, "I think they'd look nice on you. Why not buy them?"

"Oh, I'm not the type," protested Norene.

"What type?"

"You know—the type for fashion jewelry like this. Some women . . . you, for instance . . . can wear it and look smashing. But me . . . well, librarians usually stick to plain pearls or something equally boring."

"If you think pearls are boring, why not break out and try something different? Librarians don't have to fit the outdated stereotype these days. Try them on, go ahead."

Norene allowed Kate to gently bully her into buying the earrings and even left them in her ears and wore them out of the shop. The only concession to guilt she made was to purchase a large topaz brooch for her mother. Somehow Kate doubted if the smoky gold stone would appease the woman much if she noticed any sign of burgeoning independence in her daughter.

The White Stag public house had a whitewashed facade that in the summer would have been covered with wisteria vines. Now loops of Christmas lights were draped above the main door, and the old hound lying on the front step had a red bow around his neck.

Jared Harwood and O'Rourke had already met and were waiting at the bar when Kate and Norene entered. After ordering four pints of bitters, Jared immediately ushered them up a cramped and crooked staircase to a tiny room on the second floor.

"I took the liberty of reserving the private dining room," he explained. "It will be a bit quieter, and I thought you might like to see the interior of an authentic medieval inn."

"It's charming," Kate exclaimed, "but so small!"

The room at the top of the stairway barely had enough space for a round table and chairs and the high-backed oak settle placed against one timbered wall. A brick fireplace stood opposite, its mantel decorated with shiny green holly. The heavy beams overhead only emphasized the small size of the room.

"This looks like a drawing from a children's fairy-tale book," Norene said, coloring at her own temerity in speaking.

"And not a thing like the inns in the historical romance novels I've read," Kate agreed.

Unexpectedly her gaze tangled with O'Rourke's as his deep voice filled the chamber. "Yes, I'd have thought a fellow would need a tad more room when there was serious ravishing to be done."

His comment and the intense look in his eyes assured her he had been thinking along the same lines as she. Chagrined, Kate looked quickly away.

Somewhat dazedly she stacked her packages on the settle with the coats and seated herself at the table between Norene and Jared. She took a sip of the bitters and grimaced. To her surprise, Norene swallowed a hearty quaff and delicately patted her mouth with the napkin lying beside her plate.

Kate sneaked another look at her ex-husband. He had hardly said a word since their arrival, and yet he didn't seem to be angry, though grudgingly she admitted he probably had several good reasons to be.

He looked bigger than life, his rangy physique an incongruous contrast to the miniature room. He was wearing a blue heather tweed sport coat over federal-blue wool slacks and a sweater. The jacket made his eyes the same hazy color as distant mountains at twilight, Kate thought, promptly castigating herself for such an idiotic flight of fancy.

O'Rourke grinned a grin that told her he knew precisely what she was thinking. Kate wondered if it would be possible to kick him beneath the table without doing bodily harm to the others.

Jared asked a timely question about their shopping spree, and conversation revolved around that until a waitress brought their lunch.

Kate had not realized how hungry she was until that moment and eyed the food with approval. Steaming bowls of homemade vegetable soup and thick sandwiches made from freshly baked bread and sliced roast beef arrived. In addition, there were cheeses, pickles and pots of spicy English mustard.

"Mmm, this looks delicious," she said. "Much nicer than the fast-food lunches I grab back home when I'm at work."

Her comment prompted Jared to pose a question about her job, and for the next ten minutes, while the others ate quietly, the two of them discussed everything from jurisprudence to conditions in British prisons. Finally O'Rourke broke in with a different topic.

"I was disappointed not to encounter the ghost of the infamous highwayman last night. I wondered—would any of you know the details of the legend?"

"Sorry, old man," Jared replied, returning his attention to Kate.

Norene spoke, a little breathlessly. "I...I have done some reading...."

"Great," responded O'Rourke. "What have you learned?"

"Well..." She glanced at the others in hesitation. "Are you...will this be too boring for you?"

"Of course not," Kate assured her, despite the fact that Jared indulged in a rather exasperated sigh. She gave him a severe look, wishing he would pay more attention to Norene. It couldn't help the poor girl's insecurities to be so totally ignored.

Well, Kate conceded, at least O'Rourke was treating her politely.

"It does seem the story of the highwayman and the lady is a true one," Norene said. "Naturally, it happened so long ago that the legend has become distorted, but authorities know its origins were factual." She looked up, her voice fading, but O'Rourke nodded encouragingly and she continued.

"The lady was a young noblewoman who lived here at Cross Coombe Manor with her parents. Her father was some sort of officer in Henry VIII's court and spent a good deal of time in London. At eighteen, she was nearing the end of the journey home from school in France when her coach was stopped by a highwayman—a highwayman so smitten by her beauty, they say, that he gave back the booty and allowed her safe passage." She paused.

"That can't be all the legend, surely?" Jared muttered. He seemed interested in spite of himself.

"No, there's more," Norene said apologetically.

"Then please tell us," urged O'Rourke. "I, for one, am enthralled."

She smiled shyly. "Well, it seems that later her father was instrumental in sentencing one of the highwayman's comrades to death, so in an attempt to save his friend, the outlaw waited until the father was in London, then broke into the manor house and made the lady his captive. He barricaded himself and the girl in the large bedchamber and . . . vowed to . . . well, to . . ."

"Ravish her?" O'Rourke kindly supplied.

"Uh . . . yes, that's it. Uh, if her father wouldn't release his friend."

"What happened?" asked Kate.

"The father refused to be bullied and ordered the man to hang."

"Oh, my God! He certainly didn't have much regard for his daughter, did he?" Kate commented.

"He probably thought upholding the law was more important than a mere girl-child. Oh, not that I'd ever feel that way!" O'Rourke winked at Jared. "My wife is a diehard feminist," he explained, putting only the slightest emphasis on the phrase *my wife*.

"What happened then?" Kate asked, ignoring him.

"It's purely a matter of speculation from that point on," Norene replied. "When her father's men battered their way into the bedchamber, both the girl and the highwayman were gone. No one knows what happened to them, but of course, legend has it that they had fallen in love and she went with him. Other versions say he killed her and did away with the body."

"Not the most romantic version, obviously," Kate said with distaste. "I'd like to think they ran away together. . . ."

"And lived happily ever after?" inquired O'Rourke.

She met his gaze squarely. "I'm not that much of a romantic," she said. "They'd have been lucky to have a few good months of happiness."

He shrugged and turned back to Norene. "Tell me, how were they supposed to have escaped the bedchamber? Surely the father's men would have been posted outside?"

"I read that there was believed to have been a secret passage the girl knew about. It was her room, you see, so historical researchers think she must have known of the passageway, even though her father did not."

"Where did you find all this information, Norene?" asked O'Rourke.

"Oh, there are some wonderful books in the hotel library."

"Could you show them to me?"

"I'd . . . I'd be delighted. Perhaps this afternoon?"

"Great." O'Rourke drained his glass of bitters. "In fact, no time like the present. Have you finished your lunch?"

She nodded eagerly, rising.

"You two coming?" O'Rourke asked blithely, helping Norene with her coat.

Kate eyed him suspiciously. What new tactic was this? she wondered.

She was still wondering as Jared held her coat and escorted her down the narrow stairs. Once they reached the street, they paired off, she and Jared following the amiably chatting Norene and O'Rourke.

She heard him say, "By the way, Norene, those are very pretty earrings. Are they new?"

Kate experienced a distinct pang of anxiety. Lord knows, she should have expected O'Rourke to pull something shady—such as using an innocently unsuspecting Norene to try to make her jealous. But, good heavens, not once had she even considered that he would be decent enough to like the woman—to treat her with friendliness and respect for her intelligence—and to be genuinely interested in all that highwayman nonsense.

She sighed, vaguely wishing that Jared would be quiet and let her think about this latest turn of events.

Thieves weren't supposed to be kind, damn it. How could she persevere in her campaign against him if he was going to do something as underhanded as turn out to be a sensitive human being.

Chapter Six

Kate was upset. Upset with O'Rourke because he hadn't done the obvious and tried to use Norene to make her jealous—upset with herself because, despite everything, she *was*!

In the middle of the afternoon she had gone down to the writing room, a small study next door to the library. Lord Harwood had informed the guests that a supply of boxes and Christmas paper would be left there for those wishing to wrap items for the gift exchange. After wrapping the rose-colored sweater for Norene, Kate couldn't resist a quick peek into the library as she passed by.

Seeing O'Rourke's head bent close to Norene's, she experienced an uneasy twinge. He was pointing out something in the text of an old book open on the table in front of them, and Norene was gazing raptly...not at the book, but into O'Rourke's face. For a moment, Kate forgot she had given up the right to resent him receiving attention from another woman. She tried to tell herself there was nothing of a flirtatious nature between the two of them—but she was envious of their newfound closeness nonetheless.

O'Rourke looked up and saw her standing there. "Hello, Kate. Have you come to join us?"

She could swear he was aware of what she was feeling, so she made a concentrated effort to appear nonchalant.

"No, I just came down to wrap a gift." She held up the silver foil box. "Thought I'd look in on you as I passed. Finding anything of interest?"

"Oh, my yes," Norene assured her. "Your hus—I mean, O'Rourke is such a clever man. He has ferreted out all sorts of clues."

"Oh?" Kate's enthusiasm left something to be desired. "How fascinating."

He grinned, the dimple taunting her. "Sit down, and we'll tell you all about it."

"No, really, I can't," she protested. "I've got to do a few things to get ready for this evening."

"Well, whatever you say." O'Rourke turned back to the book. "What do you think of this theory, Norene? If the secret passage extended all the way to..."

Kate stood in the doorway several seconds longer, feeling like a pesky child who had just been dismissed by her elders.

It's my own fault, she thought, walking briskly to the lounge where she placed the package she carried beneath the tree. O'Rourke invited me to join them, and I made the decision not to. Therefore, I shouldn't feel so damned left out!

Restless, Kate put on her coat and walked into the village to a shop where earlier she had seen a rack of books. She suddenly felt in need of a diversion. Passing up the thick family sagas popular with the British, she chose two contemporary romances from the States and, in a moment of weakness, a bag of hard candies.

As she walked back to the hotel, she realized the day had grown much colder. The overcast sky seemed to promise some sort of precipitation before evening, and Kate hoped for snow. It would provide the perfect touch for such a beautiful holiday setting.

Lazily she spent the rest of the afternoon curled up in a chair before the fireplace with a pot of tea and one of the novels she'd bought. Her thoughts strayed to O'Rourke once or twice, but each time they did, she silently renumerated her grievances against him, dredging up the old feelings of distrust and betrayal. She needed to make herself remember exactly who he was and not be won over by what he now seemed to be.

Kate had bathed and was already dressed for the theater before O'Rourke came back to their room. As much as she might despise herself for it, she admitted she had begun to be concerned because he hadn't acted like the same man since morning when she had so haughtily returned her wedding ring to him. Deep in her heart, she knew he had not given the ring lightly; perhaps he would not take its return lightly, either.

She stood at the cheval mirror, fastening tiny silver bell earrings in her ears and wondering why she felt so badly about giving back the ring. She should have done it ages ago. Couldn't, in fact, really say what had prompted her to keep wearing it. Maybe it was that she hadn't wanted to admit the failure of her marriage, a basic human relationship that other members of her family seemed to manage so well.

She glanced down at her left hand; its bareness made her sad somehow. By taking off the ring, she apparently had stumbled onto the fastest method of convincing O'Rourke she no longer wanted to maintain any connection between them. But to be honest, she had not expected it to be so difficult for *her* to accept. Watching him draw away from her in the way he had, made her question whether she was as ready to end matters as she thought.

When he walked into the room and stood looking at her, admiration in his eyes and a slow smile on his face, something twisted inside her and she was filled with relief. Even the discovery of such vanity within herself did not diminish the pleasure she felt in knowing his attraction to her had not suddenly vanished.

"You look beautiful, Kate," he said. "The most beautiful woman in the world."

"Oh, come now," she murmured with a small, embarrassed laugh. "Surely not the world?"

"*My* world." He came a step closer and took her hand. "No, I was right the first time. The whole damned world."

Kate feared he was going to kiss her, and she didn't know how to react. It had been a strange day, and her emotions were terribly jumbled. But instead of kissing her, he began turning her so that he could view her from every angle.

"That dress is perfect for you," he stated. "Makes you look like a maiden of old."

"Are you sure you don't mean an old maiden?" she quipped, but he didn't respond in the expected way. He merely put his hands on her shoulders and faced her toward the cheval mirror again.

"Look at yourself. Don't you see what I mean?"

In a way, she thought she did. The gown she wore was full-length, of velvet the same midnight blue as her eyes. The dress itself had a square neck and fell in a slim, straight line from a high waist that started just below her breasts. The jacket was hip length with a small stand-up collar and modified leg-of-mutton sleeves, full above the elbows and tight at the wrists. It did indeed give her an aura of the past, an illusion heightened by the softly poufing hairdo that framed her face. For once, as she studied her reflection, Kate was not startled by her appearance. She was beginning to get used to the fact that she looked completely different outside than she felt inside. Kate Callahan was obviously a complex woman...or women, she thought with a faint smile.

"Kate, what's your middle name? I seem to recall it's something a little unusual."

She glanced up to see him staring intently at her. "You know I never discuss my middle name! It's awful...."

"Kathryn Aurelia...am I right?"

"You sneak—you knew it all the time. Lord, I'll never forgive my mother for giving me such an...antiquated name!"

"*Antiquated* is a good word for it," he said casually.

He started toward the bathroom, then turned to regard her once more. "Did you know that the woman kidnapped by the highwayman was named Lady Aurelia? Odd coincidence, don't you think?"

But before Kate could determine what she actually did think, he had disappeared behind the closed door.

Lord and Lady Harwood entertained their guests royally at a festive Theater Supper in the main dining room. A sparkling white cloth covered the long table, and centerpieces of white carnations with asparagus fern and red streamers were placed on top at intervals. Strewn here and there were papier-mâché masks representing tragedy and comedy. The menus had been printed to look like antique playbills. Young men and women wearing harlequin costumes of black, white and scarlet served the meal of roast wild duck with apricot stuffing.

When the after-dinner coffee and mints had been brought, Lord Harwood rose and signaled for attention by tapping a spoon on a crystal water glass.

"Now, ladies and...harrumph...gentlemen," he announced, "we will be transported to the Theatre Royal in Bath by two minibuses. Not the most elegant way to go, but the...ahem...coziest." He stroked his bristling mustache. "And, I daresay, the most economical."

"Oh, and Cornie, don't forget to warn everyone to bundle up," his wife added. "They tell us the weather is turning a bit nasty outside. I'm certain I shall need something more substantial than this light shawl over my shoulders."

Carolyne Harwood let the fringed shawl slip backward to reveal a gown of jarring fuchsia. She then rested one hand on the broad shelf of her bosom, drawing attention to the brilliance of the necklace she wore. For a few seconds, it was as if every eye in the room were affixed to the artful arrangement of diamonds.

"What a wonderful piece of jewelry," exclaimed Mrs. Phillips, Norene's mother. "It looks very much like the—"

"Star of Pretoria?" questioned Lady Harwood smugly.

"Why, yes. Didn't we read a magazine article about it, Norene? Just recently."

"Yes, in *World Business Weekly*, I believe," Norene replied. "The star-cut diamond around which the necklace was designed is one of the most valuable diamonds to be discovered in the last fifty years."

Lord Harwood rocked back and forth on his feet, beaming proudly.

"Well, you're all simply too clever for us," Lady Harwood said. "This *is* the Star of Pretoria. Cornie read that same article and decided it would be a marvelous investment. He..." she favored her husband with a fond, toothy smile, "...presented it to me for our anniversary. This is the first time I will be wearing it in public."

O'Rourke leaned to whisper into Kate's ear. "Those stones flash like searchlights at an airport. If she isn't careful, she might—"

"End up with a 747 on her chest?" Kate finished with a chuckle.

"Something like that," he agreed, pleased she had fallen into their old repartee with such ease.

"Well, it's certainly stunning," one of the Australian women commented. "I do hope you are well insured."

"Absolutely." Lady Harwood nodded, causing the fat curls pinned atop her head to quiver frantically. "One wouldn't dare be without adequate insurance these days."

Mrs. Phillips leaned forward for a closer inspection of the jewels. "My, they are lovely! So elegant and tasteful." She straightened and cast a severe glance at her daughter. "Not at all like the gaudy jewelry some people prefer."

With the disappointment, Kate noticed that Norene had taken off her gold hoops and replaced them with the more sensible pearls. Norene caught her eye and offered an apologetic smile. Kate smiled back, but the ugliness of the tailored brown suit the librarian was wearing upset her. She had hoped Norene would dress more attractively for the theater—had hoped she might be able to capture Jared Harwood's attention. She was certain that if he would actually *look* at the woman just once, he would see her for the special person she was.

At that moment, Jared came through the doorway, his face reddened by cold despite the heavy topcoat and gloves he wore. "I've just been out to check, and the drivers are ready for us, Dad," he announced. "Before we leave, I want to impress upon everyone that the temperature has plunged. It is quite frigid out there."

"Frigid? What a nasty choice of words," O'Rourke muttered, taking Kate's coat from her. She flashed him a stern look, and he grinned. "You're warning me to behave after that remark you made about the 747? Oh, all right, I'll be good. And you may take *that* any way you please."

"My goodness, you do a longer monologue that Johnny Carson," Kate muttered.

He held the three-quarter-length faux fur coat so she could slip into it, chuckling as he noticed the bold label sewn to the satin lining. Kate herself had designed and commissioned the labels so that she could place them in each of the three furs she owned. In flowing script it read, "This fur is one hundred percent synthetic. I do not believe in the destruction of animal life for human vanity."

O'Rourke had always enjoyed the stir that sentiment caused in certain areas of society. Kate was a hell-raising crusader about such things—about a great many things that really counted. It was one of the qualities he admired most about her, and ironically, the one that had made their marriage an impossibility.

The minibuses were smart maroon-and-tan vehicles with Christmas wreaths hanging from the front grills. As O'Rourke stood assisting several of the ladies so they could manage the high step up, he could feel the sting of icy rain on his face and idly wondered if anyone had bothered to catch a weather forecast.

By the time he got into the bus, he assumed the only seats left would be those directly behind the driver, but to his surprise, the other guests had very thoughtfully left the seat next to Kate empty for him. He had to smile as he settled into it and Kate angled her head away, pretending to stare out the window. He couldn't tell if she was really upset or not.

The sixteen-kilometer journey to Bath did not take long, and they were soon rumbling along the busy streets near the heart of the elegant old spa city. The stately Georgian buildings looked especially pretty decked out in colored lights for the holiday season. O'Rourke leaned forward to point out several famous landmarks as they passed.

"I'd like to bring you back during the day sometime to see the Roman baths," he said. "We could take the waters, as they say, or, if you prefer, have coffee in the Pump Room. And there's an excellent costume museum I think you'd enjoy."

"That would be nice," Kate said mildly, surprising him. Was it his imagination or had she mellowed since yesterday? He smiled to himself as he considered the possibility.

The minibuses stopped in front of the theater, and the passengers dashed inside to avoid the chilling rain now coming down steadily. They were ushered into seats in the balcony only minutes before the first curtain.

The pantomime, long a tradition in England, especially at Christmastime, was a great success. The play enacted on that particular evening was *Cinderella*, but it was a version completely dissimilar to the children's tale. Because this was adult night at the theater, the songs and jokes were exceedingly risqué, causing the ladies to blush and the men to laugh uproariously. The play was a fast-moving combination of story, music-hall revue and variety show.

Kate laughed until she cried over the antics of the three ugly stepsisters, all portrayed by men in garish costumes complete with ludicrous bloomers. At the point in the play when Prince Charming—also an unlikely character, as he was played by a pretty young girl—allowed the stepsisters to try on the glass slipper, she became so amused she automatically turned to O'Rourke to make a comment. She laid a hand on his knee and leaned toward him . . . and then suddenly remembered all the things that had transpired since last they shared an evening at the theater. She would have withdrawn her hand had he not clasped it in his own larger one and drawn it up to rest on his thigh.

"Enjoying yourself, Kate?" he asked in a low voice, a mesmerizing glow in his eyes. She swallowed deeply, then nodded and settled back in her chair. Not wanting to spoil the rare moment of camaraderie between them, she did not pull her hand away, but left it where it was, in the delicious warmth of his. He only released it later when the end of an act called for applause.

The good spirits engendered by the pantomimes very nearly disappeared as the group emerged from the theater into a shockingly cold winter night. The temperature had fallen to a new low, turning the rain to sleet. Ice glazed the streets and buildings, even the trees and fence railings.

"The trip back to Cross Coombe . . . ahem . . . is bloody likely to be treacherous," observed Lord Harwood, handing his wife into the first bus. "Dastardly weather, this."

O'Rourke nodded his agreement. "Good thing we don't have too far to travel."

"Fortunately these minibuses have efficient heating systems," put in Jared Harwood. "Brr, it feels arctic out here!"

The drive around the city was not as bad as anticipated, because the volume of traffic had kept the pavement fairly ice free. Once they got into the countryside, however, the drivers slowed their speed considerably, able only to inch along.

Kate and O'Rourke were seated at one end of the long bench across the back of the bus. Farthest from the heater and with cold air filtering in around the rear window, they soon began to feel the chill. Kate huddled in her coat, won-

dering if it would be too unladylike to kick off her shoes and
sit on her feet. She wriggled her numbed toes, wishing she
had worn boots instead of evening pumps. She shivered, and
O'Rourke responded by moving closer. The contact between their shoulders and thighs generated a comforting
heat.

About halfway back to the hotel, as the bus crept around
a wide curve in the road, a car coming from the opposite
direction lost control and slid into their lane. With a curse,
the bus driver swerved to avoid the vehicle careening toward them, and the minibus skidded dangerously. The tires
struck the edge of the pavement, and the impact was enough
to spin it around and send it sliding into the ditch at the side
of the road. Narrowly missing a huge beech tree, the bus
came to a jarring halt against an earth embankment.

O'Rourke had thrown his arms around Kate and pulled
her away from the wall of the bus, hoping to cushion her if
they crashed.

"Are you all right?" he asked anxiously in the moment
of stunned silence that followed the accident.

Shaken, she nodded and glanced at the other passengers,
relieved to find no sign of injuries.

"Blimey," exclaimed the driver, his eyes wide with fright.
"Blimey!"

"You did a good job," O'Rourke assured him. "If we'd
have hit that tree . . ."

From the outside, Jared and the other driver wrenched
open the sliding door at the side of the bus.

"Is anyone hurt?" asked Jared anxiously.

"No one's injured," the driver answered, "but we're
stuck in this ditch. It'll take a tractor to get us out."

Jared nodded. "The fellow who caused the accident
stopped to say he would phone up a garage, but it may be
hours before they can get someone out here."

"It's too cold to wait for that," O'Rourke stated. "We'll
have to come up with an alternate plan."

"Yes, and a swift decision is imperative," Jared agreed.
"It's getting colder by the minute, and it is dangerous to

leave the other bus stopped on the edge of the carriage-way."

O'Rourke started counting heads. "We're going to have to crowd everyone who'll fit into the other bus and send it on to the hotel. The younger or more warmly dressed of us can wait here until it comes back."

Kate was impressed by the competent manner in which O'Rourke organized the exodus of passengers from the stalled bus. He swiftly determined which passengers most needed to be sent on to the safety of the hotel and then helped them off the tilted minibus.

When the bridegroom from Canada, Weldon Blake, told them his wife, Denise, had struck her head against the win-dow and was experiencing the onset of a painful headache, O'Rourke insisted the two of them be sent with the first bus load.

"You make sure the hotel manager phones a doctor to take a look at your wife," O'Rourke called after the young man. "We don't want to take any chances on spoiling her Christmas."

"Well, Dad says that's about all they can squeeze in," Jared finally announced. They had taken just over half the passengers. "I'll send them on and then come back to keep you company. It may be a long wait, so sit tight."

O'Rourke made his way back to the corner where Kate sat, somewhat warmer since she had succumbed to the temptation to take off her shoes and tuck her feet beneath her. He dropped down beside her and flung an arm along the back of the seat.

"Cold?" he asked.

"Positively frigid."

He chuckled, and his breath fanned her ear. "No, I'll be-lieve anything but that," he murmured suggestively.

She tossed her head and the bell earrings tinkled faintly. "You haven't felt my toes lately."

His dimple flashed in the dim light. "No, I haven't. Per-haps we'll have to remedy that situation."

Jared ducked back into the bus, sliding the door shut behind him. After a brief discussion with the driver, it was decided to keep the engine running, but with one window slightly open to guard against carbon monoxide poisoning.

"Don't want anything to turn this into a real tragedy," Jared said. "It'll be colder that way, but infinitely safer. For the time being, I suggest that everyone find a seatmate and cuddle up for warmth. Nothing like sharing body heat with someone to instigate new friendships."

"Or renew old ones," added O'Rourke just loud enough for Kate to hear. "Care to share a little body heat, Kate, my girl?"

She would have declined on principle had not a violent shiver racked her frame. Before she could object, O'Rourke hauled her onto his lap, sliding into the corner to brace his back against the rear wall of the bus.

"What do you think you're doing?" she whispered.

"Trying to keep my vital parts from freezing," he replied calmly. "Even you have to admit this is better."

"Better than what?" she snapped, but, despite herself, snuggled closer to his overpowering warmth.

Jared watched them for a few seconds with a rather resigned expression on his face, then slid into the seat ahead of them, his broad shoulder brushing Norene's. The librarian gave him a startled glance, then looked hastily away. Sharing body heat was obviously not something she was familiar with.

"You know," O'Rourke observed, "I think we might be warmer if we'd use your coat as a blanket. Here, slip your arms inside my topcoat and let me throw yours over us."

His instructions gave her a legitimate excuse to do something she had thought about all evening long, Kate realized. She half turned, fitting her body against his, her arms sliding inside his coat and then, of their own volition, around his waist. Her head came to rest just below his chin, and her nostrils were filled with the wonderfully masculine, exciting scent of the man who held her. He always had the faintly spicy odor of a subtle, expensive men's cologne, but tonight there was also the clean smell of soap and the starched freshness of the shirt he wore. Kate rubbed her cheek against the brushed wool of his suit and permitted herself one small, silent sigh of contentment.

O'Rourke tucked the fur around them both, then brought his hands back beneath it, letting them settle lightly around Kate. The feel of her in his arms again filled him with a variety of emotions, not the least of which was a guilty gratitude for the circumstance that had brought about their present closeness. Something in the way she clung to him seemed to indicate her motives went beyond merely warming herself.

"Didn't I tell you body-to-body contact would be better?" he whispered.

"I'll admit I'm warmer," she conceded.

"So am I," he heartily agreed.

"Except for my feet. They're like two chunks of ice."

"Here, let me rub them." Keeping one arm curved around her, he used his free hand to pull her stockinged feet close to the outside of his thigh, gently massaging them.

"Mmm," she purred. "That feels wonderful."

"You should have worn something more sensible on your feet," he growled.

"You're right," she said amiably.

Movement in the seat ahead of them caught their attention, and they watched in surprise as Jared, murmuring something inaudible to Norene, slipped an arm about her shoulders and pulled her close to his side.

"Good. She's not objecting," Kate uttered in a low voice.

"She's far too intelligent not to accept aid when it's offered," O'Rourke returned.

Kate drew back to look into his face. "You really admire Norene, don't you?"

"Of course. She's got a lot of admirable qualities."

"And she certainly admires you."

"I did mention that she is intelligent, didn't I?"

Kate stiffened. "Why didn't you perpetuate your mutual admiration society by volunteering to keep her warm?"

She could feel a laugh rumble deep inside his chest.

"Katie, are you disgruntled—maybe even a little jealous—because I spent time with Norene this afternoon?"

"Don't flatter yourself!"

"For a woman with blue eyes, yours sure are looking green tonight," he commented dryly. "You can't blame me for wondering."

"Maybe not, but I can certainly blame you for a number of other things."

He smiled down at her. "Now you sound more like the old Kate. Testy as hell."

She made a face at him. "Testy, maybe. But not jealous."

"Good, because I like Norene too much to use her friendship that way."

"Friendship?"

"That's all it is, Kate, believe me."

"Not that it matters, but if you weren't trying to make me jealous, what were you trying to do?"

"Make Jared jealous."

"What?"

"Well, actually, I was trying to get him to take a good look at Norene...and leave you alone."

"Really?" Pleased that their minds had been operating in a similar vein once again, she nestled even closer to him.

O'Rourke's hand stopped moving over her feet while he savored the sensations created by her motion. As she pressed the softness of her breasts against his chest, the hardness of her hip was brought into contact with his own and a sharp flash of desire spread upward, threatening to overpower him.

This is not the time or the place, he thought.

"Katie, darlin', please don't wiggle," he pleaded. "You don't know what it is doing to me."

"Oh, yes, I do," she whispered.

Her eyes were dark and fathomless as she looked up at him, her lips softly parted. The invitation was unmistakable, and O'Rourke was in no mood to deny himself. He lowered his mouth to hers just as the driver let out a loud shout.

"Thank the Lord, they're back for us. All right, folks, prepare to abandon ship."

O'Rourke favored Kate with a rueful smile. "To be continued later..." he promised.

Once they had transferred to the other minibus, the journey back to Cross Coombe Manor was accomplished without further difficulty. Though it was no longer necessary, O'Rourke insisted Kate remain on his lap, and she offered no objection.

As he cradled her, O'Rourke grew increasingly more daring, letting one hand creep upward from her waist toward the swell of her breast, the other along her thigh and eventually over her hip to rest firmly against the soft curve of her velvet-clad bottom. Advising himself to be patient, he ventured no more, and consequently Kate slowly relaxed, falling asleep before they reached the hotel.

She awakened when the other passengers began stirring, and though O'Rourke gallantly offered, she refused to be carried inside. Yet, after slipping on her coat and shoes, she did take his arm, allowing him to escort her from the bus up the icy front steps of the manor. Inside the entryway they were greeted by the hotel manager, the Harwoods and Mrs. Phillips.

"Glad to...harrumph...see everyone arrive safely at last," boomed His Lordship. "Come on into the lounge. We've got hot chocolate waiting."

"Sounds good," said O'Rourke, looking questioningly at Kate. "Shall we?"

She took off her coat and returned his look with a sleepy smile. "You go ahead. I think I'll run along to bed if you don't mind."

"Sensible idea," affirmed Mrs. Phillips. "Norene, you really should do the same."

"Yes, Mother," Norene murmured obediently. "I do feel tired. Shall I walk you up, Kate?"

"That would be nice. Good night, everyone."

Kate's eyes lingered on O'Rourke, but he was unable to discern their expression. He wanted nothing more than to follow her up the stairs then and there, but knew instinctively that it was not a good idea. He'd better have a drink first and get his feelings under control.

But, he assured himself, I won't be drinking hot chocolate. I'd better opt for something a shade more . . . cooling.

He heard a tiny gasp from Mrs. Phillips and glanced up. Her disapproving gaze was fixed on the two women climbing the stairs. Lord and Lady Harwood were watching them also, and, with a quirk of his mustache, Lord Harwood screwed his monocle into one eye and took a second, harder look. O'Rourke followed the stare and found himself trying to stifle an emotion that was half amusement and half sensual reaction.

There, branded into the nap of the velvet gown Kate wore, was the sharply defined imprint of his hand splayed possessively across her lovely derriere!

Chapter Seven

O'Rourke forced himself to stay in the lounge for at least thirty minutes, but all the time he was chatting with the other guests, his thoughts were on Kate.

He couldn't seem to close his mind to vivid images of her getting ready for bed. He saw her unzipping the blue velvet gown and stepping out of it; he pictured her clad in a delectable undergarment similar to the red one he had hidden away in the bottom of his suitcase. His attention fully captured, he watched as the Kate in his vision lifted a hand to brush a thin strap off her shoulder, letting the teddy slide lower, revealing a tantalizing glimpse of swelling flesh. He quickly wrenched his mind away from that impression, purposely conjuring up the safer image of Kate in her mannish pajamas. But the scene playing in his head was so real that mentally he reached out to touch her and experienced the erotic sensation of jade silk sliding over petal-soft skin.

A hearty laugh from across the room disturbed his thoughts, causing him to plunge into the present once more. He felt as though he had just risen from a hypnotist's couch, a bit relaxed and groggy but aware of a rising tide of energy within himself. He knew he couldn't sit there calmly any longer. He had to know what Kate was doing.

To his disappointment, the bedroom was dark except for the fireplace and a soft glow cast by a bedside lamp. Kate must have already gone to bed.

O'Rourke quietly shut the door and stood still a few seconds to let his eyes adjust. In the silence, he could hear the brittle tapping of frozen rain striking the windows.

Though the bedcovers were neatly turned back, the bed was empty. It took him a moment to realize Kate had pulled a chair and ottoman together near the fire and was lying on them, a blanket pulled up to her chin. He knelt beside her and put a hand on her shoulder.

She stirred sleepily. "Mmm?"

"What do you think you are doing?" he softly demanded. "You can't sleep here."

"Why not?" she mumbled, turning to face him.

"If anyone is sleeping here, it'll be me."

"I think I fit better than you do."

"Don't be stubborn about this, Kate. Go get into bed."

She shook her head. "No, really. This is fine. I feel guilty about you sleeping on the floor last night...so this is my way of making it up to you."

"I can think of better ways," he teased, keeping his voice light.

"But it's all I'm offering," she responded. "Go on, you take the bed."

"Kate..."

"I'll be fine right here. The fire's warm, and this chair is actually rather comfortable."

"But you do know the bed is big enough for both of us?"

"Ha—you're saying that to someone who didn't think Kansas City was big enough!" She yawned. "I'm already settled for the night, so do me a favor. Would you please get into that bed and make me a happy woman?" She grimaced and held up a negating hand. "Strike that," she muttered. "Just sleep in the bed, okay?"

He grinned. "Okay...but promise me that if you get cold or need anything, you'll wake me up."

"I promise."

"Good girl." He tilted his head appealingly. "Want to kiss me good-night?"

She looked at him with an odd expression, "Yes, but I'm not going to. It's definitely against my better judgment."

"How so?"

She sighed and flopped back onto her makeshift bed. "O'Rourke, be a nice fellow and go to bed."

He stood, hands on his hips. "You know, it's pretty damned demeaning for a grown man to be patted on the head and told to run along. Especially when he has . . . well, when he has what I have on my mind on his mind."

"Huh?"

"Forget it."

"Toss that last log onto the fire, will you?"

For a second, he looked as if he might be considering tossing her into the flames, but finally his better nature won out and he did her bidding.

What had he expected, after all?

It was three o'clock in the morning. Lying on his side, only half asleep, O'Rourke had just heard the muted chimes of the bedside clock when he felt the mattress shift and knew someone was getting into bed with him. Suddenly a small, cold hand grazed over his shoulder, sliding down the length of his arm . . . and back up again.

"Kate?" he murmured, disbelieving.

Instead of answering, she crept closer and, to his surprise, snuggled against him, fitting her body to his. Her breasts were flattened against his back, and her hips cradled his buttocks. He could feel her legs behind his, thigh to thigh. She burrowed one arm beneath him, curling it around to let her fingers twine themselves into the thick hair on his naked chest. Her other hand rested momentarily on his hip, then moved upward to slip just beneath the elastic waistband of his pajama pants as if seeking warmth. O'Rourke's mouth went dry at the feel of her cool fingers upon his stomach.

"Katie, for heaven's sake," he whispered in agitation. He managed a small chuckle. "I'm positively rigid . . . with indignation. How's a man supposed to get any sleep?"

She didn't reply to his teasing, but he felt the warmth of her breath flutter over his spine and thought she might be trying to stifle a laugh . . . or a sigh.

O'Rourke sensed that it had not been easy for her to make the decision to come to him. She had spent far too much time vehemently denying any attraction between them for it to have been. But the sheer exhilaration of heated blood zinging through his veins made him very grateful for whatever impulse was urging her on, and he was willing to do anything it took to cooperate. He grinned in the darkness, thinking of the welcome he'd like to give Kate. It would be one neither of them would soon forget. . . .

She wriggled even closer, and all thoughts—the noble as well as the lascivious—fled his mind. How could he think when he was so overpoweringly aware of her full breasts pressing into his back? Her taut stomach and hips tightly molded to his backside? A low, involuntary groan was torn from his throat as she shifted position enough to throw one leg over his, rubbing a chilled foot up and down against the calf of his leg. The motion bumped her pelvis into his buttocks with a gently sensuous rhythm, causing him to clench his teeth and fight for control. The thought of simply rolling over and capturing her beneath him was so tempting he wasn't certain he could resist it—even knowing it would be the worst thing he could do. He had to hold himself in check, let her be the aggressor. Kate's pride was sometimes a fragile commodity, and he dared not rush this long-anticipated reunion.

"Ah, love," she mumbled, making him strain to hear her low words. "I've missed you so much."

"I've missed you, too, Katie...more than you'll ever know."

She pressed her face to his shoulder, and he felt as though he were being branded by the tiny nibbling kisses she placed there. The pleasure of her touch was mixed with remembered pain and useless regrets; he was experiencing a sweet agony, an exquisite torture.

He wanted her badly, but he'd be a liar if he didn't admit he still harbored some resentment for he way she had assumed him guilty—and for the way she had turned against him without even giving him a chance to explain. On the other hand, he recognized that the horror of her father's death had preempted rational thinking about certain matters. Kate couldn't help her reaction to something that triggered such painful memories...or at least, she couldn't at the time.

He realized there was probably only one way for them to get beyond their stalemate. It was going to take the immersion of each in the other—both physically and mentally—to break the cycle of solitary thinking, to make them a couple again. It would only be as a couple that they could sort out their differences and find the forgiveness and love necessary to heal their ailing relationship.

Kate's hand stroked lower across his stomach and, with a muffled gasp, he seized it in his own, stilling her provocative exploration. Without further consideration, he cast caution aside and turned toward her. As he did so, the bedcovers slipped, baring his shoulder and alerting him to the fact the air in the room was biting cold.

"Hell, Kate." He sighed, drawing the covers over both of them and slipping his arms about her. "You were cold, weren't you?"

She murmured something he couldn't hear and inched closer, resting her head against his chest.

"Oh, well...if that's what it took." He buried his face in the silkiness of her hair and drew a long, unsteady breath. "I'm just glad to have you back where you belong, darlin'."

The scent of her hair filled his nostrils, reminding him of a sun-hazed field of herbs and wildflowers, a delightfully elusive and fresh odor that teased his senses unmercifully.

He'd never thought of himself as an especially emotional man, but at that moment he knew he was on shaky ground. Naturally he was responding to her physical proximity, but there was something else—a whole-again feeling that made him reject the idea of ever letting her go again.

O'Rourke loved Kate, and had since the first instant he'd seen her, but even so, he found himself surprised at his sudden understanding of the depth and breadth of that love. The reality of it seemed to transcend the mere years of his life or Kate's; it stretched forward and backward as far as human imagination could project, unfurling into infinity like a shining silver ribbon. Somehow he knew that, for each of them, there would be no existence without the other. It was as simple as that.

Kate raised her face and, with eyes closed, sought his mouth. The soft crush of her lips fell first on his chin, then on the corner of his mouth. Hands spanning her ribs, he lifted her up and into the curve of his body, hungrily fitting his mouth to hers.

Despite his intention to proceed slowly, he couldn't harness the untamed energy of the kiss. The past months of lonely frustration took over and moved him beyond the reach of reason. Every thinking, feeling cell of his fevered brain was concentrated on the sensations generated by the feel of Kate's moist lips, aggressive and submissive by turns. He had been starving for this! He could no more have drawn away than a beggar could have refused a feast.

When she finally pulled back from him to rest her face against his neck, he could feel the rapid, erratic pounding of a heart, but he couldn't tell if it was his own or Kate's.

O'Rourke let his hand slide over the sleekness of the silk pajama top she wore, fingertips tentatively smoothing the rounded side of her breast, thumb searching for and finding the firm surging proof of her instinctive response. Emboldened by her reaction, he strengthened his caress and was rewarded by Kate's utterance of a low, sobbing moan. The raggedly uncontrolled sound sent a flare of desire thrumming through him, and he began undoing the buttons of her pajamas with trembling fingers. He pushed the fragile fabric aside and let his hand cup her softness.

As her stimulated nipple brushed his palm, a passionate urgency overtook him. He shifted her onto her back, pressing her into the pillows and raising his own body so that it half covered her. He began whispering mindless love words into her ear, arching his hips against her.

"Oh!"

"Katie," he muttered, lost in sensation and need.

"O'Rourke," she gasped, struggling violently. "What . . . what is going on? Let me go!"

The scattered threads of his sanity twisted about in his mind, trying desperately to weave themselves back into some kind of order. He heard her shocked exclamation and felt the heels of her hands slamming into his chest, but his first inclination was to ignore her protest. Damn, they had been so close to . . . *something*! Something that, at this moment, seemed absolutely and utterly essential to his survival. He needed her, needed the release she offered . . . needed the fulfillment of being with her again.

With a despairing groan, he moved away and flung himself back onto his own pillow, one arm across his face.

"Damn it, Kate," he rasped. "What are you trying to do to me?"

"To you? What were *you* trying to do to *me*?"

"I thought it was rather obvious."

"How could you?" She sat upright in bed and, when her open pajama top fell away to reveal breasts heaving in indignation, gave a small horrified scream.

"You...you maniac!" she ground out between clenched jaws.

He removed his arm and stared at her, puzzled. "How is it I'm the maniac when you're the one who crawled into my bed? Hell, practically into my pants, if you want the truth."

"I did nothing of the kind!" she stormed, fumbling with the pajama buttons. Then, more uncertainly, "Did I?"

"How else would you have gotten here?" he queried less than patiently.

"You didn't . . . ?"

"No, I didn't."

"I don't understand. How could I have crossed the room and gotten into this bed without remembering it?"

"Did you know that you walk in your sleep, Kate?"

"I do not! At least, I don't think I do."

"You did last night. I didn't say anything because I didn't want to worry you."

"Didn't want to worry me . . . or didn't want to flub up a chance to . . . to get me into your bed?"

"For what purpose?" He sat up, also. His tone was dangerous.

"For the usual reason men lure women into their beds."

"Being a little Victorian, aren't you? You should remember that I don't have to *lure* bed partners." He seized her arm and pulled her face-to-face with him. "And when I make love to a woman, I'd prefer that she be awake and responding, if you don't mind."

"I don't mind," she said sarcastically, "as long as *she's* not me."

"You know, maybe I'm the one being duped," he drawled. "I'm not sure you really were asleep. In fact, speaking of responding, you were doing a damned good job of it for a while." A nasty grin twitched the corners of his mouth. "You're a clever woman, Kate—did you pretend to be sleepwalking so you'd have an excuse to creep into bed with me?"

She jerked her arm free, eyes blazing. "What a horrid insinuation!"

"Well, considering your actions, what else am I supposed to think?"

"I couldn't care less."

"You surely don't deny that you acted like some aggressive little passionflower, do you?"

"My God, of course I do! I couldn't possibly have acted like that."

"Oh? And why not?"

"Call me foolish, but maybe, just maybe, there has to be something to respond to!"

"Meaning . . . ?"

"Meaning that there isn't anything you could possibly do to . . . well, to sexually stimulate me."

"Oh, yeah?" he growled. "Care to put it to the test?"

"Don't be ridiculous," she snapped. But he noticed she had begun a stealthy retreat to the edge of the bed. Tossing the covers aside, he followed. With a cry of alarm, Kate leaped to her feet and started backing away.

"Don't come near me," she cautioned harshly. "Don't you dare lay one hand on me."

"Coward," he taunted softly.

"I'm not. I have nothing to fear from you."

"Who's talking about me? You're really afraid of yourself."

"I am not."

"Prove it."

"I don't have to prove a thing to you."

"I'd have agreed . . . before you challenged my abilities," he commented dryly, stalking her as she retreated.

"I take it back, then. Leave me alone, will you please?"

"Surely you're interested in the outcome of this experiment?"

"No, I'm not."

"And you pride yourself on being a modern woman," he chided. "Where's your sense of adventure? A mere man is calling your bluff. Doesn't that inspire you?"

"Look, O'Rourke, I'll give you my answer in words of one syllable . . . so you'll understand. No! No, but hell, no!"

"No? Where's all your big talk now, Katie?" He backed her right into the wall, his hands moving swiftly to capture her shoulders. "Put your convictions where your . . . mouth . . . is."

His eyes lingered on her slightly parted lips, his gaze searing in its intensity. Kate felt the old familiar liquid heat rising from the pit of her stomach to spread through every limb, undermining her resolve, weakening her so that she sagged beneath his hands.

"O'Rourke!" Her pleading whisper revealed her vulnerability, her fear.

He contemplated her pale face, framed by tumbled chestnut hair. It was dominated by her eyes, huge and dark, the blue nearly obscured by the wide pools of her pupils.

Deliberately he brought his gaze back to her mouth and slowly, purposefully lowered his head to take her lips with his own. In that second, all fight went out of Kate. She was mastered, albeit willingly. She was conquered and claimed....

The kiss was like a draft of cool water after parching thirst, and when it ended, they were both gasping for breath, their eyes locked in mutual realization. Though nothing had altered the difficulties they faced, *this* was still between them. This attraction, this drawing together...this love.

Light from the window struck the lower half of O'Rourke's face, leaving the upper part in shadow. As Kate stared up at him, she was suddenly stricken with the somewhat incoherent thought that, with the strip of darkness across his eyes, he looked very much as the highwayman would have looked. And, like poor Lady Aurelia, it wasn't the loss of her life she had to fear. Rather, it was the loss of her heart, her reason... very possibly, her mortal soul. The thief who took those things was far more dangerous than the one satisfied with mere gold and jewels.

O'Rourke's hands had fallen from her shoulders to her waist. Now they spread across her back, drawing her into his embrace again. Something of the chill in the room penetrated her abstracted mind, and she pressed herself into his warmth. This time when he kissed her, her arms crept upward to encircle his neck and her fingers sought the thickness of his hair.

Hot and ardent, his mouth played over hers, wringing an almost frenzied response from her. She struggled closer, and he pulled her high against his chest so that she was nearly hanging in his arms. With a minimum of effective moves, O'Rourke lowered her to the upholstered fainting couch along the wall.

Kate felt the unyielding couch beneath her and O'Rourke's weight on top of her.

"Oh!" she exclaimed with a throaty laugh. "I didn't realize it was so hard!"

He groaned. "No time for jokes, Kate."

"Who's joking?" she gasped breathlessly. "It's like a rock! No wonder you couldn't sleep on it—that can't be good for a person."

"You're telling me," he muttered, rolling away from her.

"O'Rourke...?"

He sat on the edge of the couch, head in his hands.

"What's wrong?" she queried, closing the distance between them and laying an arm over his shoulders.

He turned his head and looked at her. "You know, we're worse off than a pair of teenagers in the throes of puberty."

"What do you mean?"

"Hell, look at us. Here we are, hot to trot, or so you'd think, by the way we've been cavorting around this room for the last thirty minutes. So why don't we go ahead and get it over with?"

"Because it's not something to be gotten over with," she stated.

"Exactly."

"You're agreeing?"

"It's not unheard of."

"But rare, you have to admit."

"Look, Katie, let's just lay our cards on the table. I want, like hell, to make love to you. Here and now. But..."

"But?"

"But the time isn't right. I believe I effectively proved my ability to...stimulate you...." An amused glow came and went in his blue eyes. "But to make things right between us, you're going to have to decide you want me."

"I do want you," she whispered in voice so low he could barely hear it.

"No, I don't mean just that way," he said. "We could spend the night making up for the past six months, but in the morning, chances are, you'd still be angry and upset and distrusting. We've got to settle our other differences before we turn our libidos loose."

"I'm not convinced those things can be settled."

"They can't be if you're not willing to hear me out. To give me a chance to explain."

"Right now?"

"No, it's too late, and we're too aroused by other, more earthy issues. I think we'd better call it a night and work on our problems tomorrow. It's going to take a long, long talk…and then some. You'll have to be willing to trust me."

She wrapped her arms about herself and shivered in the cold night air. "You don't ask for much, do you?"

"Look, darlin', I happen to think it's important. You don't know how easy it would be to simply take you back to bed and do what my body is telling me I'm a blasted fool for not doing." He reached out to take one of her hands in his. "But, sweetheart, I'm going for broke. If we talk first, before we sleep together, there's every chance we can salvage our relationship…and our marriage. I want that more than anything else."

"I think I understand what you're saying."

"Katie, there's only one thing more appealing than the thought of having you tonight . . . and that's the thought of having you for the rest of my life." He pulled her close and, with a hand at the back of her neck, moved her face to his, brushing a softly tender kiss upon her mouth. "Nothing less could keep me from you, darlin'. Nothing."

Using their old signal, he gave her hand three short, quick squeezes, then before she could speak, stood up and scooped her into his arms. He carried her across the room and dropped her onto the rumpled bed.

"Now, I don't want any argument from you, woman. You're sleeping here . . . with me. It's too cold to sleep anywhere else."

"But I thought you just said . . ."

"I did, and I meant it. You stay on your side of the bed, and I'll stay on mine. What could be easier? We're adults, for God's sake!"

"All right," she said meekly, burrowing beneath the covers. "Good night, O'Rourke."

"Good night, Katie. Thanks for another stimulating evening."

"Humph."

An hour later, as he tossed and turned, tormented by the faint, perfumed aroma of her sleep-warmed body stretched out next to him and her fragrant hair spread over the pillow close by his head, he cursed himself for the worst idea of his life. But . . . as bad as it was . . . he lacked the strength of will to remove himself from the bed and sleep by the nearly dead fire.

Sleet rattled on the glass as a wintry wind tore at the eaves. He could hear the creaking of the hotel sign in the gale.

With a shiver, he allowed himself to inch a little nearer to Kate, and she stirred in her sleep, sidling toward him. Their companionable closeness evoked memories of married life. Memories that were both poignant and promising.

O'Rourke stared upward into the darkness of the tester bed. He'd made considerable progress, or he wouldn't be here beside her now. And even though tonight's gamble might cost him hours of sleeplessness and the nagging ache of unfulfilled passion, something—some cheerful, singing, confident *something* deep inside told him it was going to be worth it.

Chapter Eight

Drowsily Kate opened one eye and peered at the bedside clock. It was already a quarter past nine, though if the darkness of the room was any indication, the day outside must be gloomy and overcast. The thought sent a chilling shiver through her, and she snuggled deeper into the cozy warmth of the bed. She could stay there all day....

The nudge of a knee against her hip startled her, causing her head to whip about on the pillow.

O'Rourke! How could she have forgotten that she was lying in bed with O'Rourke? She had to get out of there....

But before she could fling the covers aside, some stubborn perversity in her soul made her pause. Made her take advantage of the moment to fill her heart with the once-familiar image of him asleep beside her.

He lay on his stomach, with his arms beneath him. She wanted to believe he was trying to prevent himself from reaching for her in his sleep, but instead of malicious satisfaction, the thought merely filled her with a soft stirring of pleasure.

His face was turned toward her, his profile clearly defined against the whiteness of the pillow. His hair tumbled forward, enticing in its unruliness, and long black lashes swept the high plane of his cheekbone. Kate thought he looked tired, as if he hadn't rested well, and an undeniable sympathy rose within her.

Ruefully she had to admit to herself that no matter what, this man had always had the ability to elicit powerful emotion from her. In the beginning, love and passion; later, despair and distrust and, she had thought, hatred. Now—though she was still confused that such a thing could be—his reappearance in England had made her realize they had come full circle. Not sure if she wanted to acknowledge it or not, she knew they were back to love and passion.

Somehow, the passion was easier to accept. But the love was still there, maybe stronger than ever.

It would have to be stronger, she told herself, easing from the bed, because I must love him enough to overlook what he is and what he has done.

Though the hotel brochure had boasted central heat, it simply wasn't what Kate had expected. The bedroom had been so chilly that she had dressed in the bathroom, practically standing on top of a small heater in there. She had draped her clothing over the heated towel rack, a luxury she would enjoy having back home, and dressed in a mad scramble. She simply wasn't acclimatized yet.

She put on the warmest things she had brought—a burgundy cowl-neck sweater with a matching thigh-length cardigan and navy wool slacks with faint burgundy pinstripes.

Downstairs, as most of the other guests who were up and about, she gravitated toward the blazing fire in the lounge. Just as she decided her slacks were probably at the point of bursting into flame, she saw Norene hurry past the doorway and decided to catch up with her.

"Norene, wait," she called. "Where are you going?"

The librarian's face lit up. She held out a flat cardboard box.

"I'm off to the study to wrap this for the gift exchange."

"I'll tag along, if you don't mind."

"Of course I don't mind. In fact, if you would, I'd like for you to tell me what you think of the gift I purchased. I'm not certain it will do."

Inside the small study, Norene opened the box and drew forth a crisply starched Victorian nightgown with a low, embroidered lace neckline and a wide ruffled hem.

Kate stroked the soft ecru cotton. "Why, it's lovely!"

"Do you think so? I got it for Denise Blake...you know, the newlywed. But it came from an antique shop. It's not new."

"That shouldn't matter a bit. I'll bet Mrs. Blake will be thrilled you found such a treasure within the price range."

"Well, I wouldn't have if it hadn't been for O'Rourke."

Kate's eyes widened. "O'Rourke? What does he have to do with this?"

"While we were reading up on the highwayman legend, I happened to mention that I hadn't finished all my shopping and he offered to help me find something for Denise. Said he had a few things of his own to buy."

"Are you telling me that you and O'Rourke went shopping together? And that he helped you choose this nightgown?"

Norene nodded. "Actually, he saw it first and suggested it might be nice for a new bride." She blushed. "I would never have thought of it."

"Trust O'Rourke to have his finger on the pulse," Kate said dryly.

"The wonderful thing about it is that the gown looked rather rumpled in the shop, lying in a heap of old garments. Not really something you'd even notice. But your hus—excuse me, O'Rourke convinced me it could be washed and pressed. The hotel laundress just got it back to me a short while ago, and I have to admit, he was right. I only hope Denise Blake will think so, too."

"If she doesn't, she's a pretty poor excuse for a romantic."

Norene refolded the gown and placed it back into the tissue-lined box. Reaching for a roll of wrapping paper printed with holly leaves, she smiled. "A romantic—how nice to be that sort of person. I must confess, I envy you, Kate."

"Me? You think I'm a romantic?"

Norene giggled softly. "I don't know about that. What I meant was, I envy you having a romantic in love with you."

Flustered by the casual remark, Kate turned away to look out the window. A weak wintry sun struggled to force its way through a thick layer of gray clouds. A coating of ice still covered every tree limb and blade of grass.

"Norene, I thought I explained the situation between O'Rourke and me."

"Oh, you did," the other woman answered over the rustling of paper. "I know you're not married anymore, and I know you aren't certain of your feelings for O'Rourke. But, Kate, I'd have to be even more naive than I am not to see how much he loves you. Good heavens, he reveals it in every word he says, every look he casts in your direction."

To conceal the erratic beating of her heart, Kate didn't speak. Instead, she concentrated on drawing designs on the frosted windowpane.

"He's a fascinating man, Kate," Norene continued. "I can't think why you risk letting some other woman get her hands on him."

"Is there...some other woman?" Kate heard herself ask.

"Lord, there'd be dozens of them if he ever gave any indication he was interested. Fortunately for you, he only wants his wife."

Kate turned to face her. "Norene," she said sternly, "did O'Rourke recruit you to plead his cause?"

Norene unrolled red ribbon from a spool. "No, he did not," she said calmly. "But it's evident how he feels. And something tells me you are beginning to find yourself in a similar frame of mind."

"Don't be silly. What would make you think that?"

With a smile that looked suspiciously like a smirk, Norene pointed to the window. "Your artwork, for one thing."

Kate spun around, dismayed to see she had drawn a series of hearts across the frosted window. Inside each one were the initials *O'RC*.

"Oh, my Lord," she sighed, hastily rubbing out the incriminating evidence. "How adolescent!" When she faced Norene again, it was with a wry grimace. "Oh, all right," she admitted. "Tried and convicted. But what in the hell am I going to do about it?"

"Just tell him."

"How can I?"

"I'm positive you'll find an appropriate moment."

"It isn't the timing that bothers me. I meant, how can I simply forget the past? What he did?"

"You can . . . and you should."

"But you don't know what—"

"Yes, I do. He told me. And I think you should put it behind you, Kate, and go for what is really the most important thing—your happiness and O'Rourke's." She flung down the scissors she held. "Oh, listen to me, giving advice! As if I . . . as if I know the first thing about living or being happy. . . ."

"Norene, what's wrong?" Kate felt helpless in the face of the frustration she sensed the other woman was feeling.

"Oh, I don't know. Everything, it seems."

"What do you mean?"

"Since meeting you and O'Rourke, I've realized how utterly worthless and dreary my own life is. I've taken a good look at myself, and I hate what I see."

"You shouldn't feel that way."

"There's no need to be kind," Norene said stiffly. "I'm a plain, mousy, dishwater-dull *librarian*. And no matter how much I might want to be, I'll never be like you. And I'll never find a man like O'Rourke to love me. And I never knew before how darned much I want that!"

Kate was appalled by the tears that had sprung into Norene's eyes. Her own psychological state was such that if the woman really started to cry, there was no guarantee she could prevent herself from joining in. It could turn out to be a pretty soggy Christmas Eve!

"Norene," she said in her best imitation of a prosecuting attorney's voice. "Get ahold of yourself. It isn't like you to be so maudlin."

Norene managed a watery smile. "See what I mean? Not even you can believe that I am capable of indulging in the usual human emotions."

"It isn't that at all. I just don't understand why you think of yourself in such an unflattering way."

"Because I'm homely...."

"You are not!"

"And have the personality of a piece of chalk..."

"You do not!"

"And the sex appeal of a ... of a ... baked squash!"

"Oh, for crying out loud," Kate exclaimed, exasperated. "Look, I've known O'Rourke long enough to know he would not spend an entire afternoon with anyone who even faintly resembled baked squash! Now, if he thinks you're fascinatingly intelligent and interesting, why can't you believe other men would, too?"

"Maybe he is just kinder than most."

"Or maybe you're used to selling yourself short?"

"No, it's more than that. I'm not attractive in any way."

"How can you say that?"

"I've heard my mother say it often enough."

"That's no reason."

"Then what about Jared Harwood? He doesn't even know I exist."

"He seemed to do a good job of keeping you warm last night."

"It was freezing out there in the minibus. He was worried about himself as much as anyone. I'm sure he won't give me a second thought."

Kate laid a hand on Norene's arm. "Does it matter that much to you?"

Norene composed her face and went back to her gift-wrapping. "No, not at all."

"Talk to me, for heaven's sake," Kate remonstrated. "Listen, Norene, if it does matter, if you really want Jared to notice you, I think I can help."

Norene's hands stilled instantly, but she refused to look up. After a moment, she began to fuss with the bow she had created. "Wh-what do you mean?" she managed to say. Her hazel eyes widened. "You're not going to say anything to him, are you? Oh, please don't!"

"Trust me," Kate said, tapping her chin with a slim forefinger. "I'm not going to say a word to Jared. But I have an idea...."

"An idea?"

Kate beamed at her apprehensive friend. "Norene, I want you to come up to my room at least an hour before dinner tonight."

"All...right."

"And be prepared to put yourself entirely into my hands."

"But...how is that going to affect Jared?"

"My dear, just be patient and you will see. I have a feeling it is going to affect him very much." She winked broadly. "And he deserves it. He's an attractive man, but a bit dense and self-contained. I think we should put an end to all that."

"I really don't understand, Kate. Couldn't you explain what you have in mind?"

"You'll see soon enough."

Norene coughed lightly. "Uh, Kate, this plan of yours...is it something my mother will approve of?"

"I'll be honest with you, Norene. I doubt very much whether your mother would approve of any scheme that might cause you to get involved with a man."

"Yes, she does seem to discourage such things. But she's afraid of being left alone, you see."

"I can understand that, but you cannot sacrifice your own freedom for her sake. Look, I know it's a tough decision to make, but the only way my idea will work is if you have already made up your mind you will go along with what I say, regardless of your mother. Promise me you'll think about it?''

"I promise." Norene laughed halfheartedly. "I doubt very much that I shall think of anything else the rest of the day."

"If you don't come to my room, I'll assume you've changed your mind. But, oh, Norene, I hope you'll come. I think tonight could be so important for you." Kate glanced down at her left hand, seeing the pale circle where her wedding band had been. When she looked up again, her eyes were dark with determination. "In fact, unless I am terribly mistaken, I think tonight is going to be very important for both of us."

At midmorning the hotel manager, Mr. Smythe, called all the guests into the lounge. There they were greeted by a solemn-faced Lord Harwood, his obviously distracted wife and a tall, grouchy stranger in a greatcoat and deerstalker hat.

Kate and Norene had been sharing a cup of tea and a plate of toast in the dining room when the summons came. As they approached the door to the lounge, they encountered O'Rourke. Seeing her mother across the room, Norene dutifully went to join her, leaving Kate to face her former husband alone. So much was expressed by his vivid blue gaze that she had a difficult time meeting his eyes.

"Good morning," she murmured, feeling unaccountably shy.

"Good morning, Katie. It seems you're making a habit of slipping away and leaving me asleep."

"It just proves I am a thoughtful person," she said with a small show of spirit.

"Or a coward," he returned softly, a glint of laughter in the warm look he turned upon her.

"Sorry, old man, but you're blocking the doorway." Jared Harwood showed no remorse at interrupting what might have become a rather intimate moment.

O'Rourke merely smiled, then with a possessive hand at the middle of her back, guided Kate to one of the overstuffed chairs and settled himself on the chair arm beside her. He draped his own arm along the back, barely brushing her neck.

"Any idea what's going on here?" one of the other men from the States asked as he escorted his wife to a second chair.

O'Rourke shook his head, but for an instant, Kate thought she discerned a glimmer of suppressed excitement in his eyes. A sudden uneasiness began to steal over her.

"Er, harrumph!" barked His Lordship. "Could I have your attention, please?"

The room grew silent almost immediately.

Cornelius Harwood tugged at his luxuriant mustache. "I'm afraid a rather unusual circumstance has arisen. A circumstance that requires the presence of this gentleman, who will explain matters forthwith. Permit me to introduce Inspector Reginald Snelling of Scotland Yard."

Scotland Yard? A low murmur ran through the room, and Kate was aware of the tension in the arm behind her. She glanced up to find O'Rourke carefully scanning the faces of the other people in the lounge.

Inspector Snelling took his time making his announcement. He dragged off his heavy coat and the Sherlock Holmes hat, handing them to a maid hovering nearby. Then, smoothing thin gingery hair with long, knobby fingers, he turned a somber look on those gathered. His eyes had the saddened droop of a bloodhound.

"We've had a nasty piece of business at this hotel, my good people. A theft." He hunched his bony shoulders. "And someone here knows exactly what I'm talking about."

What *was* he talking about? Kate silently wondered. She had a sinking feeling that somehow O'Rourke knew precisely.

"Someone posing as a guest in this hotel is a thief," Snelling said dramatically. "A thief who used the confusion of last night's motor accident to cover up his dirty little shenanigans."

Kate stirred restlessly, and O'Rourke's hand dropped to her shoulder. Whether he intended to soothe her or warn her to sit still, she couldn't tell. She wished the inspector would simply cut to the heart of the matter. Then he did, and she wished he hadn't.

"Someone has stolen Lady Harwood's diamond necklace." He paused. "Yes, the priceless Star of Pretoria— purloined!"

Kate was ashamed of her sudden flare of suspicion. Refusing to even consider the possibility that O'Rourke might have something to do with the theft, she made herself concentrate on the dramatic Inspector Snelling.

The man is such a cliché, she thought. She tried to dredge up a laugh, but she felt too much like crying.

Oh, God, she prayed, please don't let O'Rourke have had anything to do with this . . . please!

"How is that possible?" asked Chester Rand, the Australian man who had been O'Rourke's seatmate at dinner that first night. "When was it taken?"

"Sometime during the shuttling of the guests back to the hotel after the bus went into the ditch. Lady Harwood discovered it missing as soon as she removed her coat."

"Obviously," spoke up Lady Harwood, "the bugger is an experienced thief. He had to take the jewel right off my neck."

"But why weren't we told of this earlier?" asked Mrs. Phillips, a look of avid excitement on her plump face. "The robbery took place quite some hours ago."

"You see, madam," growled Snelling, looking ferocious, almost canine, "the hotel authorities kept the information mum hoping the villain would attempt to make a getaway. Had anyone turned up missing it would have been easier to point the finger of guilt. . . ."

"But . . . harrumph, it seems the thief is too clever by half," broke in Lord Harwood. "By brazening it out, he sheds no light on his identity."

"Therefore, we are asking each of you to do what you can to assist us in this investigation," stated Snelling. "If you witnessed anything strange or unusual last night, we'd appreciate hearing about it. If you have any information at all that you think might aid in the search for this criminal, we want to know it. In the meantime, before you leave this room, my assistants and I will check your persons."

A man and woman in police uniforms, bored expressions on their faces, left their post at the back of the room to flank the door to the hallway. An excited buzz rippled through the lounge.

"At some time during the day, your rooms will be thoroughly gone over. Now, people, be forewarned. I am asking for your full cooperation. If I don't get it, I can become one rather nasty individual."

And what does that mean? Kate thought grumpily. That you'll bite us? Or chase us up the nearest tree?

"Looks so much like a bloodhound, I'll bet he has fleas," O'Rourke whispered, giving her a wicked smile.

She couldn't help it—she smiled back and felt his hand tighten on her shoulder.

No, she decided, caught up in the incredible blue of his eyes, he couldn't have had anything to do with the theft of the necklace. It was surely an unfortunate coincidence. This time she was going to believe in O'Rourke.

One by one, as the guests began to drift from the lounge, the uniformed pair at the door routinely frisked them. Though the female officer gave the women only the most cursory of body searches, she was diligent about going through purses or knitting bags. Because Kate's work had made her familiar with police procedures, she submitted with good grace, but several of the others protested vigorously. Mrs. Phillips was scandalized, only acquiescing after O'Rourke flattered and cajoled her into doing so. Even then, she was indignant, her bosom thrust out like that of a pouter pigeon.

With a faint smile, Kate started up the stairs. Halfway up, it occurred to her that it might be possible to make use of O'Rourke's uncanny knack for pacifying unhappy females when she set her plans for Norene into motion. Making a quick decision to take him into her confidence and ask his help, she turned around and started back to the lounge to find him.

She came face-to-face with him in the corridor, but before she could even speak, he seized her arm and, opening the nearest door, dragged her inside.

Because of the darkness and the scent of lemon oil, Kate realized they must be in a broom closet of sorts. She barely had time to form the thought before O'Rourke pulled her into his arms. When he spoke, his breath stroked along the side of her neck.

"I know you're a stickler about the law, Counselor...."

"What...what do you mean?" It annoyed her that her voice should sound so weak.

"It must have disgusted you to observe the namby-pamby way those officers conducted the body searches."

"N-no..."

"Come now, I know you better than that."

She was suddenly aware that his hands had slipped between the two sweaters she wore and were now moving over her back in slow, sensual circles.

"Hmm?"

"I thought I should show you that someone still knows how to frisk a lady."

His hands spanned her waist and rib cage, and she could feel the branding heat of each fingertip.

"Really, it's not necessary," she murmured, resisting an urge to arch her body against him.

His hands sculpted the curve of her hips, then moved lower to possess the softness of her buttocks, pressing her close to his own solid frame, holding her there in an intimate embrace.

Kate, feeling like a wax candle left outdoors in July, was afraid she would simply melt, dissolve into a puddle of pathetic nothingness at O'Rourke's feet.

This is ridiculous, she lectured herself. How can you so casually dismiss the fact that a serious crime has been committed? And that, considering his past record, this man may have been the one who did it?

She had no answer, so with her last ounce of strength, she raised her arms and let them fall heavily about his neck. Her cheek rested against the scratchy wool shirt he wore, and she calmly waited to see what he would do next.

Not one to disappoint, O'Rourke backed her deeper into the closet, until her hips gently bumped a cupboard. Keeping their lower bodies in direct, devastating contact, he bent her slightly backward, letting his hands delve beneath her clothing to bare flesh. Slowly his caress moved upward, along the flatness of her abdomen to the firm swell of breasts restrained by the flimsiest of lace bras. Just as the heat of his hands closed over her breasts, the heat of his mouth claimed hers, and she gasped with a combination of dismay and delighted surprise.

His mouth tenderly savaged her own, leaving her uttering soft, sighing little cries of passion. Her hands meshed in the thick hair at the back of his head, and she struggled to strain closer. She could feel the hardness of his knuckles as he curled his fingers over the edge of her bra and for a wild moment, she wondered if he was preparing to rip it to shreds. Not that she could have stopped him... or would have, for that matter.

"Hmm," he panted, sliding his lips from hers, to catch his breath. "The search is a success. I think I've just discovered a couple of very valuable jewels, madam." He let his hands spread wide over her breasts. "You should have known you couldn't keep anything hidden from me."

She wriggled her hips invitingly. "Just as you can't keep anything hidden from me?"

He gasped. "Damn it, Kate..." His lips crushed hers again, roving restlessly, feverishly. "We've got to talk...!"

She was so busily engaged in returning his frantic kiss that she did not hear the door open. It was only as the small room was flooded with light that she uttered a faint shriek and they leaped apart.

A cleaning lady was observing them with a puzzled expression.

"I can't believe you Yanks," she said with a shake of her curly gray head. "Why would you pay a hundred pounds a night for a nice room and then do your grappling in a broom closet?"

Still shaking her head, she leaned the mop she held against the cupboard and, with a clatter, plunked down an empty pail. Kate and O'Rourke, clutching each other like two guilty teenagers, simply stared at her.

"Well, go back to what you were doing," she grumbled. "Don't let me disturb you."

She switched off the light and shut the door.

After a few seconds, Kate could feel a rumble of laughter from deep within O'Rourke's chest. Despite the heated blush creeping all the way to her hairline, she hid her face against him and gave in to her own amusement.

"She's right, you know," O'Rourke finally managed to say. "This doesn't make much sense when we have that wonderful room upstairs."

"We've got to talk," she reminded him. "You said so yourself."

He heaved a somewhat impatient sigh. "All right, let's do it as soon as possible. Have tea with me this afternoon?"

Kate knew the Wiltshire Cream Tea was one of the special events planned for the guests, and though she was not certain they could conduct a private conversation in the midst of holiday merrymaking, she was more than willing to try. She had waited long enough to hear O'Rourke's explanations.

"Whatever you say."

"Then meet me in the dining room at four."

"Where are you going now?" she asked.

"I've got to conduct a bit of business," he said offhandedly. "In fact, I'd better get going." He dropped a light kiss on her mouth. "I suggest we leave the closet one at a time— to avoid further embarrassment."

Kate was still wondering what kind of business O'Rourke could possibly have to conduct on what was supposed to be a holiday when she heard the door click shut behind him.

Chapter Nine

Kate stood at the window, gazing out into the rapidly darkening afternoon. Even though the thick glass slightly distorted the wintry view, she could see a few feathery snowflakes drifting lazily from the pewter sky.

A large hand fell upon her shoulder, and she turned with a delighted smile. "Look, it's starting to snow."

O'Rourke leaned to peer around her, bringing their faces within inches of each other. His distracted gaze never made it to the view outside the leaded panes. It met hers and clung there for a long, breathless moment.

"It...uh..." stammered Kate, nervously moistening her lips. "It will seem more like Christmas now."

O'Rourke's eyes moved down to rest on her lips with such intensity that Kate's own eyes closed, as though he were already kissing her. He made a tiny sound in his throat.

"Lord, but you look inviting, Kate," he murmured with regret. "I must remember where we are."

Her eyes flew open and slowly refocused on the dining room behind them. Most of the tables were occupied by other guests, a great many of whom seemed to be watching the two of them—some covertly, some with undisguised curiosity. Kate felt hot color creep into her face.

"Why does it seem that people are always looking at us?" she whispered as they seated themselves at the isolated table in the back.

"It's probably just your imagination," he replied evenly. "And anyway, you're a rather watchable woman, Kate."

"No, that's not it." She shook her head in puzzlement. "I can't figure it out. It's almost as if they—"

At that moment a waitress in mobcap, voluminous black skirts and a frilled apron approached to serve their tea. In addition to the steaming teapot, there was a plate of cheeses and sandwiches, a tiered stand filled with scones and a dish of preserves.

As O'Rourke poured out the tea, Kate glanced around the room again. It looked like a color photograph from *In Britain* magazine.

A cheerful fire danced on the hearth beneath a cedar-laden mantel; a kettle of wassail hanging from an iron crane filled the room with the scent of simmering spices. There were snowy cloths and dark green napkins and Spode Christmas china. The low strains of popular holiday music muffled the noise of lively conversation.

O'Rourke handed her a cup of tea. "Just think," he mused, "a year ago I didn't even know you existed. No, let me amend that. I knew you existed, I just hadn't found you yet."

Avoiding his eyes, Kate stirred sugar into her tea. "An odd way to put it."

"Not for a man who believes in fate. And I do. I believe we were meant to find each other...again."

"Again? Here in England, you mean?" She busied herself by taking a thin crustless sandwich from the plate on the table.

"Yes, here in England. Again."

"Your words sound as if they have a double meaning," she observed. "Must you always be so mysterious?"

"It isn't intentional. As a matter of fact, I'd like nothing more than to be finished with all the mysteries between us."

"I'd like that, too."

"And that's why we've got to talk."

"Yes."

She toyed with the sandwich, breaking it into pieces and littering her plate with shreds of watercress. "What really happened six months ago, O'Rourke? What was that all about?"

"The arrest, you mean?"

"Yes, that whole awful business." She raised her eyes to his at last and saw nothing but compassion in his face.

"I know it has been hell for you, Kate. It's been hell for me, too."

"I don't think you paid for your crimes as much as I did." For the first time, she realized, there was no bitterness in her voice. She was merely stating a fact.

"I know. And I'm sorry about that. Your mother told me—"

"My mother? When did you speak to her?"

His eyes were intent. "Your mother called to tell me you were coming to England. And to remind me that I had a ticket, too."

"How could she have done that?" Kate's eyes turned stormy. "She knew I wanted to be alone."

"Katie," he said, suddenly reaching across the table to take her hand, "did you ever think that your mother knows all about being alone?" His thumb made a slow, circling caress of her ringless finger. "That she doesn't want that for you?"

"Maybe my mother should concentrate on her own...affairs." Kate's voice was cool and clipped. "I'd hardly think she'd have time to interfere in my life."

"Mothers don't interfere in our lives—they're just naturally there to start with. Kate, I know how you felt about your father, and I understand your reaction to your mother's remarriage."

"You do?"

"I understand it, yes. But, darlin', it's not your place to approve or disapprove."

"You're right." She sighed, gently easing her hand from his. "And I know Mother has lived alone longer than many women would have. One of the reasons I came here was to get used to the idea of she and Charlie getting married."

"And the other reasons?"

She pushed her plate away. "Mainly to forget about you—about the scandal. I needed to think of á way to get on with my life. A way to start all over."

"Without me?"

She nodded. "Without you."

"And?"

"And you complicated everything by showing up here."

"Maybe my showing up didn't complicate things, Kate. Maybe it actually simplified them."

"Believe me, nothing has been simplified."

"Are you certain? I was hoping you'd come to the conclusion that having me back in your life might not be so bad after all." There was a long silence before he spoke again. "Kate, look at me. Would it be so bad?"

"I'm not sure...." She sighed wearily. "I can't understand a lot of things that happened between us."

"They're in the past now."

"They'll never be in the past until I learn the truth. Until I know something of your motivation."

"I think you still care for me."

"That's beside the point. You *owe* me an explanation."

"Then you're not denying you care?"

"There was a time I might not have seen what you were doing," she said, reaching for a beef and onion sandwich, which she promptly riddled. "Now I recognize your tactics."

"Tactics?"

"Twice now we've come close to touching on the subject of your arrest, but each time we do, you smoothly steer the conversation in some other direction. We'll never resolve anything this way."

She flung down her napkin and started to push away from the table. His hand on her arm detained her.

"Stay . . . please, Kate."

"Will you answer my questions?"

There was a grim look on his face. Finally he said. "I'll try. But this isn't as simple as you think."

"Of course it is. I ask a question, and, for once, you give me an honest answer."

"Just like in the courtroom?"

"Exactly."

"Only this time, Kate, you'll be judge and jury, as well as prosecutor. Something tells me I don't stand a chance."

"Why were you arrested?" she asked abruptly.

"You know that as well as I do."

"I want your version of it."

"All right. The police got a tip that I was some kind of jewel thief. A melodramatic situation, to say the least. They acted on the tip and—"

"Found the stolen jewelry," Kate finished.

"Yes."

"Yes? Is that all you have to say?"

"What else would you like for me to say?"

"I'd like some explanation. I'd like for you to tell me how the jewelry got there. To tell me that you're—"

"Innocent?" he queried with a crooked smile. "Isn't that it? You want me to be able to tell you it was all a huge mistake and that I didn't do it."

"Yes!" she hissed, leaning forward. "Yes, that's exactly what I want."

"Why? Because a woman of your renown couldn't lower herself to love a man who's less than perfect?"

"A man who's a thief, you mean."

"A man who doesn't measure up to her very high standards is what I mean. That's it, isn't it? That's the part you can't stomach."

"Your arrest was a humiliation to me," she said fiercely. "Surely you can see that?"

"I see that you were too busy worrying about your own reputation to give me a thought. You nursed your wounded pride and just assumed I was guilty. Well, that hurt, too, Kate."

They stared at each other without speaking until Jared Harwood distracted them by stepping up to their table.

"So sorry if I'm interrupting anything," he said, looking anything but sorry. "I was wondering, Kathryn, if you'd care to join me for whist this evening? Some of the others are getting up a tournament after dinner, and I need a partner."

Ignoring the set of O'Rourke's jaw, Kate replied, "I'm afraid I don't know how to play whist, Jared."

"Not to worry. I'd be happy to teach you."

Irritated by Jared's quiet forcefulness, Kate allowed herself to compare the two men facing her. The Briton, impeccably dressed as always, was an aristocratic country gentleman—good looks, good breeding, but almost too perfect. Boring, in other words, she realized. O'Rourke on the other hand, his lean frame slung insolently into a high-backed Windsor chair, represented unknown dangers. He was virile, mysterious...exciting. A tender smile curved Kate's lips as she silently admitted that this paragon of masculinity looked more like a pouting little boy than anything else at this particular moment. The dark hair tumbling forward onto his forehead shadowed the stubborn expression in his eyes, but his mouth was definitely petulant. For some odd reason, his reaction to Jared warmed and reassured her.

"I'm sorry," she said, turning to the Englishman, "but I've already made plans with my...with O'Rourke. Perhaps you might ask Norene? I understand she is excellent at whist."

"Very well." Jared shrugged, conceding victory to O'Rourke, and walked away.

Kate looked up to find blue eyes staring at her with an unnerving intensity.

"What?" she muttered, stirring restlessly beneath his appraisal.

"I can't believe it—you turned down Prince Charming!"

She prevented a smile by grimacing. "Maybe I just like frogs better," she said.

His deep, rich laugh filled the room, and his hands captured her own in a hard embrace. Heads turned, but this time Kate barely noticed.

O'Rourke grew serious. "Look, darlin', I wish there was some way I could magically fix all that's wrong between us, but I can't. I can only hope there is enough that's right…."

"Just tell me what I need to know."

He sighed. "Ask your questions, Kate."

"Were you guilty?"

"Yes … and no."

"Did you steal the jewels?"

"I can't tell you that."

"What about the phony credit cards? What was their purpose?"

"I can't tell you that, either."

"Why did they arrest you and then let you go?"

"There are circumstances I'm not at liberty to discuss, Kate."

"Is there anything you can discuss?"

He pressed her hands tightly between his. "Please believe me, there is nothing I'd like more than to get the whole story out in the open, but I can't. I can only ask you to trust me for just a while longer."

"There's no reason I should."

"I know."

"I have a right to the truth."

"Yes, you do."

"What about Lady Harwood's necklace?" she finally asked. "Can we discuss that?"

Silently he shook his head.

Kate sighed. "No compromise, huh?"

"I would if I could."

There was a momentary silence and then, incredibly, Kate heard herself saying, "I believe you."

And that was the damndest part—she did believe him. He hadn't answered a single question, he'd been evasive and noncommittal. She knew no more now than she had when they first sat down. But somehow, somewhere along the way, her faith in O'Rourke had been restored.

And the worst of it was that this time, if he chose to make a fool of her, she had no one to blame but herself.

He was smiling at her, the disarming dimple scoring his lean cheek. "I don't think you've properly enjoyed your meal up to this point." He nodded at the pile of ruined sandwiches on her plate. "Fortunately, we're just getting to the best part of a cream tea."

She watched in fascination as he sliced a scone and spooned strawberry preserves onto half of it. Then, with a wink, he piled it high with clotted cream, the thick cream for which England was famous.

"Here," he said, handing the scone to her, "try it. It's guaranteed to be delicious."

Kate took a bite and chewed enthusiastically. "Mmm, it *is* delicious."

If only everything he said came with such an easy guarantee.

No, she reasoned, I'm not going to think that way anymore. I've made a decision to trust him, and that's what I'm going to do.

"Katie," he said softly, topping his half of the scone with cream, "thank you."

She knew what he meant. "You're welcome."

They ate in companionable silence for a few seconds, each studying the other, aware they had reached a new plateau in their relationship.

"If we weren't in a public dining room," O'Rourke suddenly warned her, "I'd be vaulting over this table in an instant."

"Why?" She raised innocent eyes.

"To help you tidy up the whipped cream you've got all over your mouth."

"Oh!" Self-conscious, she touched her lips with her tongue, tasting the sweet stickiness.

O'Rourke groaned deep in his throat. "Kate, only you could make teatime an erotic event. Have a little mercy, will you?"

She smiled complacently until he took a bite of his own scone. Then, as his tongue darted forth to dispense with a residue of whipped cream, her smile slowly died and she swallowed deeply.

"You're right. I've never known dessert to be so extraordinarily sensual."

"It could merely be our frame of mind."

"Do you think so?"

"I'm not sure. But it does seem farfetched to think there could be anything so stimulating about a simple scone and a spoonful of strawberry jam."

"Hmm."

"Of course, it could be the clotted cream."

She drew in a deep breath. "You might be right. Fix me another one, just in case, will you?"

Kate realized she had been staring unseeingly at the book on her lap for at least the past five minutes. With a sigh, she concentrated her effort on the page of glossy photographs again, acknowledging the beauty of moated castles and medieval towns. Someday, maybe even next summer, she would like to come back to England. She and O'Rourke had once spent hours making plans to tour the countryside at leisure, driving through the narrow lanes of Devon and across the wind-sculpted moors of Yorkshire.

O'Rourke—what was she going to do about O'Rourke? Getting to her feet, she returned the travel book to the library shelf and walked to the long window. She pulled aside the heavy draperies. Though night had long since fallen, she could see the steady snowfall in the golden wash of light bathing the front of the hotel. The walkway and lawn were now a smooth, unmarred expanse of white, and soft drifts of snow had begun to pile up against the sill.

Kate sat down on the window seat and let the draperies fall back into place, shutting her into a cool, dark privacy. She hugged her knees and laid her head against them, remembering the words O'Rourke had spoken to her as they had paused outside the dining room following tea.

He'd leaned close, brushing her cheek with the back of one hand, tucking an errant strand of hair behind her ear. "Come upstairs with me, Kate," he'd whispered urgently.

She'd been tempted—oh, how she'd been tempted! But she knew without doubt what would transpire should the two of them end up alone behind a locked door. The mood that had been building throughout teatime would simply take over, flourishing into something inevitable. Something that would sweep them along helpless in its wake. Something that would again change their lives. And Kate wasn't ready for it . . . not yet.

She still didn't know her own mind, didn't know what it was she wanted from O'Rourke or from their relationship.

Despite his inability to reassure her, she found she wanted to trust him. Did, in fact, believe him when he said there were circumstances that kept him from being completely open with her. What those circumstances might be, or whether they would ever be resolved, she had not bothered to ask. Somehow she knew he would not have had an answer for her anyway.

When she had made some excuse for not going upstairs with him, there had been undeniable disappointment in his eyes, but he had not pressed her. It was as if he knew she was wavering, still struggling with the decision she must make, and he was trying his best to give her time. He'd merely smiled and said, "I'm going to take a nap. If you change your mind, you know where I'll be."

Yes, she did know, and the thought was subtly torturous. She pictured him in the big tester bed, limbs sprawled in sleep, hair dark against the pillows. His breathing would be steady and slow in the darkened room. The fire would snap and hiss on the hearth, while snowflakes brushed softly against the pane. She imagined slipping beneath the covers, putting her arms around him and awakening him with a deep, unhurried kiss. When he opened his eyes, she knew they would reflect the fires of a passion too long banked. Her mouth went dry at the thought.

"For heaven's sake, Denise, at least listen to me!" The harsh words cut into Kate's thoughts, startling her. She heard footsteps and the angry closing of the door, and knew she was no longer alone in the room.

"Why should I listen to you again?" The girl's voice was shrill, whining. "You lied to me."

Recognizing the voices of the young newlyweds, Kate didn't know what to do. She certainly didn't want to eavesdrop on what was probably their first marital spat, but neither did she wish to embarrass them by making her presence known. She could only hope they would decide to continue the quarrel elsewhere.

"I did not lie to you. Besides, you knew as well as I did that there were no guarantees. Things can't always turn out perfectly."

"Yes, but I didn't expect them to go wrong so soon!"

"As usual, you're just being hysterical."

"How dare you call me hysterical? I think I'm being pretty calm considering the situation."

Kate couldn't stand it any longer. The argument showed no signs of abating, and she didn't want to spend the next thirty minutes lurking behind the curtain—or worse yet, take the chance of being discovered. She parted the velvet draperies and peered out.

"Uh, excuse me," she said with a bright smile, "I thought maybe I should . . . er, warn you that you're not alone."

The couple turned their angry glares upon her. Flushing, Denise Blake cried, "What do you think you are doing, spying on us?"

Kate's smile faltered. "I wasn't spying. In fact, I was here first."

"You should have made your presence known immediately," the Canadian man said stiffly. "My wife and I were having a personal discussion."

"Precisely why I thought I should say something. It wasn't my intention to eavesdrop."

"Come on, Weldon," Denise said, taking her husband's arm. "Let's go up to our room. Maybe we'll have more privacy there."

Kate stared after them, fighting to control her temper. They were an unappealing couple if she'd ever met one, but at least venting their wrath on her seemed to have made them forget their quarrel with each other. Hopefully they would see how foolish it was to waste precious time with anger and hurt pride when they should be enjoying their honeymoon.

Kate clasped her arms about her waist, hugging herself. Wasting time...wasn't that exactly what she and O'Rourke had been doing? There didn't seem to be any question that they still cared deeply for each other. Did it really matter who had been to blame for what had happened to them? Or who had suffered the most because of it? No matter what the future might hold, shouldn't they simply enjoy being together while they could?

The image of O'Rourke lying asleep in bed...or possibly emerging from the shower came back to haunt her with devastating clarity. She was an idiot for whiling away the early evening hours here in the chilly library when she could have been warmed by O'Rourke's loving arms. She glanced at her wristwatch. Perhaps, if she hurried, there would still be time for a romantic interlude before they had to dress for dinner.

Kate almost ran from the room and up the stairs, her heart taking up an accelerated hammering in her throat. Her palms felt damp and tingly. Her breath caught on the excitement pressing upward from the pit of her stomach.

She had so much to say to O'Rourke, so much to show him! She fully intended to make up for lost time.

She reached the second-story landing and rushed the few yards down the hallway to their room. There, knocking politely on the bedroom door, was Norene Phillips. A crippling wave of disappointment and dismay nearly caused her knees to buckle. Damn! She had been too late....

As Norene turned to her with a smile, the door opened, and there stood O'Rourke, shoulders glistening with drops of water, a brief towel slung around his lean hips.

Norene gasped, and her face began to flame. "Oh!"

"Sorry." He grinned. "I just got out of the shower."

Kate dragged her eyes away from O'Rourke's splendid near-nudity and took Norene's arm. "Don't mind him—he tends to be something of an exhibitionist. Come on in."

As she brushed past him, he leaned forward and said, "Damn. I thought you'd changed your mind."

Kate threw him an arch smile. "I did," she replied. "But..."

Norene eyed them nervously. "Have I arrived too early?"

"Yes," answered O'Rourke.

"Of course not," Kate assured her. She made a face at O'Rourke. "Behave yourself for once."

"I'll just leave and come back later," Norene suggested, starting for the door.

"No, there isn't much time before dinner," Kate said. "O'Rourke, why don't you finish getting dressed and go on downstairs?"

He shrugged. "Whatever you say."

"Really, I don't want to interrupt...anything," Norene stammered miserably.

"You didn't. Besides, I'll deal with O'Rourke later."

O'Rourke stuck his head around the edge of the bathroom door. "Is that a promise?" he asked, his expression devilish.

Kate met his gaze and her chin lifted. "Yes," she responded solemnly. "Yes, it is."

Chapter Ten

Christmas Eve! Kate didn't think she had been so excited since she was a child.

Pausing outside the lounge, she gave Norene a thumbs-up gesture of encouragement, then preceded the other woman into the crowded room, pausing so that Norene was momentarily framed by the cedar-hung door. There was a dramatic lull in the conversation as all eyes were drawn to the furiously blushing librarian from York.

Kate proudly surveyed her handiwork, noticing with triumph that most of the men in the room were doing the same. Even Jared Harwood had looked up from the newspaper he'd been scanning, and now it lay forgotten in his lap.

It had taken thirty minutes of threats and cajolery to get Norene into the simple but daring red dress Kate herself had worn that first night. But once she had seen how it flattered and enhanced her figure, she had ceased protesting, putting herself fully into Kate's hands.

She confessed that she had never worn such a garment, and that the accompanying silk hose and spike-heeled shoes made her feel exotic, even decadent. It was, she admitted, a singularly pleasant feeling.

Foundation and blush had given Norene's face subtle color, now further emphasized by the rosiness of her embarrassment. Eye shadow and eyeliner made her hazel eyes wide, and mascara thickened lashes that cast mysterious shadows on her finely boned face. The brunette hair had been shampooed, then fluffed with a blow dryer into a casual, windswept style that framed her face and left her long, slender neck enticingly bare.

Looking at her friend made Kate clasp her hands in delight. Norene was pretty—no, more than pretty! She literally glowed, thrilled to find that she could be attractive. Kate caught her eye, and the two of them smiled conspiratorially.

From across the room, O'Rourke watched Kate. It amused him to see her acting like a mother hen, shepherding Norene into the lounge, positioning her so that her new loveliness could be shown off to its best advantage. Norene did indeed look wonderful, but O'Rourke's eyes refused to desert Kate.

She was wearing a two-piece sweater dress, whose long skirt fell in graceful folds, brushing the floor. The dress was winter white, with a spray of iridescent sequins sweeping over one shoulder. To O'Rourke, the glitter of the sequins paled beside the gleam of Kate's big dark eyes, and faded in contrast to the soft rose glimmer of her smiling mouth. It took more self-discipline than he was accustomed to exercising to keep himself from striding across the floor and placing a very proprietary kiss on that beautiful mouth. He would wait, he decided, knowing full well that the wait would be worthwhile.

Kate glanced up and caught him watching her. Her smile was unapologetically smug. To his intense pleasure, she murmured a few words to Norene, then made her way across the room to his side.

"Isn't she gorgeous?" she breathed, taking his arm as if it were the most natural gesture in the world.

"The second most gorgeous woman in the room," he replied gazing down at her.

Kate lowered her lashes, and he chuckled softly.

"Don't be modest," he said.

"I'm not. It's just that look in your eyes." She dared a swift glance. "If you're not careful, I may humiliate us both by flinging myself upon you here and now."

"Well, well. Will wonders never cease?"

"Hmm?" She was again preoccupied by the mesmerizing expression in his eyes.

"Let me put it another way," he whispered. "Yes, O'Rourke, there is a Santa Claus!"

Giggling like mischievous children, Kate and O'Rourke managed to slip into the dining room and rearrange the place cards.

"Did you see the look on Mrs. Phillips's face when Norene came into the room?" Kate asked. "I think she was in a state of shock."

"And feeling very threatened, no doubt." O'Rourke seized a holly-edged place card bearing the older woman's name and carried it to the end of the table. "Let's put her by Colonel Westcott. He's a widower here with his sister."

"Really? I thought most of these people were couples."

"Well, darlin', there are couples, and there are couples. Now, shall we permit Jared to sit by Norene?"

Kate thought for a moment. "No, let's make him suffer a bit. Why not seat her next to Inspector Snelling? He's about the only other unattached man who'll be here."

"What about me?" he teased.

"You?" Kate bristled. "Well, certainly you should sit by Norene, if that's what you want."

She put the place card she held back onto the table with unnecessary force and started away from him, unreasonably hurt.

He was right behind her, his arm snaking out to curl around her waist and draw her back against his chest. His breath stirred the tendrils of hair in front of her ear.

"Katie, I was only teasing. You know I'm about as attached as a fellow can be."

She had to laugh. "Yes, as I recall, you certainly are."

He grinned. "Frankly, I didn't expect such a reaction."

"Hell hath no fury..." she reminded him.

"Believe me, you definitely are *not* a woman scorned." He dropped a kiss onto the side of her neck. "Did I say I liked your hair this way?"

"Oh, it looks awful!" Kate's hand moved instinctively to pat the hastily contrived hairdo. "I was so concerned with Norene's appearance, I didn't spent much time on my own."

"You look adorable as always." He brushed her neck with a second kiss, and this time she turned in his arms.

"You have a very glib tongue, Mr. Callahan."

"Now that is an interesting statement." He lowered his head.

"Ahem, excuse me," said one of the waitresses from the doorway. "Mr. Smythe has just called the guests to dinner." She flashed a broad smile. "I thought you might like to know."

"Thanks for the warning." O'Rourke reluctantly stepped away. "Foiled again, Kate, my girl."

She merely smiled and inclined her head.

Dinner was a success in every way. The food was marvelous, from the cranberry-glazed capon to the sugar-crusted pecan tarts. Red wine in crystal goblets looked festive in the glow of candles whose light shimmered from every corner. The scent of fresh cedar brought a breath of outdoors to the room.

For the first time in months, Kate experienced a feeling of peace. Looking down the length of the table, she thought that everyone else seemed to be feeling the same sense of contentment.

Except for an occasional puzzled glance in her daughter's direction, Mrs. Phillips appeared to be relaxed, obviously enjoying Colonel Westcott's attentions. It pleased Kate to see that Reginald Snelling had taken to his task of entertaining Norene with great relish. Norene herself mostly smiled or nodded, managing to maintain her new aura of sweet sophistication. Seated close to his parents, Jared Harwood had long since abandoned the effort to engage in conversation with his dinner partners and, in fact, kept forgetting to eat as he watched the heretofore unnoticed librarian. Kate felt a sense of satisfaction on Norene's behalf.

Turning her head, she saw that even the Blakes seemed to have solved their differences and were again looking like newlyweds.

For the night at least, Cross Coombe Manor was filled to the rooftop with Christmas spirit.

When dessert was served, the waitresses placed small red-and-green foil boxes beside every plate. These were gifts from the hotel management—red for the ladies, green for the men. In a noisy gabble of sound, the guests hastily dispensed with the wrappings and revealed the contents of the boxes. Like the other men, O'Rourke received a pair of holiday cuff links, and Kate, like the other women, discovered her gift box contained a narrow silver bracelet. She slipped it over her hand and looked up at O'Rourke with a soft smile.

"It will always be a reminder of this night."

He leaned close. "Personally, I won't ever need a reminder. I'll never forget this was the night the two of us began to smile at each other again."

The front doors of the hotel opened to admit a group of carolers, who came in on a gust of frigid snow-sparkled air. They brushed snowflakes from their colorful Dickensian costumes and led the way into the lounge in a burst of cheerful song.

"We wish you a merry Christmas. We wish you a merry Christmas!"

As the singers positioned themselves around the decorated tree, the room fell silent.

"We wish you a merry Christmas, and a happy New Year!"

A burst of applause met the end of the song, and the singers immediately began another.

"God rest ye, merry gentlemen. Let nothing ye dismay...."

O'Rourke dropped onto the couch and, grasping Kate's wrist, tugged her down beside him.

"Now this is how I'd always imagined Christmas with you would be," he murmured, his thumb softly caressing the inside of her wrist, sliding the silver bracelet back and forth.

"Yes, it has been a nice evening." For an instant, she let her head rest against his shoulder. "Christmas carols always make me nostalgic," she said, by way of explanation as she moved away from him. "I wonder what everyone is doing at home."

"All the last-minute things, I expect. It's late afternoon there, so I can imagine your mom cooking, as usual. And no doubt Beth is frantically trying to keep the older kids away from the tree and bathe the baby."

"I miss them," Kate confessed.

"So do I."

She gave him a puzzled look. "You do?"

"You may not have realized it, but marriage to you provided me with the only real family life I've ever had."

"But you have a family...."

"Yes, I have a family," he agreed. "They just aren't close like yours. They never bothered with the usual family traditions."

"They didn't?"

"No." His eyes twinkled. "I always enjoyed the stories about your famous Christmas Eve soup suppers—about how your mother serves the vegetable soup no one has ever had the nerve to tell her they can't abide. And how you and Beth—"

"Fight over who gets to open the first present?" She had to laugh. "I'm afraid that's one of our more childish traditions. You'd think we'd have outgrown it by now, or else have gotten ashamed because Beth's children are so much more patient."

"And doesn't your Uncle Harve play Santa Claus? In a suit that's so—"

"Moth-eaten it's nearly in tatters! Yes, he truly does...and even though everyone knows who he really is, they play along."

"I looked forward to being a part of all that, Katie."

"You did?" she asked in a small voice.

"Yes. Selfishly, I wanted us to have our first Christmas alone, but after that, I envisioned us and our children spending the holidays with your family."

There was such sincerity in his voice that Kate knew he was speaking the truth. A truth she hadn't even suspected. It had never occurred to her that O'Rourke could be lonely, could feel there were things he had missed in life. And the thought that she was capable of meeting this need of his generated a warming sensation that began in the bottom of her stomach and moved upward, spreading throughout her chest.

"Well," she said with a tremulous smile, "you never know how things will turn out, do you?"

His arm went around her shoulders, and he pulled her to him in a hard hug. "Kate, are you saying what I think you're saying?"

Her eyes reflected the candlelight like stars in a midnight sky. She didn't have to speak a word for him to know her answer. It was there on her face for him to plainly see.

"Oh, tidings of comfort and joy, comfort and joy...oh, tidings of comfort and joy!"

Kate dressed hurriedly in preparation for Midnight Mass in the village church. She stepped into wool slacks, pulling them up over borrowed thermal underwear.

Norene had assured Kate that the underwear was not only practical, but very nearly essential. They would be walking to the service through falling snow, and once they were there, the interior of the centuries-old church was sure to be frigid despite strategically placed electric heaters. Kate thanked her lucky stars that Norene had brought extra underwear.

Slipping a wool sweater over her head, she savored memories of the evening just past. She had been so proud of the cool way Norene accepted Jared's invitation to be his partner at whist. Some innate spark of femininity had surfaced, giving the basically retiring woman the ability to be a tad ruthless. After all, Jared apparently hadn't thought her worth pursuing before her transformation. On the other hand, Reginald Snelling had barely seen her prior to Christmas Eve, so he could be more easily forgiven. In fact, Kate was uncertain about Norene's reaction to the tall, sad-faced man. She had a niggling suspicion that Norene was not merely pretending interest in him. And he obviously intended to keep a close eye on her. Though she was Jared's partner, he hovered near her elbow the rest of the evening, bringing her glasses of punch or giving her advice on how to play her hand. Unless Norene was the prime suspect in the theft of the diamond necklace—unlikely in the extreme— Kate couldn't think of any reason the inspector would be so attentive except that he was more than a little taken with the woman herself.

Smiling faintly, Kate tugged her boots on over heavy woolen socks. Christmas really was a wonderful time of the year! She had only been at Cross Coombe three days, and already she had seen things begin to change for the better. Of course, the biggest change of all concerned her own attitude toward her ex-husband. Unless she was temporarily blinded by the shine of holiday candles or rendered sense- less by the overpowering scent of pine and Christmas roses...unless she had merely imagined the miracle taking place within her heart and mind, she was more deeply in love with O'Rourke than ever before.

All right, he has been...possibly *is*...a thief, she silently admitted. He has lied to me and is still evasive and secretive. I don't understand what went on six months ago, and I sure don't understand what is going on now. Nevertheless, I love him.

And every intuitive cell in her body insisted he loved her in return. In fact, it was becoming harder and harder to ignore the joyous clamor set up by those same cells.

Kate shrugged. Sometimes it was best not to fight these things, she reasoned. Sometimes the only intelligent thing to do was simply give in.

With a happy laugh, she snatched up her furry coat and a pair of earmuffs, then flew out the door and down the stairs to find O'Rourke.

Only about a dozen of the hotel guests had chosen to attend the Christmas Eve service in the village. A few others had braved the snow to drive to the Roman Catholic church in Chippenham, but most were content to share a last cup of wassail by the fire before seeking their beds.

Kate emerged from the hotel to find O'Rourke waiting for her. Behind her came Norene and the inspector who, securing the door, smugly announced, "Jared is sulking as usual, so this is the lot of us, it seems."

The front steps and walkway had recently been shoveled clear, although they were quickly being covered again. A sharp breeze sprang up, riffling the powdery snow on the pavement, swirling it into their faces. Kate felt an unmistakable surge of excitement. She had never been out in a midnight snowstorm before.

Mr. Smythe lit and distributed lanterns to the guests who were making the chilly pilgrimage into the village. The brass lights looked like genuine antiques. Panes of glass shielded the wax candles inside. Each was topped by a large ring handle decorated with a sprig of holly and red ribbon streamers.

O'Rourke took a lantern and held it high, his eyes seeking hers. "Walk with me?" he asked.

She took his free arm, "I'd be delighted."

The group formed a procession, and, as soon as they had gone a short distance from the hotel, it became apparent why the lanterns were necessary. For the most part, the village street was dark and silent, with lights shining from only one or two houses. In one of the row houses, an elderly lady in a fuzzy robe stood at the window and waved at them as they passed.

Kate kept casting sideways glances at O'Rourke, fascinated by the play of shadows on his face. The mellow lantern light caressed slightly hollowed cheeks, flared over a sensuous mouth and turned deep-set eyes to molten silver. Kate's mittened hands, thrust deep in her coat pockets, curled tightly in response to the desire to touch him. She had waited this long, she reminded herself. Surely she could wait one more hour.

Not at all certain she could, she heaved a sigh and sank her chin into the scarf wrapped around her throat.

When they reached the end of the narrow lane and started toward the village square, they were no longer as protected from the wind and O'Rourke threw a steadying arm about Kate's shoulders, tucking her close against his side. Now they began to be joined by villagers on their way to Saint Matthew's, and the crisp night air rang with shouts and laughter. As they approached the wooden gate that opened into the churchyard, the boisterous mood quieted into a more reverent one.

In a sheltered corner near the church's ancient front doors, appropriately costumed members of the congregation were enacting the Nativity. The sounds of sheep and cattle mingled with the harmonious notes of "Silent Night" from inside. Huddled against O'Rourke, Kate stared, feeling a child's wonder at the realistic scene. It stirred her deeply.

After a few minutes, bells began to toll, announcing the start of the service, and the spectators extinguished their lanterns and moved indoors.

Lighted only by candles, the thirteenth-century church had been beautifully decorated for the holiday season. Even the monument of a reclining knight in armor along the north wall was decked out in greenery and ribbons, and the altar was a mass of brilliant poinsettias.

Kate and O'Rourke squeezed into a wooden pew with Norene and Snelling, but they didn't mind being crowded, because the air was so frigid. Kate stretched her toes toward a small electric heater, but found there was more warmth to be gained by pressing closer to O'Rourke. The elusive dimple appeared at the side of his mouth, making her confident he wasn't displeased by her move. And a quick glance at the couple beside them seemed to indicate that Snelling also found no fault with Norene's decision to snuggle nearer to him. In fact, his face was positively animated as he raised his excellent baritone voice in song.

"It came upon a midnight clear, that glorious song of old...."

The music was emotional and uplifting, the sermon simple and concise. Kate found herself hanging on every word. For the first time, sitting in a little stone church far from the competitive professional world in which she normally existed, she really understood the meaning behind the clichéd phrase: It would be wonderful if everyone kept the Christmas spirit alive all year long.

She felt O'Rourke's gaze upon her and reached for his hand. Without looking at him, she squeezed his fingers once, twice...three times.

I-love-you!

It was still snowing when they left the church, but now the flakes were thicker and drier. They drifted down in a leisurely fashion, clinging to everything they touched.

The guests from the hotel relighted their lanterns and, after wishing the villagers a good holiday, started along the lane that led back to Cross Coombe Manor. The wind had died, leaving the air sharp and brittle; overhead a few stars could be seen, heralding the end of the storm.

After spending an hour in the cold church, trudging through the snow had lost some of its appeal. To everyone's surprise, Inspector Snelling managed to boost spirits by suggesting they sing carols to take their minds off their numbed toes. He got things underway with a rousing rendition of "Good King Wenceslas," and even though Norene laughingly warned him he would awaken everyone in Cross Coombe, it was evident she thought the man extremely clever.

Kate and O'Rourke lingered for one last look at the snow-covered village.

"It looks like a Christmas card, doesn't it?" she asked.

O'Rourke wasn't looking at the village any longer. "Kate," he questioned softly, his breath a cloud of steam in the night air, "back in the church—did you mean it?"

There was no need for him to further explain the query. "Yes."

He lifted the lantern higher, letting its golden light flicker over her face. Her eyes were wide and dark and somber, sending a tiny thrilling shiver down the back of his neck.

"I do love you, O'Rourke," she whispered. "I always have." And that's the problem, she thought.

He raised a gloved hand, cupping her face and gently rubbing the side of her jaw with his thumb. "I wish it weren't so cold. I'd like to feel the heat and softness of your skin," he commented. "Right now. Without these damned gloves."

She smiled demurely. "Let's go home then. It'll be warm there."

He drew a deep uneven breath. "Are you sure, Katie?"

"I'm sure."

Just then a large feathery snowflake brushed her face, settling with tantalizing precision on her bottom lip.

Without hesitation, O'Rourke tilted her face upward and touched the snowflake with the tip of his tongue. As surely as the snowflake melted beneath the heat, so did Kate's lips. She willingly surrendered to him. His mouth slid tenderly over hers, chasing away the chill of the winter night, healing the chill of an estranged heart.

"I love you, darlin'," he murmured into her ear. "For all eternity."

The words floated freely in the icy night, spiraling heavenward like a swirl of smoke. Right then, Kate believed in them as much as she believed in her reply.

"I love you, too."

On their return to the hotel, they were served mulled wine and hot mince pies before a smoldering log fire in the lounge. Kate and O'Rourke stayed only long enough to be polite.

When O'Rourke looked up for the dozenth time to find Kate watching him, he decided it was foolish to waste a minute more making small talk. Stifling a somewhat contrived yawn, he winked at her and said, "Don't you think it's time to retire for the night, Mrs. Callahan?"

She set her wine aside and stood. "As a matter of fact, Mr. Callahan," she replied, placing her hand in his, "I do."

As they left the room, they heard Norene's soft laughter and knew they hadn't fooled anyone.

"Happy Christmas," she called after them. The sentiment was echoed by Inspector Snelling's deeper voice.

"Happy Christmas!"

Chapter Eleven

When Kate and O'Rourke reached their bedroom, a sudden shyness overtook them. They hung their coats in the closet and arranged wet boots and gloves on the hearth, all the while studiously ignoring the looming specter of the huge tester bed.

O'Rourke, barefoot but still dressed in camel-colored sweater and corduroys, sat down in one of the chairs and stretched his long legs toward the fire. Unobtrusively he watched Kate.

She stared into the flames as if lost in thought. Finally she seemed to sense his eyes upon her and turned.

"It's much warmer here than in Saint Matthew's," she said, pulling off the heavy woolen sweater she wore. "Thank heavens."

"But it was a nice service, wasn't it?"

"Yes. All in all, this was one of the best Christmas Eves I've ever spent."

"Me, too."

A small silence fell between them until O'Rourke suddenly asked, "What's that you've got on under your blouse, Kate?"

Her slim fingers rose to her collar, feeling the rough weave of the thermal underwear. "Norene loaned it to me. It's underwear."

He grinned. "Long underwear?"

"Yes," she answered somewhat defensively. "Is that so unusual?"

"It is for you, Counselor. Long johns have never been exactly your style," he said. "Come here and let me see."

She hesitated a few seconds, and then slowly she approached him. "There's nothing to see. It's plain, ordinary underwear."

"No, it's not. I can see flowers or something on it." He reached out and took her arm, pulling her between his knees.

"Okay, so it's plain, ordinary, *flowered* underwear. Nothing to get excited about."

"Who said I was excited?" he countered.

She dropped her eyes at the suggestive note in his voice.

"Come on, Katie. Let me see your . . . roses?"

She shook her head, but her hand had moved to the top button of her shirt.

"Pansies?"

"No . . . not pansies." She unbuttoned the blouse and let it hang open.

"They're blue," he protested. "Are you sure they're not pansies?"

"Actually, I think they're asters." Kate slipped the blouse off her shoulders and gave it a toss.

O'Rourke's hand found the fastener at the waistband of her slacks. "Let me see the bottoms, too."

"I never knew you had a thermal underwear fetish," she stated, trying to conceal a smile. She unzipped and quickly stepped out of the slacks.

"Neither did I—until now. Lord, but you look good, Kate."

His admiring eyes feasted greedily on the sight of her slender body attired in the form-fitting knitwear. "I take back what I said about not being excited," he muttered. "Damn, you are the sexiest woman I've ever seen."

"And just how many women have you seen in long underwear?"

"Sit down and I'll tell you all about it."

She made a face at him. "I'm not sure I want to hear this."

"Kate, you know I haven't really looked at other women since I met you." He patted his knee. "Now plant your pretty little asters right here. I want to talk to you."

She laughed as she settled herself on his lap. His arms went around her immediately, dragging her close against him. His mouth sought hers in a long, gentle kiss.

"You do have a way with words," she breathed when he finally raised his head.

"We'll talk in just a minute," he assured her, bringing his lips back to hers. As his hands began languorously massaging her back, her own arms encircled his neck and she shifted closer, tucking her feet up into the chair with them.

O'Rourke's face was still cool from the midnight walk; in contrast, the inside of his mouth was blessedly warm and its touch spread heat throughout Kate's body. She gave herself up to the sheer enjoyment of the moment, her contented sigh brushing softly against his lips. As though he understood her mood exactly, O'Rourke pressed his cheek against the top of her head and tightened his arms in an almost painful embrace.

"It feels so wonderful to hold you again, sweetheart," he murmured, kissing her temple. "There were times when I thought it would never happen."

"I know. If someone had told me we'd be sitting here like this, I'd never have believed it."

"Never?"

"No, not even after you had the nerve to show up at the hotel."

"You scared me then, you know."

"*I* scared *you*?"

"Yes—when you told me to get out. For some odd reason, I had hoped you'd be happier to see me."

"I wasn't expecting you. Besides, I thought I hated you. And my God, you should have seen and heard yourself. You looked so fierce! Poor Jared didn't want to leave me alone with you. He thought you were some kind of madman."

"I was, Katie. For six long months, I had been out of my mind missing you. And then to see you in another man's arms like that. Damn, I nearly lost control." He smiled down at her. "But then you sent him away and looked at me—really looked at me—and I began to have a little hope."

"What do you think I saw?" she questioned.

"I think you saw something that reminded you this thing between us is grander and more important than any mistake either of us could ever make."

"You believe that?"

"I do." He rubbed a light kiss across her mouth. "You can't fight destiny, darlin'." His next kiss was deeper and intensely erotic. Kate responded with an ardency that surprised her.

O'Rourke stroked her back, letting one hand slide around her rib cage to cover a breast. His thumb made an exploratory survey. "Mmm, these asters have very nice buds," he whispered into her ear.

"O'Rourke," Kate all but groaned, "let's go to bed."

"I was about to suggest the same thing. Shall I carry you?"

"No, wait. I want to change into...something else."

"Something more comfortable?" he asked, one black brow quirking upward.

"You could say that."

"You know you don't have to change on my account, don't you?"

"Yes. I just want to."

"In that case..."

"I'll undress in the closet," she said, getting to her feet. "You can have the bathroom."

"Will you be long?" he asked.

"Give me ten minutes."

"Ten minutes?" he protested. "What am I supposed to do for ten minutes?"

"Take a hot shower and get warmed up."

"Honey, I'm already about as warm as I dare get."

She smiled demurely. "Then take a cold shower."

His hands closed about her upper arms. "Kate, you aren't teasing me, are you? I mean, I'm not going to come back out here and find my bed made up on that damned fainting couch again, am I? Or you wearing a chastity belt?"

She laughed softly. "I've never thought of chastity belts as particularly comfortable. And no, you won't be sleeping on the fainting couch. Unless of course, you faint. In that event it might be best."

He pulled her close and kissed her firmly. "I have more stamina than that, I promise you."

"Even at two in the morning?"

"Remember—it's only eight o'clock in the evening back home. I think my hormonal clock is set on that time."

"What about jet lag?" she asked. Then, with a downward glance, she conceded, "No, you definitely aren't suffering from that."

Laughing, he turned her toward the closet and swatted her bottom. "Go get undressed, you shameless hussy."

Ten minutes later O'Rourke, clad in the black pajama bottoms, emerged from the bathroom to find the room lighted only by the bedside lamp and the fireplace. He could see that the bedcovers had been turned back neatly, invitingly. And then his eyes sought and found Kate herself.

She was standing near the small double windows at the end of the room. Enough light came through the thick glass to vaguely illuminate her figure as she stood gazing at him, hands behind her back, head tilted slightly as she waited for his reaction.

O'Rourke's heart seemed to stop and then slowly flutter to life again. He had never seen Kate look so beautiful or desirable. She was regal in a full-length, midnight-blue nightgown that hugged the upper part of her body and fell to a graceful swirl around her bare feet. The bodice, no more than two triangles of sheer lace held up by thin straps, did little to disguise the beauty of her breasts, and the skirt, which flowed smoothly from a high waist, clung lovingly to her curving hips and long slender thighs. Her thick chestnut hair tumbled about her shoulders, and her eyes glowed like dark sapphires in the shadows.

As he took a few steps toward her, she smiled and murmured, "See? No chastity belt."

"I see." He gave a rueful laugh. "But, oh, darlin', I feel light-headed just looking at you. I may faint after all."

"What? And miss all the fun?"

"You're right. I'll have to pull myself together."

"O'Rourke," she said a trifle impatiently, "will you please get over here? I have a surprise for you."

The corners of his mouth lifted. "I guess this means Santa got my letter." As he grinned, the solitary dimple danced into view. Without further ado, he strode across the carpet toward her.

When he was about ten feet away, Kate removed her right arm from behind her back and launched a missile that unerringly found its target.

Splat!

"What the...?"

A slushy snowball had struck O'Rourke in the center of his bare chest. For a long moment he stood staring in disbelief at the splatter of snow that was beginning to melt and run down his stomach to the waistband of the pajamas. Then he looked up, and one eyebrow arched dangerously. "Okay, lady," he declared, "this is war!"

Kate shrieked and darted away as he approached. She eluded his grasp and raced across the room, fully expecting him to catch up with her at every step. Instead, he cranked open the window and scooped a handful of snow off the ledge. Then, when Kate paused to look back at him, he hurled it in her direction.

She ducked, and the snow crashed against the bedpost. "Ha!" she cried triumphantly. "You missed."

"I won't miss next time," he warned.

Seeing him turn to get another handful, Kate scurried to the windows on the opposite side of the room and rapidly pushed one of them open. She had only bent over to scrape the snow off the sill when O'Rourke's snowball smashed with deadly accuracy against her thinly clad derriere. She yelped in surprise and his laugh echoed through the bedchamber.

"You beast!" Kate turned to face him, brushing the snow off her bottom with both hands.

"You started this," he reminded her, striding toward her. "Now, do you care to tell me why?"

"Gladly. Did you think you could win me over so easily? That I would fall for your blarney just like that?" Her words were softened by a teasing smile.

He came nearer. "It seemed to me that you were rather enjoying the... blarney, as you call it."

"I just can't believe I gave in so easily." She whirled to fill both hands with snow. "Don't come any closer!"

He leered. "You liked my attentions, and we both know it."

She began to shape the snow into a ball, plainly displaying her intent. He preferred to take note of the way her eyes sparkled with mischief.

Suddenly he lunged forward and caught her arms, pulling her to him. "Admit it, Katie. Admit you like being kissed like this...."

His mouth swooped down to capture hers, and for a moment she swayed against him. Then swiftly she jammed the snowball down the front of his pajamas, letting the elastic waistband snap back against his taut navel with a loud pop.

Muttering a curse, O'Rourke leaped away from her and began shaking the snow out of the bottom of his pants legs.

"That does it, you little witch," he ground out between clenched teeth. "You're going to get it now."

Giggling, Kate sprinted away. "Oh, I am so scared!"

"You'd better be, because when I catch you, I'm going to teach you a lesson you won't forget."

O'Rourke paused long enough to gather up more snow before following her. He tossed the first handful as she stopped in front of the fireplace, but the sight of her body so enticingly silhouetted against the flames was an undeniable distraction. For that reason, he rationalized, his aim was completely off, and the snow sizzled in the fire.

Kate began running again, feinting first to the left and then the right, causing his next effort to smatter harmlessly against the cheval mirror.

Using a new tactic, she doubled back in the direction of the fireplace, and he lunged after her, overturning a chair in his haste. Pushing it aside, he continued the pursuit, laughter pressing upward into his throat and threatening to spill out.

Kate skimmed more snow off the sill of the open window and tossed it carelessly over her shoulder as she fled again. It struck O'Rourke in the side of the neck, causing him to growl in mock displeasure.

"Come here," he softly ordered, but she grimaced and dashed out of reach. Executing a rather clumsy flying leap, she landed in the middle of the bed, rolling to the other side and coming up onto her feet again.

Behind her, O'Rourke's long legs easily cleared the bed, and he trod up and over it. As he gained ground, Kate began to laugh helplessly, knowing the moment of surrender could not be far away. She headed for the open windows, but as his reaching fingers brushed her hair, she veered to the right and raced back toward the bed. Again she dived for the middle and rolled quickly to the other side. But this time when she bounded to her feet, she came up against a solid rock wall with the most incredible blue eyes.

"Oh!" she cried, her chest heaving. Eyes widening, she focused on the handful of fresh cold snow he was holding. "You cheated!"

"I did not." His breath was coming in quick pants. "I finally outsmarted you. And now...no mercy!"

She pushed against his chest in an attempt to escape, but he stood his ground, encircling her waist with a steely arm to flip her backward onto the bed. In an instant, he was beside her, one leg thrown over her hips to insure her capture. He seized her hands with his free one and secured them above her head, teasing her with the snow.

"If we were kids, I'd wash your face with this," he said menacingly.

"But we're all grown-up now, aren't we?" she pleaded. "Sensible, mature adults..."

"Of course. And surely a sensible, mature *man* can be pretty inventive!"

Catching one of the thin straps of her nightgown in his teeth, he tugged it off her shoulder, edging the lace aside to bare one round ivory breast. As his eyes stared deliberately into hers, he brought the handful of snow down and rubbed it briskly over the soft mound of flesh.

Kate felt a sensation like a cold shock of electricity, but she didn't know if it was from the chill of the snow or the heat of O'Rourke's hand. She uttered a small scream and writhed beneath him.

His hand slipped to her waist, holding her steady as his mouth lowered to remove the rapidly melting snow from her breast. As his tongue lapped at the iciness, it softly battered the tightly budded nipple, causing Kate's faint scream to turn to anguished moans of pleasure.

He raised his head. "I'd forgotten snowball fights could be so much fun. I'm glad you thought of it, Kate."

When the last of the snow was gone, he moved upward, pressing short, sweet kisses along her collarbone, into the hollow of her throat and beneath her chin, coming to rest upon her slightly parted mouth. He released his hold on her wrists to bring his hand down to cup the nape of her neck, crushing her mouth even closer. Kate lowered her arms to his shoulders, her fingers kneading the hard muscles of his back.

She sighed. "I didn't mean to make this so easy for you."

"Easy?" he groaned. "I feel like I've run a marathon."

She brushed his lips with her fingertips. "But it was fun, wasn't it?"

"Yes...though I've always preferred making love to making war," he murmured, nipping at her fingers.

"Is that what we're doing?" she asked faintly. "Making love?"

"What did you think, sweetheart?"

O'Rourke's mouth caught hers again, stifling any answer she might have made. She molded her body to his, suddenly anxious to do away with the distance that had been between them for so long. She had underestimated the charismatic power of the man who had been her husband. Now it was far too late to deny her real feelings for him, and she abandoned all pretense and admitted to herself how much she wanted him. She wanted to rediscover his masculine strength, wanted him to fill her heart, her body, every aspect of her life. And it was important to her to let him know.

"I missed you," she whispered, stirring against him. "I missed this."

"So have I."

He twisted onto his back and took her with him, pulling her on top of him. Her hair fell forward over her face, and she tossed her head, unconsciously arching her back as she did so. The disheveled hair and glowing navy-blue eyes presented an image diametrically opposed to the one of coolly professional lady lawyer.

O'Rourke's hands strayed to her waist, then upward, thumbs brushing the full underside of her breasts. The blue lace gaped invitingly, and he raised his shoulders from the bed to allow himself access to the tempting rose-colored nipples. He teased first one, then the other, touching them with his tongue and grazing them lightly with his teeth before finally taking them into his mouth. The moist heat of his firmly tugging lips sent shafts of pure pleasure streaking through Kate, centering her concentration on the intense joy he was creating within her.

Of their own volition, her fingers ran through the coarse hair on his chest, stroking along an iron-thewed belly to the waistband of his pajamas. Gripping the elastic, she began inching them down, leaving no doubt about her desire. O'Rourke assisted by lifting his hips, then kicking free of the encumbering garment. Kate wriggled against his nakedness, and they both gasped.

"It has been too long, Katie," he apologized breathlessly. "I don't think I can wait...."

"I don't think I can, either," she assured him with a shaky laugh.

His big hands swept aside the crumpled gown, then cupped her hips and carefully slid her down over his body. With a soft cry of pleasure, Kate allowed herself to collapse upon his chest. O'Rourke's hands became restless, ranging up and down her back. She lay quietly for a moment as his fingers stroked the nape of her neck, her shoulders, the sides of her breasts. Then they spanned her hips again, moving her against him.

Kate clutched his shoulders and raised up to look at him. His eyes were closed, his face set in the definitive lines of passion. Only his mouth was relaxed, his lips slightly open. She dipped her head and swiftly kissed him.

Just as swiftly, his arms cradled her to him, and, without leaving her, he rolled to position himself above her.

They were overwhelmed by the sheer gloriousness of once again making love. And now, by some unspoken agreement, they rushed headlong toward the release they both needed so desperately. O'Rourke's fevered kisses and Kate's frantic little cries of passion seemed to promise there would be time later for tenderness, for slow, leisurely lovemaking. But now, stormed by desires too long unreleased, they surrendered themselves to the breathless race for fulfillment. They clung together, buffeted by an explosive climax that was a blinding, soul-searing liberation. Freed at last from lonely frustration, from anger and hurt and fear, they drifted together, peacefully content.

Kate didn't know how long they lay without speaking, or how long they might have done so, had the cold wind pouring in through the open windows not ruthlessly touched her overheated flesh. She shivered and burrowed closer to O'Rourke.

"My God, the windows," he moaned, reluctant to move from the warmth of the bed. "It'll be a miracle if we don't catch pneumonia."

"Would that be so bad?" she murmured. "We could spend the rest of our vacation in bed."

"A splendid idea," he agreed. "Only, I'd rather be healthy to enjoy it."

He reached for his pajamas. "I'll close the windows if you'll straighten the bed."

Kate's laugh was decidedly bawdy. "Is it really necessary? I'm almost certain we'll soon be in the mood to rumple it again."

"Darlin', if we don't get some sleep, we won't be in the mood for anything. Remember, tomorrow...I mean today's Christmas. We'll be expected to make an appearance downstairs sometime."

"So true," she sighed, rearranging her nightgown and combing her snarled hair with her fingers.

"My God, look at this place," O'Rourke exclaimed as he shut the window and fastened the latch. "I've never trashed an expensive hotel room before."

He crossed the room to set the chair upright and close the other windows. Just then there was a discreet rap at the door. Kate and O'Rourke exchanged startled looks, and Kate dived into the freshly straightened bed, drawing the covers up to her chin.

O'Rourke unlocked the door, opening it enough to see Reginald Snelling looking a great deal like Basil Rathbone in a green satin dressing gown.

"Snelling? Something wrong?"

"That's what I came to ask you," Snelling said, a faint smile tugging at one corner of his mouth. "The people in the next room complained to the night clerk about a frightful to-do in your room. Said they heard a woman scream."

O'Rourke felt his face turn red, and Snelling actually laughed.

"Seems none of the staff wanted to come up here and . . . er, disturb you, but they thought someone should make certain a murder wasn't taking place. I was elected—due to my position with the Yard, I suppose."

"I see. Well, there's Kate," O'Rourke said, opening the door a bit wider. "So you see, neither of us has been murdered."

"I didn't think so. But now I can report downstairs that all is well with the Callahans." He turned to go. "It is, isn't it?"

O'Rourke appreciated the concern behind the man's words. "Never better," he said with a bold wink.

To his surprise, Inspector Snelling winked back. "Well, enjoy the rest of the night."

When O'Rourke returned to bed, Kate snuggled into his arms, stifling her laughter against his chest. "We'll never be able to show our faces tomorrow."

"Maybe not, but it was worth it, wasn't it?" He nuzzled her ear.

"Absolutely."

They kissed good-night, and she turned in his arms, so that they fell asleep just as they always had when they were married, with Kate's back against his chest, her bottom tucked into his lap and his leg thrown over hers.

Faintly, from the snow-covered village came the sound of church bells marking the hours throughout the long, dark night before the dawning of Christmas Day. The bells tolled three times and fell silent again.

Chapter Twelve

Kate lay quietly, wondering what it was that had awakened her. It came again—the muffled noises of someone moving quietly about the room. She forced open one eye. It was five o'clock in the morning and still very dark outside.

Because she no longer felt the warmth of O'Rourke at her back, she knew he must have gotten out of bed for some reason. But there was something so stealthy about his movements that she didn't want him to see she was awake. She turned her head on the pillow, burrowing deeper into the bedcovers and flinging one arm across her face to disguise the fact she was watching him.

He stood at the side of the bed, wearing a robe over his pajamas. As she peeked through her lashes, she could see him come to an abrupt halt and stare down at her. When she showed no further signs of awakening, he seemed to relax and went back to the task at hand.

O'Rourke was running his fingers over the stone wall to the left of the bed. Right before Kate's startled eyes, a six-foot section of the wall swung inward and O'Rourke walked though, disappearing. In a matter of seconds, the wall swung back into place and looked as it had for over five hundred years. She sat upright, unable to believe her own eyes.

So there really was a secret passage from the Highwayman's Chamber to...where? And how did O'Rourke know about it? It scared Kate to imagine what had drawn him from the warm bed into the dark, forbidding tunnel.

Fired by the conviction he might either be in danger or about to get himself into real trouble, she dashed into the closet to find her robe and slippers, intending to go after him whether he liked it or not.

Kate rummaged through her suitcase for the small disposable flashlight she had brought with her, all the while wishing she had a weapon of some sort. When nothing more deadly than her umbrella came to light, she abandoned the idea.

After spying on O'Rourke, it didn't take long to locate the spring triggering the mechanism that opened the wall. *Spy*—she grimaced at the word. It was an ugly way to describe her real motivation in following him. All she was interested in was protecting O'Rourke, even from himself.

With determination Kate stepped through the gaping hole in the wall and saw the familiar shapes of the bedchamber disappear from view as the wall automatically swung closed. Standing alone in the darkest dark she had ever experienced, Kate's heart started beating in double time. She prayed this was not the silliest mistake of her life. Switching on the flashlight, she played it over the stone wall before her and, with relief, quickly found a lever that silently reopened the section of wall. Convinced escape was possible, she pressed the lever again and turned her attention to the passageway.

As her eyes grew more accustomed to the dark and she became bolder in using the flashlight, Kate saw what was basically a narrow stone corridor, stretching in only one direction from the entrance to her bedroom. Overhead, thick dust-silvered cobwebs spanned the hallway, but at floor level, they were tattered, hanging brokenly from the stones. Obviously someone had been using the passageway with some frequency.

As she moved down the corridor, Kate noticed two or three cramped rooms—more like cells, really—to her right. She peered into one, but it was dark and empty. Had this been built as a prison of some kind? Or were these hiding places constructed on a rather more luxurious scale than the priest's holes to be found in many English manor houses?

The passageway was dank and cold, the floor slippery with moisture. Kate wished she had worn something warmer than her velour robe. She had no idea how long it would take to locate O'Rourke.

Not long, apparently, she thought, tilting her head to catch the distant murmur of a voice she recognized as his. Moving forward toward the sound, she discovered that the corridor ended in a narrow spiraling staircase. O'Rourke's muffled voice came from somewhere above her.

Reluctantly Kate turned off the flashlight, afraid its faint light would divulge her presence as she started up the stone steps. In the darkness, with one hand pressed against the rough wall to guide her, she very nearly lost her nerve. Imagined thoughts of coming face-to-face with some unknown terror made her heart thud high in her throat, threatening to choke her. She hesitated, considering the advisability of turning back, and then, with her next step, bumped into a solid wall.

It was wooden, rough and splintered. As Kate stared, she detected vague glimmers of light that defined its arched shape. Her exploring fingers told her it was a small door studded with iron. Suddenly O'Rourke's voice sounded from less than a foot away.

"I know I'm late, but I . . . overslept."

There was brief laughter and a muffled reply in a voice that sounded familiar, though Kate could not quite identify it.

"Come on, we haven't much time," O'Rourke was saying. "I've got something to show you."

My God, Kate thought wildly, he's about to open this door!

Something told her that, whatever her reasons for following him, O'Rourke's reaction at finding her there would be too horrible to contemplate. Not knowing what else to do, she turned and fled, unmindful of the treacherous steps or the suffocating darkness. Bumping from wall to wall, she miraculously made it to the bottom of the little staircase, finding it easier going from that point on. Gasping for breath, Kate leaned against the dusty wall and watched the end of the corridor. In only a few seconds, the beam of a flashlight stabbed the gloom and she could see two shadowy figures descend the final step, one at a time.

Kate inched her way along the passage, knowing that if she made even the tiniest sound, she would be discovered immediately—caught in the ray of their flashlight like hunters' prey. Her throat was so dry that breathing had become an effort, but her hands were drenched with icy perspiration. What in hell had she been thinking of to set foot inside this medieval monstrosity?

She passed the entrance to the first two cells and was at the third when O'Rourke spoke again, his voice filling the hall with ghostly echoes.

"In here." O'Rourke and the man who accompanied him stepped into the first cell, and she breathed a sigh of relief. Then she heard him speak again. "The perfect hiding place, wouldn't you say?"

The muttered reply was unintelligible, sparking her curiosity. Who could the second man be? O'Rourke had never given the slightest indication he knew anyone else in the hotel.

"Let's simply leave it here for the next few days," O'Rourke said. "It couldn't be safer. No one knows about the . . ." Kate couldn't make out the rest of his words.

Unexpectedly the men emerged into the passageway, and Kate ducked into the room behind her. To her relief, they went back the way they had come, conversing in tones so low she couldn't make out what they were saying. As soon as their light vanished around the curve of the staircase, she moved cautiously toward the compartment they had vacated. Once inside, she flicked on her light and swept it rapidly around the small space. Its beam caught and held something lying deep in a square hole cut into one wall. Probably used for storage during the Middle Ages, it was now merely a home for spiders and waterbugs.

A very expensively decorated home, Kate found herself thinking as she gazed at the Star of Pretoria, Lady Harwood's fabulous diamond necklace.

Tentatively she reached out to touch it with her fingertips, recoiling at the flat, cold feel of it. Beneath the flashlight's beam, it scattered brilliant fire, but it was a lifeless fire without warmth.

Kate dropped her head against her chest, suddenly swamped by misery. So...O'Rourke had taken the necklace after all. She had desperately wanted to believe in him, but he was still a thief; and that knowledge would break her heart if she let it.

Kate knew she probably should take the necklace with her, but somehow didn't think she could bear to touch it again and decided to leave it there until she could think what to do about it. There had to be a way to rectify the terrible mistake O'Rourke had made...but at that moment, her mind was preoccupied with renewed sorrow. She could only hope something would occur to her in the morning.

There were no lights or voices in the passageway, so she made her way back to the bedchamber. As soon as the wall closed behind her, she dropped her robe and slippers and got back into bed.

She had lain there long enough for her breathing to slow to normal when she heard O'Rourke slip into the room. She feigned sleep as she listened to the rustle of cloth when he removed his robe, then felt the mattress give under his weight. He crawled beneath the bedcovers, sliding close to her; the chill of the secret passageway still clung to him. Kate had an intense longing to warm him, to draw him into her protective embrace and never let him go again, but her dreadful new knowledge held her back.

O'Rourke dropped the lightest of kisses on her shoulder and slipped an arm over her waist, gently pulling her back against him. His open palm spread over her stomach and reassuringly pressed three times.

I-love-you!

Kate bit her lip, fighting the pain that welled inside. Right now she needed nothing so much as his reassurance, his affirmation of love for her. His belief in their happy future. She turned in his arms and laid her head upon his broad chest.

"I'm sorry, I didn't mean to wake you," he whispered, kissing the top of her head. When she made no reply, he placed a finger beneath her chin and raised her face. "Katie? You're crying...darlin', what's wrong?"

She managed a weak smile. "Nothing," she murmured.

"It doesn't look like *nothing*."

"I'm being silly," she lied. "I was just thinking that...that tonight was so beautiful. God, O'Rourke, I don't want to lose you again!"

"You're not going to lose me," he promised. "Not ever again."

"Prove it," she challenged softly. "Prove to me that you love me...that we're always going to be together."

His arms tightened around her. "Gladly, sweetheart. It will be my pleasure."

His mouth was sweetly tender as it descended upon hers; his hands were warming and consoling as they roamed over her, stroking and soothing, using passion as a balm. And she allowed it, because she loved him desperately and wanted to ward off the fearful sadness that had crept into her heart the moment she had seen the diamonds.

Their lovemaking was fiercely ardent, achingly compassionate, healing. It was the restorative her soul needed.

This time when she fell asleep in his arms she was filled with a renewed sense of love and purpose. And a new dedication to her vow to save O'Rourke from himself.

* * *

Hours later, Kate opened sleepy eyes and was greeted by a slow smile from O'Rourke.

"Merry Christmas," he said softly, pulling her close for a languid kiss.

"Merry Christmas yourself," she replied, rubbing her palms back and forth across the lightly furred breadth of his chest. She curled into his arms with a sigh. "Want to stay right here all day?"

He kissed her again, with feeling. "Yes, I do," he stated emphatically, "but I'm afraid it's already noon."

She struggled to a sitting position. "Noon! Oh, my, we've got to get up."

"No problem for me." He grinned wickedly, tugging her back down beside him.

She fended him off with both hands. "You know we're having dinner at one, and I have a dozen things to do before then."

"Then we'd better get started," he purred, nuzzling his lips against the arch of her throat. Her laugh was only a little unsteady as she pushed him away.

"O'Rourke, be serious. We've got to get out of this bed."

"But you're the one who suggested we stay in it."

"I didn't know how late it was." She gave him a rueful smile. "I'm sorry, sweetheart. Will you take a rain check?"

"I suppose I'll have to. I recognize that look of determination in your eyes."

Kate placed a brief kiss on his chin. "Thanks," she whispered. She threw back the covers and slipped out of bed, bending to pick up her robe. She turned to give him a level look. "Of course, you know how quickly my determination always falters in the face of your... amorous insistence."

He made a grab for her, but she evaded his hand and dashed for the bathroom.

"You're a merciless tease," he accused as she slammed the door behind her.

Arms crossed behind his head, O'Rourke smiled and lay back against the pillows. With a feeling of satisfaction he realized that things were finally beginning to come together for him. It seemed he had waited a long time.

Kate showered, then dried her hair and applied makeup while O'Rourke took his turn in the bathroom. They had fallen back into the companionable intimacy of married life with surprising ease. She loved the way he winked and smiled when he caught her gaze in the mirror, the casual hand he placed on her shoulder as he leaned forward to pick up his wristwatch and wallet from the dressing table.

The feeling that she would fight if necessary to salvage what they had together was stronger than ever. It was actually something of a relief to know for certain what obstacles she would have to overcome. Nothing could be worse than battling unknown and unseen enemies. Now she knew what she had to deal with, and she discovered a wellspring of inner strength she had never known she possessed. They were going to survive this thing. She could feel it!

Dressed in a hunter-green sweater and dark slacks with a Harris tweed sport coat, O'Rourke was disturbingly handsome. He bent over her and lifted her chin with a forefinger to give her a lingering kiss.

"I'm going on downstairs, Kate. I've got a couple of things to do. I'll meet you in the dining room at one o'clock, all right?"

"All right," she said evenly. "See you then."

When he had gone from the room, Kate rested her chin in her hand and sighed at her reflection.

Secrets. It seemed O'Rourke's eyes were full of them. And, she suspected, they weren't the ordinary, innocent secrets of Christmas Day.

Unexpectedly a thought registered with startling clarity, and suddenly she knew what she was going to do about the stolen necklace.

They had only been apart thirty minutes, and O'Rourke couldn't believe how much he was looking forward to seeing Kate again. Some insecurity within himself—a throwback to an uncertain childhood, he supposed—made him need to see and touch her.

But, anxious as he was, when she appeared at the door to the dining room, he didn't rush to meet her; rather he momentarily enjoyed the pleasure of simply watching her.

She was wearing a red turtleneck sweater and a floor-length red-and-black tartan skirt. Her hair had been swept up on one side and fastened with a sprig of holly. A slight frown marred her forehead as she paused to scan the room, but to O'Rourke's intense satisfaction, it disappeared as soon as she caught sight of him. Breaking into a wide smile, she wove her way through the crowded room to his side, and he moved to meet her.

"You look sensational," he informed her. Then, leaning closer, he added, "Not as deliciously wanton as last night, maybe, but very elegant and ladylike." He led her to the table and held her chair as she took her seat. Bending over her, he added, "But you can be certain that each time I look at you, I'll be remembering how lovely you looked leaning out the window for more snow."

He took his own seat, adding in a quiet voice, "Or standing in front of the fireplace." He laid his hand over hers. "Or wriggling beneath me . . ."

"O'Rourke," she gasped, coloring. "For heaven's sake, stop it. They haven't even served the first course and you've already got me wanting to go back upstairs!"

"That was the idea, sweetheart."

"I see." Smiling, she unrolled the linen napkin at her place. "Well, you'd better just behave yourself. I'm famished."

"So am I," he heartily agreed, though his tone left some doubt as to the exact meaning of his words.

Lord Harwood commenced Christmas dinner with a short prayer, but the mood swiftly became relaxed, even jolly in the English tradition.

Christmas crackers, small rolls of foil and tissue paper, had been placed at each plate and were opened with mildly explosive bangs and shouts of laughter. Inside the crackers were paper hats or crowns, which the guests immediately donned, and a variety of candy, toys and strips of paper containing fortunes or silly sayings.

Kate and O'Rourke traded hats, deciding his red scalloped one matched her clothing better, and that the black-and-gold pirate's hat was more suited to him.

As he raised his wineglass in a silent toast to her, Kate couldn't help but think that he did indeed make a devilishly charming buccaneer. Perhaps, she concluded with resignation, he was simply one of those renegade souls never designed to be an ordinary, law-abiding citizen. Though the thought made her a little sad, it did not repel her as it once would have done.

As the waitresses ladled out bowls of Scotch broth, Kate glanced down the table and caught sight of Norene. It pleased her to see the librarian had done her best to duplicate the new hairdo they'd created for her. She had also applied makeup and was wearing the gold hoop earrings purchased in the village. Her peacock-blue suit flattered her, and though her appearance was not as dramatic as it had been the night before, she was still transformed into a pretty woman. It seemed that Jared, seated on one side of her, and the inspector, seated on the other, agreed on that point. Even Mrs. Phillips seemed to treat her daughter differently, more with pride than disapproval. Her own relationship with Colonel Westcott probably had a great deal to do with her change of attitude, and Kate found O'Rourke's pairing off the two of them inspired.

The main course consisted of both roast turkey with chestnut dressing and stuffed goose. Mashed potatoes, carrots, brussels sprouts, a variety of gravies and sauces, and yeasty dinner rolls completed the meal.

"Harrumph," Lord Harwood said as he wielded the carving knife, "when I saw all the snow this morning, I knew we must have been living right. Can't think when we last had a white Christmas...."

"I believe Jared was just a lad," mused Lady Harwood.

"Oh, we've had spots of snow," commented a round-faced gentleman with a sparse gray mustache, "but it has been some time since we've enjoyed this amount."

"You know the saying—Christmas in England is more often green that white," Mrs. Phillips added. "That's what my grandfather always used to say."

"My grandfather used to say the very same thing," spoke up Colonel Westcott. The two exchanged a pleased smile.

"Well, whatever brought the snow, we're certainly grateful for it," stated Weldon Blake. "It wouldn't seem like Christmas without it. Back home in Canada there would be several feet on the ground by this time."

"Egad," gasped the Australian man next to him. "I should think you'd have gone to Jamaica for the holidays!"

His remark was met with a round of laughter, prompting someone to propose a toast to warmer climates.

Kate turned to find O'Rourke watching her. She arched a brow. "Something wrong?" she whispered.

"Not a thing," he assured her, caressing her knee beneath the table. "I'm just so damned happy I can't believe it."

The look in his eyes was so intense that Kate blushed, feeling as if she had been thoroughly kissed. She suddenly found it difficult to keep her mind on the sliced turkey and brussels sprouts on her plate.

The meal concluded with Christmas cake and brandy butter, followed by hot coffee and mints. Then, at Lord and Lady Harwood's insistence, the entire company moved into the lounge to await a visit from Father Christmas.

As usual, Kate sat in the easy chair with O'Rourke perched on the arm, his fingers laced through hers and resting against his thigh.

Father Christmas, when he appeared, was a slight, genteel figure straight out of Victorian times, with none of the jovial characteristics of the modern Santa Claus. He wore a long robe of sumptuous red velvet trimmed with white fur. There was a crown of holly upon his head. His long hair was the same pure white as the beard that reached halfway to his waist. Leaning upon a twisted walking stick, he had a burlap bag draped over one thin shoulder, and from this he drew gifts for everyone—boxes of chocolates for the women, bottles of wine for the men.

Then the elegant old gentleman began handing out the packages the guests had wrapped for the gift exchange. Almost instantly the room filled with excited chatter and the rustle of paper.

The rose-colored sweater pleased Norene greatly, and instead of denying it was her style, as Kate had expected, she declared her intention of wearing it the following day. Inspector Snelling presented Norene with a vial of French perfume, and, not to be outdone, Jared immediately invited her to London for an evening at the theater.

"I think Harwood might as well throw in the towel," O'Rourke whispered to Kate. "Snelling's going to win out. Norene's one choice bone that old bloodhound won't abandon."

"I agree. He has been so preoccupied with his pursuit of Norene since he arrived at Cross Coombe that I can't think he has devoted much time to solving crimes." Kate cast a sideways glance at O'Rourke, but his expression didn't alter.

"I was thinking the same thing. I wonder where he found French perfume in this little village."

Father Christmas approached with packages for each of them, ending the speculation. O'Rourke eyed Kate over the box he held.

"Hmm, I wonder who this can be from?" he murmured. "Lady Harwood gave me driving gloves for the gift exchange."

"You know perfectly well who it's from." Kate smiled, laying a hand on his arm. "But please don't expect too much. I...well, I didn't have time to shop after I finally decided we were no longer enemies. I thought I might get you something more after we get home."

"Home? As in going home together? That sounds damned good, Kate."

She felt unaccountably shy. "Just open the present, will you?"

O'Rourke obliged, discovering the carved wooden figure of the highwayman inside. "Where did you find this?" he asked. "It's wonderful."

"I saw it at a shop in the village. At first, I really didn't know why I bought it, but the more I looked at it, the more I realized it reminded me of you somehow."

"I can't think of a single thing I would rather have had. You know my fascination with the highwayman legend. Thank you, darlin'."

Kate couldn't wait another second to begin ripping the paper from her own gift. She uncovered a jewelers' box and found an antique gold locket inside.

"Oh, it's beautiful," she exclaimed, lifting it. She looked up, her eyes glowing with pleasure. "It's the most beautiful thing I've ever seen."

O'Rourke reached forward and pressed the hidden spring that opened the locket, revealing two miniatures, their colors faded and mellowed by the passage of time.

"Lady Aurelia . . . and her lover," he explained.

"The highwayman?"

"That's who the fellow at the antique shop believes it to be."

Kate brushed the tiny paintings with her fingertips. "I can't say why, but I feel certain he's right. Though, of course, this locket can't be that old . . . can it?"

"It's actually believed to be a reproduction of an earlier locket. This one is only about two hundred and fifty years old."

"Only?" Kate laughed. "O'Rourke, I adore it! I'll treasure it forever."

She undid the elaborate clasp and placed the locket around her neck. O'Rourke moved closer, his hands covering hers.

"I'll fasten it for you, shall I?"

She nodded and turned her head to kiss one of his hands.

"Kate, I have one other present for you," he said suddenly. "But I'm not sure you'll be willing to accept it yet."

He reached into his jacket pocket and produced the wedding ring she had so unceremoniously dropped into his tea.

Kate rose to her feet, her eyes wide and solemn. "My ring?"

He nodded. "Will you marry me again, Katie?"

"I thought you'd never ask," she breathed. "Of course I'll marry you!"

He slipped the ring back onto her finger. "We can get married here in England if you like, or wait until we get home so your family can be there."

"Let's get married at home. And they'd better all be there," Kate said fiercely, blinking back tears, "because this is absolutely the last time I intend to do this."

He put his arms around her waist. "Ah, Katie, I love you so much."

"And I love you." She leaned into him and lifted her mouth for his long and loving kiss. She wished everything could really be solved so easily, but that wasn't the case. There was much to be done before they would be free to marry again, but knowing their love was strong would give her the will to go on.

When they ended the kiss and broke apart, the room was filled with enthusiastic applause.

"I didn't realize we had an audience," O'Rourke remarked good-naturedly.

"Not to worry," Father Christmas said succinctly. "'Tis the season . . ."

The laughter generated by his statement was interrupted by a shrill scream.

"Cornie, look at this!" Lady Harwood's face was the same puce color as her dress. She peered into the open box on her lap and clasped one hand to her bosom. "I can't believe it."

"My dear, what's the matter?" Lord Harwood charged to her side with the grace of a wounded rhino. It was obvious he fully expected to find a ticking time bomb nestled amid the tissue paper.

"There was no card or anything," Carolyne Harwood went on, "but someone has returned my necklace!"

She lifted the Star of Pretoria from the box and held it up for all to see. As it flashed fire, a series of gasps went around the room.

"Oh, my God," Kate heard O'Rourke moan. She dared a brief glance at his face and felt a pang at the shock and disbelief mirrored there.

Forgive me, love, she silently prayed. I had to save you somehow, and I didn't know what else to do!

Chapter Thirteen

Kate steeled herself against the doubt she was suddenly feeling as she stared at O'Rourke. After all, she had already reasoned it out—there really was nothing else she could have done but return the stolen property to Lady Harwood and hope the woman would take better care of it this time!

She laid a tentative hand on O'Rourke's arm, and he tensed as if aware that his reaction to seeing the recovered necklace had been too strong. With an effort, he wrenched his attention back to her and smiled.

"A stroke of luck for the Harwoods, don't you think?"

"Yes, of course," Kate replied. But she couldn't help wondering what he would say if he knew her part in the matter.

There was a general stir over the necklace, a mixture of hearty congratulations and much speculation on the thief's current state of mind.

"Blimey, the chap must have gotten a grand dose of the Christmas spirit," speculated one of the male guests, shaking his head in disbelief. "Never heard of such a thing."

Lady Harwood was completely at a loss. "Wh-what should I do with it, Cornie?"

"Why, er... harrumph... blast me, I don't know." Cornelius Harwood fingered his mustache in consternation.

"Now that you have the Star of Pretoria back," O'Rourke said smoothly, "why don't you simply put it on and enjoy wearing it?"

"No!" Even to Kate's ears, the protest sounded a bit too vehement. Realizing that all eyes were on her, she smiled weakly. "What I meant was... well, why risk anything else happening to the necklace? I think you'd be wise to put it into the hotel safe immediately."

"But if the thief has had a change of heart, are such precautions necessary?" questioned Mrs. Phillips. "I assure you I'd wear it if it were mine."

"But..." Kate's rationalization was lost in the rise of vocal approval surrounding Mrs. Phillips's declaration.

Lady Harwood cast an anxious glance at her husband and another at Inspector Snelling, who was hovering nearby, a watchful expression on his face. "Well, perhaps I shall wear it for a while this afternoon... that is, if you feel it is safe, Inspector."

"I don't see why you shouldn't celebrate the return of the Star, madam." Snelling's gaze swept the room. "Let's assume the jewel thief has repented and get on with our holiday."

"Splendid," agreed Colonel Westcott. "And if I'm not mistaken, it's about time for Her Majesty the Queen's Christmas message on the telly."

"Excuse me, but don't you think...?" Kate broke off with a sigh. It was useless to try to force prudence onto a roomful of people bent on merrymaking. Taking note of the look O'Rourke gave her, she decided it would be best to give up before she made him suspicious. All she had to do was keep O'Rourke and that damned necklace separated. With a bit of ingenuity, it shouldn't be too hard to do.

"While the others are watching the queen, I think I'll telephone Mother," she said. "Would you like to speak with her, too?"

"Yes, I would. I have a lot to thank her for, remember."

Kate made a wry face. "And I have an apology to make."

"You're right. And there's no way I'd miss that," O'Rourke stated, smiling. "Come on."

Rather than bother the staff by asking to have a phone taken to their room, Kate decided to use the old-fashioned telephone booth in the back hall.

"I applaud your decision," O'Rourke murmured as the two of them squeezed into the cramped kiosk. He sat on the low wooden stool and pulled her onto his lap. While she dialed the international operator and read off her credit card number, he occupied himself by placing tiny, precise kisses along the side of her neck bared by the swept-back hairstyle.

"That tickles," she protested. "Oh, sorry, operator—no, I wasn't talking to you. Yes, I'll hold."

She shifted the receiver to the other side and turned to O'Rourke. "The overseas lines are terribly busy."

"Hmm, it's a holiday," he muttered, blowing gently into her ear. She shivered and looked over her shoulder at him.

"Please stop—" His mouth as it came down upon hers silenced her words. The hand holding the receiver faltered, dropping to rest against his shoulder, and she pressed into him, eager for the ardent heat of his lips.

"Hello?"

A faint moan sounded deep within O'Rourke's throat, and for a instant, he increased the urgency of the kiss.

"Hello? Is anyone there?"

Kate blinked as he drew away from her, reluctant to break the spell of the moment.

"Oh, my Lord!" she suddenly exclaimed. "Mother? Hello, is that you?"

There was a delighted laugh on the line. "With all that heavy breathing on the other end, I thought I was receiving an obscene phone call," Kate's mother said. "I take it O'Rourke is there with you?"

Kate firmly placed the receiver between herself and the man in question.

"Yes, he's here."

"Hello, Mom," O'Rourke spoke up. "You know, you're one hell of a smart woman."

"Told you so," came the complacent reply.

"Mother," Kate interrupted, "I'll address your treachery when we get back home. But for now..." her voice softened "...thank you."

"I guess I don't need to ask how things turned out. I'm glad, Katie. And relieved." There was a brief laugh. "I knew that when I sent O'Rourke after you, we'd soon be attending either a wedding or a funeral."

"Hey, you were a little careless with my well-being, weren't you?" scolded O'Rourke.

"It doesn't sound as though you have much to complain about, son."

"No, nothing more than a few scars and some minor frostbite suffered that first night. Since then things have warmed up considerably."

"Mother," Kate said, smiling up at O'Rourke, "you can put away the black dress. It's going to be a wedding."

"That's wonderful, honey. I'm so happy for you."

"And...speaking of weddings..."

"Would you like to make it a double ceremony?" Kate's mother's tone was firm, warning her they were now on slightly more dangerous ground.

"No, but thank you for asking," Kate answered. "We want you to have your special day all to yourself. But I have a deal for you—I'll be your matron of honor if you'll be mine."

"That sounds terrific to me. Of course, we'll have to see what Beth thinks."

"If I know Beth, she'll agree to anything just to keep peace." Kate drew a deep breath. "I'm . . . I'm looking forward to meeting Charlie as soon as we get home. Wish him a merry Christmas for me, will you?"

"I'll be happy to."

"And when I'm back in Kansas City, we'll sit down with a gallon of coffee, and I'll tell you all about the trip."

"What she means, Mom, is that she'll tell you how I finally managed to win her over," interjected O'Rourke.

"In gory detail," promised Kate.

"I can't wait to hear. I'll even put some date balls in the freezer to have with our coffee."

"Great. Well, we'd better let you get back to your celebration. Tell everyone hello for us, okay?"

"Certainly."

"I'll let you know when to expect us home," Kate said. "I've missed you all."

"We've missed you, too," her mother responded. "But we want you to enjoy the rest of your holiday."

"We'll do our best," O'Rourke stated. "Bye, Mom. See you soon."

"Goodbye, you two. Merry Christmas."

"Merry Christmas," Kate echoed. "And, Mother, I love you! Goodbye now."

Kate hung up the phone and faced O'Rourke, a shimmer of tears in her eyes.

"I feel so much better," she confessed. "Thank you."

"Me? What for?"

"For making me face up to my problems—or what I thought were my problems." She draped her arms around his neck. "Thank you for the nicest Christmas of my life." *And I'm going to return the favor and make you face up to your problems, too*, she thought.

Slowly she moved her mouth over his, savoring the wonder of her feelings for him. He gripped her shoulders and urged her to take the kiss deeper. Gladly she complied.

A sharp, impatient rapping on the glass door of the phone booth suddenly destroyed the mood. Guiltily Kate and

O'Rourke jumped to their feet, nearly wedging themselves into the tight space.

The door was wrenched open, and they came face-to-face with the same disapproving maid who had caught them in the broom closet the day before.

"I've got to make a call..." she began, then shook her head in total amazement. "You two again?"

Kate couldn't contain her laughter. She felt O'Rourke's hand clasp her elbow, and he ushered her from the booth.

The woman stood and watched them walk away, still shaking her head.

"Kinky Americans," she finally muttered, easing into the phone booth and securing the door behind her.

"Want to go to our room and take up where we left off?" Kate asked as they approached the foot of the stairs.

O'Rourke glanced at his watch. "Sounds good to me, but there's something I have to do first. Why don't you go on up, and I'll be there as soon as I can?"

Kate didn't like the thought of letting him out of her sight. "I'll just go with you."

"Sorry, but I don't think that's a very good idea, Kate."

"Why not?"

"Look, this is business, but it shouldn't take long."

"What kind of business?"

"None of yours," he said gently. "I thought you were going to trust me, Katie."

"Can I?"

"Yes."

She sighed. He didn't leave her much choice. "How long will you be?"

"Not more than twenty minutes or so." He kissed the tip of her nose. "Then I'll join you for a long, lovely afternoon nap."

"Mmm, I'll be waiting."

Kate climbed the stairs, determined not to worry. Surely he wouldn't be able to do anything too rash in a mere twenty minutes.

She put another log on the fire, then decided to change into an ivory-colored jumpsuit she had brought especially for lounging about the hotel room. The terry cloth suit was comfortable and warm and not unflattering, she realized, eyeing her reflection judiciously. Something told her O'Rourke would definitely approve of it.

Thinking of O'Rourke, Kate checked the time and saw that he had been downstairs exactly eighteen minutes. She hoped he wouldn't be much longer.

She stood at the window, gazing out at the snowy landscape as she removed the clips and holly from her hair and brushed it.

When thirty minutes had passed with no sign of O'Rourke, Kate fought the urge to go looking for him. He'd said she could trust him, and that was what she had to do. She couldn't spend the rest of her life wondering what he was up to every time he was a few minutes late.

When another ten minutes had gone by, she lay down on the bed, hoping a brief nap would calm her nerves. Not that she had any real intention of going to sleep...

O'Rourke switched on the bedside lamp and bent over Kate, shaking her gently.

She stirred, then sat up, smiling sleepily. Almost instantly the smile died.

"My God, O'Rourke, it's dark outside!" she exclaimed. "Where the hell have you been?"

He considered telling her he had been in the room for the past three hours, resting and watching her sleep, but the idea of flat-out lying to her was patently unappealing. On the other hand, telling her the truth was out of the question, also.

"I'm sorry, darlin'," he finally said. "Things didn't go exactly as I planned."

"Yes, well, my plans didn't work out, either," she snapped. "I don't like being stood up."

"That was the last thing I intended, Kate, believe me."

Her anger faded as quickly as it had flared. "I'm trying to believe you," she said in a resigned tone. "But you don't make it very easy."

Instead of asking the questions crowding her tongue, Kate pushed past him and went into the bathroom. When she came out again, he was sitting on the edge of the bed, waiting.

"Look, I realize I screwed up our plans for this afternoon," he said quietly.

"It's really no big deal," Kate said offhandedly. She sat down at the dresser and began brushing her hair.

"It is to me. I'd like to try making it up to you."

"There's no need, O'Rourke." She shrugged and faced him in the mirror with a wry smile. "You aren't accountable to me for where you spend your time."

"I am when I promise to spend it with you." He came over to stand behind her, gently taking the brush from her fingers. "I wanted to be with you, Kate. I doubt if even you know how much." He drew the brush through the full length of her hair, and she shuddered as prickles of sensual pleasure danced over her scalp. Lightly he clubbed the soft thickness beneath his hands into a loosely held ponytail, brushing upward from the nape of her neck.

Kate closed her eyes and leaned back against him. "That feels so good," she murmured. "If you are trying to distract me, it's working."

He laughed softly and continued brushing, leaving her hair swirling over her shoulders.

"Will you have dinner with me tonight?" he asked unexpectedly.

Her eyes met his. "Aren't we having supper with the other guests? I thought they were doing something special tonight."

"They're having a Feast of Wiltshire buffet," he informed her. "But I'm a little tired of all the socializing, aren't you? I hoped you might agree to something a bit quieter."

"Such as?"

"A private dinner for two?" He laid the brush aside. "I've already made the arrangements. What do you say?"

"Well, all right, I guess. It sounds nice—even if you did take my acceptance just a bit for granted."

Since he didn't care to admit the extent of his worry about her reception of his plan, he simply smiled. "Sorry."

"I really haven't given you much reason to doubt my... eagerness." She sighed. "And privacy does sound awfully good."

"Then, shall we go?" He offered his arm.

"Now? Shouldn't I change clothes first?"

"Not on my account," he assured her. "I think you look beautiful. Besides, this is strictly private, so you may wear whatever you please."

"I suppose the thing to do is just put myself into your hands," she said, rising.

"You won't regret it," he promised.

On the stair landing, they met the Harwoods, who were on their way down to dinner. Lady Harwood wore a rainbow-hued dress that bordered on gaudy, but Kate was effusive in her praise.

"You look wonderful tonight, Lady Harwood. What a gorgeous dress!"

And, she thought with a smile, that rope of brilliant diamonds strung around your aristocratic neck has never looked more stunning.

However O'Rourke had spent the afternoon, he obviously hadn't used the time to steal back Lady Harwood's necklace. With that knowledge, Kate could relax and look forward to the evening ahead.

Leaving the Harwoods at the dining room, O'Rourke led her farther down the deserted hallway to a plain door with a Do Not Disturb sign hanging from the doorknob.

"There's a sign—we can't go in here," Kate protested.

"Don't worry. I put the sign there myself."

"*You* did?"

"Yes, my love. And I have this...." He brandished an old-fashioned brass key with which he locked the door behind them. "When I said a private dinner, that's precisely what I meant."

"Hmm, sounds interesting."

"More interesting than beef roast and Wiltshire cheese? That's what they'll be having in the dining room."

"What will we be having?" she asked.

"Leftovers, I'm afraid."

"Ah...well, that sounds interesting, too."

O'Rourke's dimple leaped into view as he smiled wickedly. "And I believe I can safely promise you that dessert will be...very special."

To hide the pleased look on her face, Kate turned to observe the room in which they were standing. "Why, this is a conservatory! I didn't know the hotel had one."

"Do you like it?"

"It's lovely."

"I thought it would be perfect for a romantic evening."

"But are we supposed to be here?"

"I have a key, darlin'—I didn't steal it."

"Sorry, just asking." Kate smiled inwardly. With O'Rourke, you never knew for sure....

"Let's have a look around," he suggested, dropping the key into his pocket and taking her arm. The conservatory was a Victorian garden room with a flagstone path that wound through the landscaped areas. There were shoulder-high ferns, and flowering trees and palms draped with liana, luxuriant tropical vine that transformed the small room into a veritable jungle.

"That path winds around to a door that goes into the greenhouse," O'Rourke said, pointing. "We want to go this way to the pool."

"There's a pool?"

"Complete with goldfish and lily pads."

"My goodness, this is quite a place. Oh, look—birds!"

As several scarlet tanagers flew overhead, a brightly colored parrot scolded them from his perch in a poinciana tree.

"Ah, here's what we've been looking for," announced O'Rourke, ignoring the bird's disgruntled chatter.

Pushing aside the fronds of giant ferns that screened the area, O'Rourke led Kate into a sheltered corner of the conservatory, which contained white wicker furniture and a blue-tiled fish pond. A small round table with two fan-backed wicker chairs was set for their supper.

"The hotel staff was efficient as always, I see," said O'Rourke. "Our picnic is ready."

"This is wonderful," exclaimed Kate. "How did you ever think of it?"

"Oh, I don't know. I just wandered into the conservatory once . . . and saw the possibilities, I guess."

"I'm so glad you did."

O'Rourke lighted the hurricane lamp on the table, then held Kate's chair. "It'll be even more romantic once I turn off the overhead lights," he warned her. "After all, the walls are glass, and we don't want to be on display should anyone wander past."

When only the dim flicker of the lamp remained, they could see out through the steamy windows of the conservatory to the snow-covered landscape beyond. A pale moon barely illuminated the foggy hills in the distance, and the stars were tiny pinpricks of light. It was an odd sensation to stare out at the chill winter scene while sitting in the almost tropical heat.

O'Rourke uncorked the icy bottle of champagne and filled two fluted glasses. "I asked for their best champagne, hoping it would make up for the main course . . . turkey sandwiches."

Kate laughed. "I love turkey sandwiches! And that luscious crumbly cheese. This is a terrific meal."

As they ate, O'Rourke found himself constantly studying the woman across the table. He had seen her in any number of lights, and she was always beautiful. Now, with the flutter of lamplight ebbing and flowing over her features, she looked so appealing his heart had started a slow, thudding beat. An unmistakable excitement had begun building, pulsating throughout his body.

As compelling as his desire for her was, it seemed to be all mixed up with a myriad of other feelings, not the least of which were gratitude and protectiveness.

Poor sweet Katie, he thought, recalling the look of relief that had dawned in her eyes the instant she saw Lady Harwood wearing that damnable necklace.

He knew exactly what Kate feared he had been doing during his prolonged absence from her. The knowledge that she still suspected him of being a thief tore at him, but it was made more bearable by her obvious decision to love him anyway. Still, it was frightening to see a normally practical and intelligent woman throw caution to the winds in favor of love and loyalty. O'Rourke hadn't wanted to ask that of Kate, and he certainly didn't relish having that kind of power over her. He'd be glad when the whole thing was finished and they could start fresh. Then, he promised himself, he would make it all up to her.

Kate sipped champagne, watching him over the rim of her glass. "Warm in here, isn't it?" she commented in a husky voice. Her fingers toyed with the tab of the zipper down the front of the jumpsuit she wore.

He understood immediately. Kate wanted tonight . . . this moment, to be very special. She was silently asking him to help her create a few hours of tranquility amid the uncertainty of their lives. She was envisioning the two of them being transported to some point beyond reality where there was no doubt, no unreasoning suspicion, no need for blind trust. A place where they could forget the gnawing fear that some unknown truth might unexpectedly surface to destroy their lives again.

O'Rourke set his glass aside and rose to his feet. This was the one thing he could give Kate right now—her longed-for moment out of time.

She half rose to meet him, and he took her into his arms, rocking her gently back and forth, comforting her.

"My strong, brave Kate," he heard himself whisper and, for a moment, feared he might have revealed too much of what was in his mind.

He leaned away to look into her face, but her expression was merely wistful. Even so, it hurt him. Damn! Why couldn't he say what she so desperately wanted to hear? That he wasn't a thief, that he'd had nothing to do with stealing the Star of Pretoria. If only he could tell her what she needed to know...

Instead, he had to settle for the one thing he could tell her. "I love you, darlin'."

Trustingly Kate's arms went around his neck, and she lifted her mouth for his kiss. She tasted of champagne, sweet and tart...and more than a little intoxicating. This was what he needed—what they both needed.

"Shall I blow out the candle?" he asked, caught unaware by the unsteadiness of his voice.

Kate nodded and stepped away from him. In a few seconds the room was dark except for the faint blue haze of moonlight reflecting off the snow. O'Rourke reached for her, drawing her down onto a cushioned wicker settee beside him.

Her skin looked luminescent in the gloom, and her eyes glowed with gentle fire. O'Rourke traced the line of her mouth with his thumb, brushing upward over her cheek, his fingers fanning out to cup her jaw and lift her face to his. The kiss began innocently enough as a sweet, searching touch, but progressed rapidly to an almost frenzied expression of growing passion.

O'Rourke's hands dropped to Kate's waist, pulling her onto his lap. He loved the various, sexy textures of the woman he held. The softness of her skin, the scented tangle of her hair as it brushed forward over his face, the slight roughness of the terry cloth beneath his roving hands. The silky heat of her mouth excited him unbearably, and he found himself filled with an urgency he couldn't explain. It was almost as if this were their first time together. But then, he told himself, whenever he made love with Kate it was always beautifully unique.

He slowly unzipped her jumpsuit and slid his hands inside. Her smooth, soft skin contrasted with the hard, beading nipples he could feel beneath the thin lace bra she wore. A sharp thrill pierced through him.

"O'Rourke," Kate pleaded. She stirred restlessly, arching against him, silently asking for more. Her honesty in expressing her need for him made his heart swell and his pulse thunder. The desire to treat Kate with gentle adoration warred with his more primitive urge to fiercely ravish her, claim her as his own and no other man's. The two impulses combined to give his lovemaking a rough tenderness to which Kate responded with ardor.

O'Rourke reveled in the aggressiveness she showed in removing his jacket and sweater. The slight awkwardness of her fingers as she unbuttoned his shirt pleased him absurdly, for he sensed her eagerness. When her hand slipped inside his waistband, he gladly lent his assistance. Releasing her, he stood and stepped out of his slacks and underwear, thoroughly enjoying the way her eyes welcomed the sight of his nakedness. Dark and glowing, those eyes made him feel utterly masculine and powerful.

Kate slipped the jumpsuit off her shoulders and down over her hips, to stand before him, clad only in her wispy underclothing.

O'Rourke felt an excited greed. She looked so beautiful, he could stare at her for hours, and yet, he also wanted nothing more than to strip away those last bits of cloth and feel her body next to his. Kate settled the dilemma by reaching behind her back to unhook the bra and then stepping out of her bikini panties.

With her name on his lips, O'Rourke dragged the thick cushion from the settee and, pulling Kate with him, dropped onto it. His arms closed about her as his mouth pleasured hers in long, drugging kisses.

His hands explored her body as if with a will of their own. They petted and stroked and stimulated, until Kate was writhing with passion, opening herself to him with frantic whispered invitations. Slowly he entered her, not certain he could withstand the intense jolt of sensation that ripped through him. Kate's arms and legs tightened around him, assuring him she felt the same pulsating rapture.

There was nothing as overwhelming to O'Rourke as the feel of this woman in his arms. She looked fragile, and yet physically and emotionally she was so strong. Her fine-boned delicacy contrasted drastically with his iron-hard muscularity, frightening and tempting him at the same time. He was at once afraid he would hurt her, but driven beyond control by her motions and by the sweetly undisciplined kisses she pressed against his neck. In a few short moments, there was no time left for caution or reserve. As his body gave itself up to ecstasy, his mind struggled, then succumbed to the all-encompassing need for fulfillment. The one thing that mattered was pleasing and satisfying Kate, taking her with him to that blissful oblivion only true lovers ever achieve.

They found what they sought, arriving breathless and spent, filled with peaceful contentment.

Instead of rolling away from her, O'Rourke merely shifted his weight so she would be comfortable. With one hand, he brushed a stray lock of hair off her forehead.

"Katie, I meant it when I said I was sorry about this afternoon." O'Rourke kissed one corner of her mouth. "All I ever want to do is spend time with you."

"So you want to do time, huh?" she teased. "Then tell me, my good man, of what are you guilty?"

He traced the line of her throat with his forefinger. "I'm guilty as hell of loving a certain lady lawyer from Kansas City. I can't think of anyone or anything else. You be the judge. Is it criminal to love someone that much?"

"Definitely. I'd say you were guilty as charged. In my opinion, the only solution is to give you a lifetime sentence."

"I accept." He kissed her eyelids.

"With no parole," she warned.

"I won't be asking for any."

O'Rourke's mouth captured Kate's as his body began moving slowly and deliberately against hers.

And once again, magically, the world retreated.

Chapter Fourteen

Kate turned away from the dining room window and frowned at O'Rourke.

"I have half a mind to go out there and give those people a good lecture on the evils of hunting," she said, dropping back into her chair.

O'Rourke peered around her to get a look at the crowd of horses and their red-coated riders milling about in the street next to the hotel. "It's mostly for show," he assured her.

"Oh? Has anyone remembered to tell the fox?"

"Katie," he soothed, "I've heard all about the Rush Vale Hunt. They are notoriously poor huntsmen. Honestly."

"Honestly?" she murmured, fidgeting with the silver ring around her breakfast napkin.

He reached across the table to pat her hand. "Honestly. Mr. Smythe tells me the club has met outside Cross Coombe Manor every Boxing Day for twenty years, and in all that time, they've only run their quarry to ground one time. And then, he swears, it was quite by accident."

Kate held up a restraining hand, even though her mouth turned up slightly at the corners. "Spare me the details, please."

Boxing Day, the first weekday following Christmas, was a legal holiday in Britain, and traditionally, at least in the countryside surrounding Cross Coombe, the hunt was on. The sight of scarlet jackets and beautifully sleek horses was a glorious one against the backdrop of a snowy landscape, but Kate's dedication to animals denied her any enjoyment in the colorful scene. She breathed a long sigh of relief when, with a last flurry of cheerful shouts and a clashing of hoofs against the cobblestones, the huntsmen rode off.

"That's one part of merry old England I can do without," she said firmly. "But..., the only part. I love everything else about this country."

"We'll come here again, shall we?" O'Rourke released her hand to return to his breakfast. "Maybe next summer?"

"I've been thinking the same thing," she concurred. "I'd like to rent a car and just wander about."

"It's a date, Mrs. Callahan."

Kate gave him a warm smile. After their evening in the privacy of the conservatory, she felt closer to O'Rourke than ever. His loving tenderness was gradually driving out all the demons that had taunted her for the past months. Trust... and hope were rapidly being renewed.

"Have you thought about our last night here?" he asked, buttering a muffin.

"About the costume ball, you mean?"

"Yes. I'd like to go, if you would."

"It sounds fine, but we'll have to find some costumes somewhere."

"I've already taken care of it," he stated. "They keep quite a stock of them on hand here at the hotel, so I put in an order for two... just in case you decided to accept my invitation to attend."

"How will we be dressed?" she asked curiously. "Something terribly original, I hope."

"You'll see. It's a surprise.... Oh, good morning, Norene. Inspector."

Inspector Snelling nodded, his admiring gaze drawn back to Norene as she smiled charmingly and replied to O'Rourke's greeting.

"Good morning, you two. Isn't it a splendid day?"

Under the table, Kate's foot gently nudged O'Rourke's. "Yes, and you're looking splendid, too, Norene," she said. "That sweater suits you perfectly."

Norene's cheeks quickly matched the color of the rose-colored sweater Kate had given her in the gift exchange. She wore it with a pair of charcoal wool slacks that flattered her slim figure and banished forever the image of a dowdy librarian.

"Told her the same thing myself," Snelling interjected. "Norene's a really smashing-looking woman. Can't think why some bright fellow hasn't carried her off by this time." He winked broadly, and again Norene blushed prettily.

"Surely you've considered it?" O'Rourke spoke mildly, the dimple in his cheek making a sudden appearance.

"I'm giving the idea my undivided attention, I assure you."

"Reginald, you embarrass me," Norene scolded, her eyes shining.

"Why don't you join us for breakfast?" Kate asked, feeling inordinately pleased with the success of her matchmaking endeavors.

"We'd be delighted, wouldn't we, Norrie?" Snelling held the chair for Norene, then seated himself across from her, beckoning to the waitress.

Norene unrolled her napkin. "Have you heard about the treasure hunt this afternoon?"

"Yes," Kate responded. "It sounds like fun, I think."

At that moment several of the other hotel guests came into the room, led by the bustling figure of Lady Harwood.

Norene lowered her voice. "Oh, my goodness! Can you believe it? Carolyne Harwood is still wearing that flashy diamond necklace."

"If she isn't careful, it could get stolen again," O'Rourke casually observed. "It could end up being the object of this afternoon's treasure hunt."

Inspector Snelling cast him a quick, grave look.

Kate drew a deep breath. "I'm...sure that's only a very remote possibility," she stated. As if to add emphasis to those somewhat unconvincing words, she began vigorously attacking her grapefruit.

The rest of the morning passed quickly. Kate and O'Rourke took a stroll around the hotel grounds, then played cards with Mrs. Phillips and Colonel Westcott until lunch. When it was time for the treasure hunt to get under way, Kate, suddenly apprehensive, suggested an alternate plan to O'Rourke.

"Would you mind if we missed the treasure hunt?" she asked. "I was just thinking...instead of running around the hotel like children, why don't we have that nice long nap we missed yesterday?"

Thank heavens, O'Rourke seemed interested.

"Yes, a much more adult activity, I agree."

They made their excuses and, arm in arm, climbed the stairs to their room, locking the door behind them. Kate was neatly turning back the bedcovers when O'Rourke emerged from the closet wearing only the black pajama bottoms and a suggestive smile. He tumbled her onto the bed and, seizing her legs, pulled off her boots and tossed them into a far corner. Then he began tugging her slacks down over her hips, while she laughed and twisted, trying to get away from him.

He threw a leg over Kate's thighs to pin her down as he stripped her sweater off over her head.

"Something about wearing those black silk pajamas turns you into a wild beast," she gasped, feebly attempting to fend him off.

"Might not be the pajamas," he panted. "It could have been the thought of you in provocative lavender underwear. I caught a glimpse of it when you were dressing this morning." He drew back slightly to admire the lacy Victorian teddy she was wearing. "And I've wanted a good look at it ever since."

"Fiend," she teased, settling into his arms again. "Don't tell me that's what you were thinking of while we were playing cards with Norene's mother!"

His blue eyes twinkled. "Can you think of anything better?"

"I'm surprised you didn't bid a bra or three undies."

"I could have said, 'I'll raise your teddy.'" He chuckled, untying the ribbon closing at the front of her undergarment. "Still not a bad idea."

Kate wiggled beneath him. "Something tells me this nap isn't going to be the least bit restful," she remarked.

O'Rourke gave a short, groaning laugh. "And to think, back in kindergarten I always rebelled when the teacher made us take naps. If I'd only known..."

His mouth swooped down upon Kate's with swift, sensual audacity, drawing an abandoned response from her. As he stroked and nipped at her bottom lip with his teeth and tongue, Kate felt an unmistakable warmth rise up within her. It began somewhere in the region of her lower abdomen and radiated outward in slow, delicious waves of sensation that reached every inch of her body. She felt as if she were being sheathed by heat, devoured by fiery pleasure. She was going up in flames....

"Fire!"

There was a loud pounding on the door and someone shouted again. "Fire!"

"What the...?" O'Rourke sat upright, dragging her with him.

"There's a fire in the hotel," came the voice again. Kate thought it might be that of the hotel manager, Mr. Smythe. "Vacate your room immediately. We're meeting outside on the front lawn. Hurry!"

"My God!" Kate cried, clutching O'Rourke's arm. "A fire..."

"Come on, let's get out of here," he said, sliding off the bed and lifting her to her feet.

"I can't go like this," she protested, tugging the straps of the teddy back onto her shoulders.

"Get your robe then," he said. "We don't have time for anything else. As old as this place is, it could go up in a real blaze of glory."

Kate dashed to the closet, fighting panic. O'Rourke slipped on his moccasins and unlocked the door. "Kate, bring my jacket, will you? It'll be cold as hell outside."

They could hear more shouts in the hallway and the sound of running steps on the stairs. From a distance came the thready hum of a fire alarm.

Kate tied her robe and hurriedly shoved her feet into a pair of slippers. She had grabbed O'Rourke's tweed jacket off a hanger and started toward the closet door when something made her stop short. She hefted the jacket she held. Why did it seem so heavy?

With a terrible, sinking feeling, she thrust her fingers into a pocket and met cold stone and metal. Her heart began to slam painfully against her ribs as she withdrew the hand that now held the Star of Pretoria necklace. She clutched the diamonds to her chest and sagged wearily.

How and when had he managed to steal it again? *Why had he done it?*

"Kate," called O'Rourke, "what's keeping you? We've got to get out of here, sweetheart."

"I'm coming." Kate looked about frantically. What could she do with the damned thing? If she left it in the hotel, it might be needlessly lost in the fire. Still, if she took it with her, someone could discover it and . . .

"Kate? Come on, damn it!"

Not knowing what else to do, she dumped the necklace back into the jacket pocket and, saying a silent prayer, left the closet.

Without a trace of guilt, O'Rourke took the jacket and slipped it on over his bare chest, all the while ushering her through the door and down the stairs.

Inspector Snelling and his police personnel were efficiently shuffling the distracted guests out the front door into the chilly winter air. Kate eyed the uniforms with dread. Why had the police lingered once the necklace had been returned? she worried. Had they suspected the thief would act again? Her mind was so numbed with fear for O'Rourke that it wasn't until they had stood shivering in the cold for several minutes that she became aware of the amused glances they were drawing.

Curious eyes slid away from hers as she gazed about the small crowd gathered on the snowy lawn, but there were hints of quickly hidden smiles and a palpable atmosphere of avid interest.

Kate looked down at her robe, suddenly convinced that everyone there could actually *see* the frivolous lavender garment under it. And if that wasn't bad enough, O'Rourke's appearance left no doubt as to his state of undress. Though the tweed jacket looked respectable enough, his hairy chest did not. Nor did the thin pajamas that the wind persisted in flattening against his body. Blatantly they advertised the lack of substantial clothing beneath.

Kate closed her eyes and swallowed deeply. With very little effort, she could begin hyperventilating—just what she needed!

She would never be able to face any of these people again. Ever. It had been bad enough when O'Rourke had kissed her under the mistletoe that first night, or even yesterday when he had proposed marriage in front of everyone, but now... she dropped her head in complete disgrace. It was three o'clock in the afternoon, for God's sake! Could there be anyone on the face of the earth too naive to realize what they had been up to? She pressed a hand to her aching forehead and petitioned the gods to let the earth open up and swallow her.

O'Rourke moved closer, dropping an arm around her shoulder. "Buck up, Katie," he murmured, a quiet laugh underlining his words. "It's not as bad as you think... look."

She raised her eyes to his, and he nodded toward the hotel's front door. There were Denise and Weldon Blake, she wearing a filmy pink negligee and he clad in a white sheet. Both were reluctant to leave the hotel, but Reginald Snelling was insisting, a slight smile hovering about his thin lips. Besides the staff, they were the last people to leave the endangered building.

O'Rourke squeezed her shoulder. "See, we weren't the only ones caught with our . . . well, you know the old saying."

She fairly snorted. "Yes, but they're newlyweds! We're middle-aged . . . well, practically middle-aged. We're supposed to be mature!"

His grin was maddening, but Kate had to admit she did feel a little better. At least knowing someone else kept them company in their painful humiliation eased her mind, leaving it free to worry that the stolen necklace would be discovered in O'Rourke's pocket.

She craned her neck, finally seeing Lady Harwood at the back of the crowd. The lady, swathed in furs, merely looked anxious, as did everyone else waiting for word on the fire. Kate decided the woman probably didn't even know her ridiculous necklace was missing again. No doubt the announcement would soon be forthcoming. . . .

A siren sounded in the near distance as Mr. Smythe stepped onto the portico. "The men of the village fire brigade will be here in a moment, so we need to clear a path for them. Because several of you are . . . ahem, clearly suffering from the cold, I suggest as many of you as possible move into the greenhouse for warmth."

"Is that sensible?" questioned Chester Rand. "Isn't it attached to the hotel?"

"Yes, but it is judged safe enough for the time being. The staff believes the fire is contained in one of the upstairs storage rooms, so the danger has been minimized. Ah, here are the firemen—move quickly, please."

Kate didn't mind being crammed into the greenhouse; it was warmer, and in the crush of bodies, she didn't feel as though she were on display. But as she stood close to O'Rourke, she was miserably aware of the bulky necklace in the pocket between them. What on earth was she going to do about that?

In a short time the relieved guests were allowed to reenter the hotel through the conservatory. Fortunately, the fire had turned out to be a relatively harmless one, easily extinguished. There was no significant damage and only a small amount of smoke on the top floor.

"Well, that's certainly good news," commented O'Rourke.

Kate merely nodded and started up the stairs.

"Where are you going?" he asked, catching up with her.

"To put on some clothes," she replied. "And I'm never taking them off again."

"Now that would be a real shame." He chuckled.

Behind them came a sudden shrill scream. "Oh, my God, Cornie!"

Kate sighed heavily. "Excuse me, but this is where I came in," she muttered, continuing to climb the stairs to their room.

What a day!

Kate hoped it would be a long, long time before she spent a worse one.

Dressed in jeans and a cable-knit sweater, she sat before the blazing fire, pulling on her boots. Pleading a headache, she had insisted O'Rourke go down to dinner without her, and now, in his absence, she was preparing to carry out a plan conceived in panic. Hours of racking her brain had produced no other solution.

Seeing that cursed necklace again had only confirmed an earlier suspicion that had niggled at Kate's mind. Obviously O'Rourke was acting out of more than simple greed. Knowing he had taken the diamonds a second time, when the hotel was still being watched so carefully, meant only one thing. It was the thrill of danger that appealed to him—the challenge. He must have some inner compulsion to prove he was capable of the kind of derring-do necessary for pulling off a reckless stunt like that.

It wasn't the money, she realized. It could never have been entirely that. He'd hinted that his family was well-heeled, and since her own yearly income was impressive, he had never been exactly poverty-stricken. The "family business" he was involved in must provide well for him, for he had never shown any inclination to let himself be supported by his wife. Nor had he ever expressed a desire for a more regular job. With his personality and talents, he could have insinuated his way into any company in town, but he obviously hadn't needed to. No, there had to be deeper, darker reasons than money or pride.

Kate stared unseeingly into the fire. O'Rourke was sick . . . mentally and emotionally ill. It was time to face the facts, no matter how much she longed to deny them. Outwardly he was one of the most handsome and personable men she had ever met. Inwardly he must be a tortured, neurotic soul. Lost and unconsciously crying out for help.

Well, she intended to provide that help, but not in the way his twisted thinking had devised. She knew that certain criminal types committed their crimes in the hope they would be caught and punished—it seemed to prove that someone cared about them, even if it was only an impersonal judicial system. She wasn't going to let that happen to the man she loved. She would see that he had help, all right, but it was going to be professional aid . . . something constructive that could never be accomplished by years spent locked up in a cell.

She had to get O'Rourke safely away from England. Once they were back home and remarried, she would calmly explain to him that she knew all about his problem and wanted to do what was best for him. If she was firm and confident, surely he would be reasonable about it. He'd understand that their new life was too precious to risk, wouldn't he?

She got to her feet with a distracted shake of her head. She didn't know. She could only hope and pray for the best. But first, before they could begin to think about professional counseling, she had to see that he was beyond the reach of the law. And the only way to do that was to get rid of the evidence linking him to the crime committed here at the hotel.

She went into the closet and studied the tweed jacket he had left so carelessly flung on a hook. Once the hue and cry went up, he had to have known they would be searching the hotel a second time. And yet, he hadn't bothered to try hiding the necklace. Why would he have been so casual about the whole thing unless he simply wanted to be apprehended?

Kate closed her eyes tightly against the sting of tears. Poor darling, she thought sadly. Why couldn't you have just told me you were struggling with such an emotional burden.

Of course, he probably didn't realize it himself. Disturbed people were often unaware of their own frailties.

It hurt her to know there was such weakness in the man she had considered one of the strongest people she'd ever met.

With renewed determination, she transferred the piece of jewelry to the pocket of her coat, which she then slipped on.

My best chance, she thought as she let herself out of the room, is now while everyone is at dinner.

She crept down the stairs, relieved not to encounter other guests. Hearing voices in the downstairs hallway, she decided she would not risk going that way, but slip out the front doors instead.

When she was certain no one would see her, Kate dashed through the circle of brilliance thrown by the floodlights and into the shielding darkness beyond. She hurried down the cleared walkway toward the greenhouse.

It was the logical place, she told herself. Because Lady Harwood had discovered her necklace missing immediately after the fire, it was assumed that the thief set the blaze as a diversion, then used the resulting confusion as a cover for the robbery. And because too many people had scattered throughout the hotel before the loss was noticed, the police had not been able to conduct a proper search.

But, Kate had reasoned, for all they knew, the person who had taken the necklace could have hidden it temporarily in the greenhouse, planning to return for it later. By putting the damned thing there herself, she hoped that thought might occur to them, prompting a search that would turn it up. All she had to do was plant it in a flowerpot or a bag of fertilizer and forget it.

Naturally O'Rourke might have a few questions of his own once he determined the diamonds were no longer in his jacket pocket, but she would simply have to deal with that if and when the time came.

Through the long windows in the dining room, she could see that dinner had ended and the guests were beginning to scatter. Her pulse sped up alarmingly. She'd have to hurry. There'd be no time for finesse in finding a hiding place. She'd pitch the miserable Star into the first compost heap she saw and get her fanny back upstairs. If O'Rourke had returned to the room before her, she'd have to lie and say she'd gone for a walk, hoping it would ease her headache.

When the greenhouse doorknob turned easily within her grip, she swallowed deeply. She hadn't considered the fact that it might be locked. Lord only knows what she would have done in that case.

The glass-enclosed building was dark, and silent except for the low roar of a heating system that pumped moist warm air through it. Kate's eyes had already adjusted to darkness, and she started unerringly down the middle aisle, past low tables filled with bedding plants. Toward the back of the room, she could see a row of trees in tubs and made that her destination. Digging into her pocket, she dragged out the necklace and held it ready for disposal.

Suddenly she heard a faint creaking noise and stopped dead, peering about in confusion.

It was only the furnace, she assured herself. Surely that was all it could be....

The noise came again, and somehow she knew that whatever it was, it had nothing to do with the furnace. At the back of the greenhouse, shadows moved and mingled, and Kate caught her breath.

Someone was coming in through the door from the conservatory, moving stealthily but with purpose. Whoever it was had seen her, she realized.

Get the hell out of here, her brain urged as her body stood frozen to the spot. *For God's sake, get moving!*

Activated by overwhelming panic, Kate whirled and ran. Just as her disbelieving eyes fastened on a second figure sidling through the front door, her feet entangled in a hose strung across the floor and she went sprawling. Her last conscious emotion was fear for O'Rourke—everything else was lost in an explosion of black pain when her head struck the stone pedestal of a birdbath.

Kate's pursuers closed ranks to stand over her.

"My God, it's your wife!"

With a strangled cry, O'Rourke dropped to his knees, shaking fingers searching for a pulse. When he found it, he heaved a relieved sigh and gently brushed stray tendrils of hair away from the swelling bruise on her temple. "Oh, Katie," he murmured in a low, tense tone.

The other man knelt and took the necklace from Kate's relaxed grip. As he held it up, it glittered icily even in the dimness. Their eyes met in reluctant agreement.

"You know what we've got to do, don't you, mate?"

Silently O'Rourke nodded.

"We have no choice," he said. "We'll have to get rid of her."

Chapter Fifteen

It took an enormous amount of concentration, but at last Kate managed to open her eyes.

"There, didn't I tell you she'd be coming round soon?"

She blinked. The blow to her head must have been worse than she'd thought. Not only did she have a terrible headache, but she could swear Albert Einstein was standing by her bed.

Bed? How had she gotten back to her room?

"O'Rourke?" she murmured fretfully.

Instantly two large hands gripped hers fiercely. "I'm here, Katie. Are you all right?"

"Wh-what happened?"

"You struck your head, Mrs. Callahan," stated Albert, cocking his head to one side. "How are you feeling?"

"Awful. Where did you come from?"

"Darlin', this is Dr. Miller from the village."

Kate gave the doctor a sharp look. Why was he lying about his name?

"If you would step to one side, Mr. Callahan, I would like to check your wife's reflexes and ask her a few simple questions."

All the while the man with the wild white hair and mustache was asking her to count his fingers or recite her name and address, Kate was aware of O'Rourke speaking quietly with another man who lurked in the shadows. When the man shifted positions, the light fell across his bony face and she recognized Inspector Snelling. Suddenly, with devastating clarity, the scene in the greenhouse came back to her. The fact that Snelling was here in the room with them could only mean one thing—he'd deduced O'Rourke was the thief.

Kate groaned, knowing the whole thing was her fault. She should have left well enough alone.

"Yes, I'm afraid you'll feel a bit dicey for a while," chuckled the doctor, "but I'm leaving some headache pills for you."

"Will she be all right?" questioned O'Rourke. "Did you find anything seriously wrong?"

"No, it seems she merely suffered a nasty blow to the temple. A bit of throbbing and bruising should be the extent of it."

"Thank you for coming, Doctor. I appreciate it."

"Glad to do it, Mr. Callahan. A call at Cross Coombe Manor gives me a chance to stop in at the bar and have a pint before I return home. Now...where did I leave my bowler?"

"I believe this is it," said Reginald Snelling, handing the doctor a felt hat.

The Einstein look-alike patted the derby over his unruly hair. "I'll be off now. Be sure to ring me if any problems arise. Cheerio."

A uniformed policeman opened the door for the doctor, Kate noticed with a sinking heart. That the room was being closely guarded confirmed her worst fears.

"Now, Mrs. Callahan," intoned Inspector Snelling, "perhaps you'd like to explain to us what you were doing in the greenhouse this evening?"

Kate's gaze flew to O'Rourke's and, unbelievably, his eyes fell.

He's just as scared as I am, she thought, heaving herself into a sitting position.

"I was taking a walk," she said coolly.

"A walk?" he queried doubtfully. "At night, in a dark greenhouse? A bit odd, don't you think?"

"I . . . I had gotten cold and was simply returning to the hotel through the nearest entrance. There's nothing unusual about that."

"Maybe not," he agreed amiably. "But what about the diamond necklace you happened to be carrying?"

Kate cleared her throat. "I found it in the greenhouse as I was passing through."

Snelling rubbed his forehead wearily. "Come now, surely you can do better than that? One doesn't *find* diamond necklaces lying about in potting sheds. Not unless one has hidden them oneself. You put it there earlier today, didn't you?"

"What? No!"

"Don't lie to me, Mrs. Callahan."

"O'Rourke," Kate pleaded.

"Snelling," growled O'Rourke.

The inspector crossed thin arms over his chest and peered at her with narrowed gaze.

"You stole that necklace, didn't you, Mrs. Callahan?"

"Don't be an ass!" she gasped.

"O'Rourke," warned Snelling. "Make her behave."

"Katie," soothed O'Rourke. "Don't upset yourself."

"I'm not upsetting myself," she snapped. "*He's* upsetting me. How dare you insinuate I had anything to do with stealing that atrocious piece of junk."

"Atrocious, indeed. But extremely valuable. Is that why you took it, Mrs. Callahan?"

"I did not take it!"

"Then would you care to shed some light on who did?"

Kate's mouth closed immediately. It was obviously a trick question. And one to which she would not give an answer.

"Kate," O'Rourke said in a resigned tone, "I think you should tell Snelling anything you might happen to know."

"No! I...I mean, I really don't know anything. I found the necklace and was returning it."

"I had hoped you would see your way clear to being a bit more helpful, Mrs. Callahan," said the inspector. "Since it's obvious you don't wish to cooperate, I have no choice. You'll be detained here until I can get in touch with my superiors in London."

"Detained?" she repeated. "Meaning?"

"Meaning you will remain in this room, with a police guard outside the door."

"But why?"

"I should think that would be elementary."

Kate wanted to laugh, but she seemed to have forgotten how. "You really think *I* took the necklace, don't you?"

"It would seem so."

"Am I under arrest?"

"You are being detained. By morning I shall know what Scotland Yard advocates doing with you."

"I protest. There are legal guidelines that must be followed."

"I haven't forgotten that you are a barrister, madam, but may I remind you this is England, not the States. We do things our own way here."

Kate glanced at O'Rourke, appalled by his strained silence. He stood with shoulders hunched, pale and miserable, apparently as much at a loss as she. Of course, if O'Rourke objected to her treatment, Snelling might turn a more watchful eye upon him. It was probably best if she kept the detective's attention on herself.

"All right, I will bow to your judgment," she announced. "But you may be sure I will have plenty to say to your superiors."

"Very well." Snelling looked amused. "We'll leave you alone now, but don't hesitate to inform the guard if, at any time during the night, you wish to make a confession."

"I would appreciate a few minutes alone with my...wife," O'Rourke said.

"Sorry, old man. I can't permit that. You know all the reasons."

"Are you saying that O'Rourke is not allowed to stay with me?" Kate got to her feet, steadying herself by clinging to the bedpost.

"That's correct. After all, this is a police detention, not a honeymoon. Your husband will be sharing a room with me tonight."

For the first time, Kate saw O'Rourke's suitcase sitting by the door. It was a circumstance for which she had not been prepared.

"But we . . . I need to talk to him," cried Kate.

"When you are in the mood to talk, it will be to the police. *Afterward* you will have the chance to speak to O'Rourke."

O'Rourke crossed to her and, putting his hands on her shoulders, gave her a quick, hard kiss. "It will be okay, sweetheart. Don't worry."

She watched as the guard opened the door for them and saw O'Rourke turn to give her a final look. Suddenly the seriousness of the situation dawned on her. They were going to lock her in this room like a common criminal. And tomorrow she would be facing a group of men from Scotland Yard who wouldn't be interested in playing games. She knew she was innocent, but she also knew who was guilty. That simplified matters.

Right. It made the whole thing about as simple as walking a tightrope blindfolded.

Thirty minutes later, Kate had undressed and put on her pajamas. She was taking one of the pills the doctor had left her when she heard a faint noise and the wall beside the bed opened up. There stood O'Rourke, the worried frown on his face failing to dominate self-pride at his own ingenuity in making use of the secret passageway.

"O'Rourke," she exclaimed, "thank goodness! I have to talk to you."

"We don't have much time," he said, crossing the room to bolt the door from the inside. "Once Snelling notices my absence, he'll know exactly where I've gone."

He closed the distance between them and took her into his arms. "Oh, Katie," he murmured against her hair, "what have you gotten yourself into?"

She raised her face for his kiss, drawing strength from his very nearness. "It will be okay," she said, as if sensing he needed soothing more than she.

"I can't let them do this to you," he said, leaning back to study her face. "I'm going to tell them that I—"

"No," she cried, "please don't do that! It would be a terrible mistake."

"Kate, you don't understand, darlin'. I haven't been—"

"Look," she insisted, "I've got this all worked out. There are two things I want you to do for me."

"Kate . . ."

"Hush now, and listen to me. We may not have much time." She stepped out of his arms and began to pace the floor. "I need you to call my law partners as soon as you can. Get one of them—I don't care which—over here to advise me. Snelling may think he has a case against me, but with my reputation in the States, it will soon be evident that I am anything but a jewel thief. However, the longer it takes Scotland Yard to find that out, the more distance there will be between the crime and the . . . the real thief."

"I can't let you do this." O'Rourke ran an agitated hand through his hair. "It's my responsibility."

"I want to do it. Don't you know that?" She put her arms around his waist and rested her head against his shoulder. "I just want us to be able to go home together and start over again."

"I want that, too, but—"

There was a loud pounding at the door. "O'Rourke! Are you in there?"

O'Rourke heaved a sigh. "Snelling. He was faster even than I thought he'd be."

"Open this bloody door!" bellowed the Inspector.

"Listen, Kate, I'm going to tell them that I want—"

"Please don't," she begged. "Promise me you won't say a word to them!"

"I can't let you go through this."

"I don't mind if it will help you."

The door fairly buckled under the force of Snelling's blows. "If you don't open this damned door at once," he shouted, "I'll break it down—even if I have to get a battering ram to do it!"

"Go quickly," breathed Kate. "If you slip out through the secret passage, they won't know for certain you were here. You'd better do what you can to stay on Snelling's good side."

"I thought we'd have time to work this out," he muttered, as another series of blows assailed the door. "Hell, I'm in over my head this time!"

"Hurry, love," she pleaded. "They could come through that door at any second. If you're found here, they'll be more suspicious than they already are."

Kate began running her hands over the rough stone wall. "Oh, where is that blasted lever?" she whispered.

O'Rourke reached out and touched the right stone, and the wall creaked open. He paused in the entrance to the passage, as if debating whether or not to leave her.

Kate threw her arms around him and gave him a frantic kiss. "You've got to go. Hurry now!"

"I don't like this," he started, but she waved an imperious hand.

"We don't have time to argue about it. Just do your best to get in touch with the firm and get me some help, all right?"

"All right," he said, making no effort to disguise his reluctance. "And what's the other thing you wanted me to do?"

"I want you to promise me that, no matter what happens, you will not make the mistake of confessing."

"I can't—"

"Promise me," she whispered fiercely.

The pounding resumed, so loud the room echoed with the sound. Inspector Snelling had obviously sent for reinforcements.

"Promise me, O'Rourke!"

"Oh, all right, damn it." He ducked into the dark passageway. "We'll talk later."

"Take care."

When the wall had swung back into place, Kate hurried across the room to unbolt the door. It sprang open almost immediately.

"Where the bleeding bloody hell is O'Rourke?" demanded Snelling, glancing at the empty room over her shoulder.

"O'Rourke? What makes you think he's here?"

Snelling uttered a four-star obscenity and issued terse orders for the guard to relock Kate's door. "And don't try your hand at the secret passageway," he warned her, "because my men are watching the other end." With that, he turned and stalked down the hall.

Kate glared at his stiff, retreating back and, just before the door slammed shut, made a horrible face at him. She felt childish, but better.

There was only one way out of the hidden passage, and as soon as O'Rourke stepped into Lord and Lady Harwood's bedchamber, he knew how unfortunate that was. Among the people waiting for him were the Harwoods, Colonel Westcott, Chester Rand, two policemen and, just bursting through the door, Reginald Snelling.

"How in the hell did you get into that secret chamber?" Snelling barked. "We know you didn't go this way."

O'Rourke shrugged. "Some of my more recent explorations turned up another entrance—through a trapdoor under the orchestra platform in the ballroom."

"You dropped from above?" gasped Lady Harwood.

"Yes. Nearly breaking both legs, I might add." O'Rourke's grin was rueful. "At one time I'm sure there was a ladder of sorts . . . but it has long since rotted away. Of course, that left me no choice but to make my exit the usual way." He jerked a thumb at the tapestries that hid the small arched doorway.

"Care to enlighten us as to what you told her, Callahan?" Snelling asked, breathing hard from his headlong rush down the hotel corridor.

"I didn't tell her a damned thing," O'Rourke mumbled. "But I should have. I went there intending to."

"But why?"

"Because, by God, I don't like the way you're treating Kate. She has a right to know what's going on."

Rand chuckled. "O'Rourke, mate, think how she botched things up when she *didn't* know! And remember, a little knowledge is a dangerous thing."

"She was only trying to help me."

"And very commendable, too," Rand agreed. "But the lady was becoming something of an annoyance. When I was sent here by Interpol to catch a jewel thief, I had no idea how matters would be complicated by a charming female determined to save her ex-husband."

O'Rourke dropped into an empty armchair near the fire. "I realize something had to be done, but why can't we simply tell her what is really happening?"

"She's been kept in the dark this long," Snelling pointed out. "A while longer can't hurt."

"Not you, maybe," O'Rourke said dispiritedly.

"You know as well as I do that your wife is going to start demanding her rights as soon as she figures out Scotland Yard isn't going to incarcerate her," Snelling reasoned. "If she raises enough fuss, we'll have to let her out of that room. Judging from her recent actions, we can't be certain she will keep quiet about this. What if she says the wrong thing to the wrong person? Her life could be endangered."

"I could explain matters to her," O'Rourke argued. "She won't say a word if I tell her not to."

"Oh, yes, she has been remarkably obedient thus far." Snelling's sarcasm hit home.

O'Rourke shrugged. "I guess you're the boss, but you have no idea what kind of hot water I'll be in when she finds out the truth."

"Nonsense, dear boy," scolded Lady Harwood. "Your wife will be pleased to learn you are not and never have been a thief."

"Yes, think on the...harrumph, positive side," concurred Cornelius Harwood. "Everything will turn out for the best."

"Wish I could believe that."

"Just give us two more days," suggested Snelling. "I'm announcing at breakfast in the morning that if the culprit hasn't been apprehended by the night of the masquerade ball, which marks the end of Christmas week, no one will be allowed to leave. Surely the thought of remaining under house arrest indefinitely will inspire the fellow to act. If he turns out to be more patient than I think, we'll release Kate, and I'll consider letting you explain everything to her."

"In the meantime, we can't take the chance of her letting the cat out of the bag," agreed Colonel Westcott. "If the real thief hears your wife was found with the Star of Pretoria in her possession, he'll realize there are *two* necklaces. It wouldn't take him long to smell a rat...so to speak."

"I can't believe he didn't give up after Mrs. Callahan foiled the first theft by finding and returning the diamonds," commented Lady Harwood. "The bugger must have a well-developed ego to think he could manage to pull off a second robbery—right under the noses of the police."

"That's what we're hoping for," nodded Inspector Snelling.

"But the thing I can't figure," O'Rourke said, "is that, from the beginning, this whole mess has had all the earmarks of a personal grudge."

"I agree with the grudge theory," spoke Westcott. "The jewel thefts have all been in hotels owned by your family. It's as if the Callahan name is under attack."

"Originally I thought it might be my cousin Nicholas Callahan," mused O'Rourke. "He was abandoned as a child, and grew up in an orphanage. When he became old enough, my parents took him in. Free help around the hotels, you know. He worked his tail off, but no matter what, my father always made sure he knew he was living off our charity."

"This Nicholas...was he the vengeful type?" questioned Snelling, tamping tobacco into the pipe he had drawn from his pocket.

"Nick never had the most attractive personality in the world," admitted O'Rourke. "He was a sniveling sneak as a kid. I could have hated him if he hadn't been so pathetic. Yeah, he was the jealous sort—always trying to prove he was as good as everyone else. His time in the orphanage and with my parents really did a number on him."

"So he has a grudge against your family?" asked Rand.

"Had." O'Rourke glanced up to meet the Australian's gaze. "We hadn't kept in touch, but after I was set up in Kansas City, I hired a detective to locate Nick. I found out he died in upstate New York some time ago."

"That puts him out of the picture, eh?" Lord Harwood stroked his mustache and rocked back and forth on his heels.

"Yes. And anyway, we know the thief has to be someone in the hotel right now," O'Rourke pointed out. "Either a guest or a worker here. Smythe has checked and rechecked the credentials of each of the hired help, so that narrows the field even more."

"One of those guests is going to make a mistake sooner or later," stated Snelling. "What we are looking for is someone who tries to leave the hotel for any reason."

"Right," said Chester Rand. "That will be a dead giveaway that he has the necklace and wants to stash it somewhere safe until he can pick it up later."

Snelling gave a short, harsh laugh. "And we'll be right there to watch when he makes his move. Yes, I can almost promise you, O'Rourke, that by this time tomorrow, the puzzle will have been solved...and you'll be able to give your wife the true story."

O'Rourke's expression was glum. "I'm not sure I'm looking forward to it," was all he said.

Kate spent a long and lonely night, her sleep troubled by vague dreams of dangerous highwaymen and beautiful, frightened ladies fleeing down endless, hidden passageways.

A policewoman brought her a breakfast tray, but other than telling Kate the rest of the guests had been informed she was indisposed, there was little conversation.

When she was alone again, Kate dressed in jeans and a sweater and, for lack of anything better to do, got out paper and pencil and began listing points of defense. She wanted to be able to get the legal ball rolling as soon as her colleague arrived in Cross Coombe.

By early afternoon she was slightly stir-crazy. She read; she wrote; she napped; she paced the floor. She stared out the window and wondered where O'Rourke was, what he was doing.

What is going on downstairs? she wondered for the hundredth time. *This hotel is too damned quiet.*

At approximately three o'clock in the afternoon, all hell broke loose.

O'Rourke had just stepped out of the library when he heard a heated altercation at the front door. Hurrying to the source of the angry shouts, he saw Mrs. Phillips striking a uniformed police officer with her umbrella.

"I demand to be allowed out of this hotel," the irate woman shrieked.

"But, madam," gasped the guard, dodging blows, "I have my orders! No one is to leave."

"I'll have you know I've errands in the village," Mrs. Phillips ranted. "And I am sick of being cooped up indoors!"

At that moment a siren shrilled suddenly, causing O'Rourke's heart to jump against his ribs. A small white ambulance van careened to a halt outside the main entrance, and two men in coveralls, a stretcher between them, raced up the walkway.

"Where's the victim?" one of them asked as they burst through the front doors.

"What the . . . ?"

"Has someone died?" cried Mrs. Phillips, letting her umbrella fall to her side. "Oh, my Lord!"

Reginald Snelling appeared instantly. "What is going on here?"

The police guard, Mrs. Phillips and both ambulance attendants began to talk at one time, creating a din that fairly rocked the narrow entryway.

"Up here!" called a new voice. "Hurry!"

"Blake?" queried the inspector. "What's up, man?"

"It's my wife," Weldon Blake called back. "She's having some sort of attack. I . . . I called the ambulance first thing."

"What sort of attack?" Snelling asked, following the attendants up the stairs.

"It sounds like appendicitis to us," one of the uniformed men tossed over his shoulder. "Vomiting, severe pain."

"Wait just a minute. This is highly irregular. Why wasn't I informed of the situation?"

A high, thin scream ripped through the upper hallway, and Weldon Blake turned on the inspector in fury. "There! Did you hear that? My wife is in pain. Why the deuce should I waste time asking your permission before calling for help?"

"Let's have a look," Snelling said wearily. "O'Rourke, will you for God's sake, get that woman to shut up?"

O'Rourke turned back to Mrs. Phillips, but before he could make an attempt to pacify her, she thrust the guard aside and strode out the door.

"I'm going into the village whether you like it or not," she blared. "You dare not stop me."

The policeman was clearly stymied.

"Let her go," advised O'Rourke. "Just follow her at a discreet distance and keep an eye on her. Make certain she doesn't have a chance to hide the stolen goods anywhere."

"You want me to follow her?"

"Somebody has to. Be reasonable—how dangerous can she be?"

The man rubbed his stinging head. "If I'm injured in the line of duty," he warned, "I'll expect compensation."

No sooner had he sprinted after Mrs. Phillips than Norene and Jared came out of the residents' lounge wearing their coats.

"Sorry, you two," O'Rourke said, "but no one is being allowed outside the hotel."

"Are you certain?" Norene asked. "I thought I just saw my mother walking down the street."

"Be a sport, old man," Jared entreated. "I haven't had a chance to be alone with Norene for days now. I thought I'd take her out to tea."

"No can do."

"That's right," Snelling boomed from above. "You'll have to take tea here in the hotel . . . or allow me to join you in the village."

Jared cursed soundly. "Your company is exactly what I am trying to avoid. As if you didn't know . . ."

"Jared, don't be rude," scolded Norene.

"Here now, you'll have to move out of the way, folks. We've got an emergency on our hands."

The two ambulance attendants were hastening down the stairs, bearing a thrashing, moaning Denise Blake on a stretcher. Her husband hovered at her side, a definite hindrance as he refused to release her hand.

"Is she going to be all right?" he asked anxiously.

Norene looked pale. "Oh, my goodness," she whispered. "How awful!"

"Let us through, please. We've got to get her to hospital in Bath. We've no time to waste here."

"O'Rourke," boomed Snelling. "You go with them."

"With the Blakes?"

"It's not necessary, Inspector," Weldon Blake insisted. "I'm not even sure there's room in the van."

"Find room," snapped Snelling. "He's going with you."

Another agonized moan from Denise Blake cut short her husband's protest.

"Oh, all right—what the hell!" Blake turned his attention back to the woman on the stretcher. O'Rourke grabbed a coat off the hall rack and glared at Snelling.

"Don't give me that look," Snelling chided. "I'll be on duty myself. Just as soon as I find another guard for this front door, I'm off to tea with Norrie and Mr. Harwood."

Precisely four hours later, Reginald Snelling faced the guests assembled in the lounge and made an announcement.

"Ladies and gentlemen, I'm rather pleased to be able to tell you that, at last, we have apprehended the person responsible for the theft of Lady Harwood's diamonds."

The room hummed with excitement as heads turned in an effort to determine what guest was missing.

O'Rourke squared his shoulders and said, "If you don't need me here, I think I'd better go break the news to Kate."

"Fine idea. Tell the guard he is released from duty, will you?"

"Sure thing."

"Oh, and O'Rourke ... good luck."

O'Rourke nodded. "Thanks. Something tells me I'm going to need it."

Jamming his hands into his pockets, O'Rourke took the steps slowly, frantically rehearsing the words he would need to make Kate understand.

Chapter Sixteen

When O'Rourke entered the bedroom, Kate sprang out of a chair by the fire and ran into his arms.

"What has happened?" she cried. "I've been going crazy with worry."

"It's all right now," he assured her, resting one cheek against the top of her head. "Everything is over at last."

She drew away. "Then...they know about you?"

"Actually, Kate, you're the one who doesn't know about me." His blue eyes were grave as they moved over her face. "I think we'd better sit down."

"O'Rourke?" Her voice was breathless. "What's going on?"

He took her hand and led her back to the overstuffed chairs. Gently he pushed her into one, then seated himself in the other, moving it so he faced her and their knees nearly touched.

"What about the necklace?" Kate insisted.

"I didn't take it," he stated simply.

"You what?"

"No, and I'm sorry I had to let you believe I did."

"I don't understand...."

"Let me start at the beginning," he said.

"Yes, perhaps you'd better do that."

O'Rourke gave her a quick look, but she seemed calm enough. He drew a deep breath and started talking.

"I guess the place to start is with my family. I know I've never told you much about them, but there's a reason for that."

Kate raised an eyebrow, but remained silent.

"There's no love lost between us, as they say. I never approved of the way my father made his money. In Ireland it's too easy for the unscrupulous to prey on the misfortunate. And I felt that was what he was doing. He began with a few hidden stills in the mountains, and, when that proved lucrative, he branched out."

Kate couldn't suppress a smile. "Your father was a bootlegger?"

"In a manner of speaking."

"I never knew you were a prude."

"Prude? Because I hated seeing him profit from men's weaknesses? How do you think I felt when he sent me and my brothers out to peddle the damned stuff? Do you think I enjoyed seeing common laborers hand over money they could ill afford for a taste of poteen when their wives and children were starving?"

"I hadn't thought of it that way...."

"It got better when Da moved his operations to the city. Eventually he made enough money to become legal, and that was something. But when I was growing up, it seemed to me my father had a finger in every shady deal going. We lived well, but I was ashamed of the way he made his money.

"When I was about sixteen, he finally got into a business I could deal with—the hotel business. For once he was involved in something legitimate."

"Wait a minute," Kate said slowly. "Hotels? Your father owns the *Callahan Hotels*?"

O'Rourke nodded. "He does. Or rather, he did. A few years ago he developed a heart problem, and his doctors persuaded him to slow down. That's when he turned the hotels over to his five children."

Kate's eyes grew huge in her pale face. "Do you...? Are you saying that *you* own Callahan Hotels?"

One corner of his mouth twisted up. "I'm saying *we* own Callahan Hotels...or at least a dozen or so of them. Your name is on the deeds, too."

"Oh, my God," she gasped, clutching the arms of the chair in shock. "Why didn't you tell me before this?"

"I didn't know how well you'd receive news that the infamous Timothy Callahan was your father-in-law."

"Oh, of course! I've read so much about him...the 'Irish Godfather'...the 'Grand Old Man of Sin'...O'Rourke, I never dreamed!"

"Everything you have read is true, I'm afraid. There's nothing my old man didn't try...liquor, gambling, prostitution. I've always thought it was fortunate he started having health problems. Otherwise, the old devil would probably be the biggest drug king in the world."

"But his hotels have a wonderful reputation," Kate pointed out. "How did he prevent his...uh, other activities from creeping into the hotels?"

"He didn't. His children did." O'Rourke leaned forward, resting his elbows on his knees. "You see, when Da expanded his field of influence, he couldn't be everywhere at once. He had to delegate some responsibility, and, though he didn't like us much, he decided his children were the most likely recipients of his...generosity. So, even back before he became ill, he put us in charge of the hotels. But when he attempted to equip them with hookers and casinos, we put our collective foot down."

"That must have gone over well."

"Yeah, like a painted woman at the church's Saint Patrick's Day parade! The old man was furious. He raged and threatened for weeks. But we all stood firm for the first time in our lives, and finally he had to back down or hire all new people. I think he was proud of the reputation the hotel chain had been building and somehow knew it would be insane to jeopardize that.''

''All right, I think I understand something of your background, O'Rourke...but what on earth does this have to do with here and now?''

''The hotels...the ones owned by my family?'' When she didn't seem to make the connection, he explained. ''For a number of years guests at various hotels around the world have been robbed of valuable jewelry. It became rather obvious that the thefts were occurring with increasing frequency at the Callahan Hotels. I heard rumors that the international police had my family under intense observation—Lord knows they've tried for decades to get enough evidence on my father to put him out of commission. Once I had satisfied myself that Da actually had nothing to do with the thefts, I offered my assistance to Interpol. Even if the thief turned out to be one of my own brothers or sisters, the rest of us needed to know.''

''Are you saying that you were working with the police?'' Kate asked, her voice a little too quiet.

He nodded. ''One of their requirements was secrecy on my part. For all they knew, *you* could have been the one behind the robberies.''

''Me? When I wasn't even aware I had any connection to the hotels?''

''The police didn't know that at first. Later, it was an easy matter to clear you...and, incidentally, my sisters and brothers. But that left a huge question mark. Who was the thief? Who had enough of a grudge against the Callahans to want to ruin their reputation and put them out of business? I figured it was some old associate of my father's—''

''Tell me about Kansas City,'' Kate demanded suddenly.

''My arrest, you mean? Well, I was working with the police, as I've said, when they got an anonymous tip that I was giving them the runaround. Hence, the search...and the discovery of the jewelry and phony credit cards. They were planted, Kate. I was set up. But that posed a couple of new possibilities. The thief seemed mainly interested in framing me, and he had to be someone who had a contact with me or with someone in my life.

"For a time I suspected my cousin Nick Callahan. As a teenager he lived with us...and worked like a dog, I might add. Nick left our little family circle after he got into a fight with my dad. Some money came up missing, and Da accused Nick. There was a big blowup, during which Nick was informed he was a charity case and there wasn't a chance in hell he'd be mentioned in the will. Well, he walked out, and we never saw him again."

"And you thought he might be exacting a bit of revenge?"

"That was my theory, but then I did some checking and found out Nick had died. That left me at square one again."

"If, as you say, you were innocent, why didn't you just tell me?" Kate leaned back in her chair and crossed her arms. "The police knew you had been framed. Didn't you think it was important to let your wife have the same information?"

"I wasn't allowed to tell you in the beginning. And when I became a suspect, you acted differently than I expected, Katie. Instead of asking for explanations or having a little faith in me, you walked out. Your first reaction was to file for divorce. I didn't know how to approach you, what to say."

"You didn't try."

"The hell I didn't! When you came to the jail to see me, I nearly pleaded with you...if you'll remember. You turned your back and walked away."

"All right, I wasn't very receptive at that moment, though you have to understand the shock I had suffered. But later, why didn't you come to me later?"

"I wanted to, but your family advised me to let you alone, to give you time."

"You were in constant contact with my family, weren't you?"

"Not constant," he hedged. "I talked to your mother occasionally. I wanted to know how you were getting along."

Kate rubbed her forehead, realizing her headache had returned. "Okay, we don't need to go into that. I just want to know what it had to do with Lady Harwood's necklace."

"I was tired of living in limbo," O'Rourke stated. "I wanted my wife back, and I wanted my family's name cleared. And everyone wanted the thefts to stop. So I met with authorities, and we came up with a plan, a plan I hoped would solve all my problems.

"Because you and I already had reservations to come here for the holidays, it was decided to make Cross Coombe Manor the base of operations. Then all the police needed was bait to lure our villain here, as well."

"The diamonds," Kate murmured.

"Exactly. When the Star of Pretoria began attracting public attention, we arranged for the Harwoods to buy it for a spectacular sum. With their cooperation, we managed a media campaign that informed people around the world the Harwoods had purchased the necklace and would be showing it off during Christmas week at this hotel."

"Weren't you taking a lot for granted? That the thief would just happen to show up here?"

"Not necessarily. Remember, the person behind the robberies always had a pretty good notion of who was staying in what Callahan hotel, wearing what priceless little bauble. And, had he not shown up, I'd still have been able to concentrate on patching things up with you."

"I see."

O'Rourke thought Kate's tone made it perfectly clear she did not especially like what she saw, and he deemed it best to forge ahead with the explanations.

"But, as we quickly learned, the thief had taken the bait. He stole the necklace during the confusion of the accident the night we went to the theater."

"And hid it in the secret passageway?"

"Yes, probably sneaking into the hidden chamber either through our room or the Harwoods'. What I want to know is, how on earth did *you* manage to find it there?"

"How do you know I did?" she queried.

"I didn't at first. In fact, I couldn't figure out what the hell was going on. Then something about the way you reacted when Lady Harwood decided to put it on and wear it, as opposed to socking it in the hotel safe, made me suspicious."

"I woke up in the middle of the night and saw you go through the wall. I simply followed you and heard you talking to another man...."

"Chester Rand."

"Oh? Well, *I* thought he was your accomplice. I hid while you showed him the necklace, then decided to go back the next morning and get it. I... I was trying to help you out."

"Because you believed I was a thief."

"Because you allowed me to believe you were a thief. My God, what was I supposed to do? Turn my back and pretend I'd never seen the damned thing?"

O'Rourke sighed. "No, you did the right thing—from your point of view. Actually, from the police point of view you screwed up an important operation."

"How so?" Kate's voice was cool.

"When the thief did not attempt to skip out of the hotel right away, we knew the necklace was hidden somewhere on the premises, somewhere he considered out of reach. Thorough searches of the rooms turned up nothing, but my own interest in the highwayman legend, and incidentally, your walking and talking in your sleep, gave me an idea. What if the secret passage of the legend existed? And what if the thief knew about it? Since you seemed so intrigued by the stone wall in our bedroom, I made that a starting place. Quite by accident, I got inside the passageway, and sure enough, there was the necklace."

"If that's true, why didn't you return it?"

"If I had removed the necklace, that's all we'd have had. But, by leaving it there and keeping a discreet watch, we'd have eventually surprised the thief when he came to get it. Once I'd found it and showed it to Rand, he began making arrangements for a hidden camera to be installed in the cell. That way we'd have the proof of who knew the diamonds were there.''

''Oh. So my returning the Star wasn't the solution I thought. . . .''

''It was a real shock to those of us who were feeling so confident about nabbing our crook! The only thing we could do was have Lady Harwood wear the necklace and hope the thief was stupid enough to try again. And he was.''

''Why then did I find the diamonds in your coat pocket? Surely you can see what I must have thought?''

''Yes, I understand. I assume you hoped the police would think the thief had stolen the jewels during the fire and that the greenhouse was the logical place for him to hide them until things calmed down. But by taking them to the greenhouse, you could have been putting the real diamonds right back into the thief's hands.''

''The real diamonds?''

''Yes, there were two necklaces all along. Colonel Westcott represents the insurance company with which the Star was insured. His superiors sent him down here with a copy to substitute for the real necklace. The plan was to let Lady Harwood flaunt the real diamonds for an evening, then substitute the fake ones, hoping the thief's actions would be so rushed he wouldn't have time to make a detailed study of the gems. Unfortunately, circumstances made it possible for him to act much more quickly than we'd expected. . . .''

''So the necklace stolen first was the real one?''

''Yes. And because we finally located it and had it under surveillance, we didn't make the substitution.''

''So I returned the real one?''

''Yes, and immediately, Colonel Westcott made the switch, giving the fakes to Lady Harwood and slipping me the real jewels.''

''The ones in your coat pocket?''

"Yes. The ones you were attempting to hide in the greenhouse. We were using the same theory you did, that the thief had to have hidden the necklace there, and that's why we were watching it. However, as it turns out, he simply hid the thing in the sheet he was wearing . . . then when he got back to his room, he stashed it on an outside windowsill and covered it with snow. That turned out to be a pretty satisfactory hiding place."

"Sheet?" Kate looked shocked. "Are you saying . . . the thief was—"

"Yeah, Weldon Blake. And he had a little help from Denise."

"The newlyweds? My God, those sweet-looking kids?"

"First of all, they aren't sweet, and they certainly aren't as young in experience as they are in years. Weldon is an accomplished pickpocket with something of a ruthless streak. He set the fire yesterday—an unforgivable act in an historic old building like this—as a diversion. And then, counting on human nature, he and his wife rushed outdoors in a state of undress and voilà! We all automatically furnished him with an alibi."

"So we did."

"I'm just glad they decided they had to make an attempt to get the diamonds out of the hotel before tomorrow. Had they not shown up by the end of the Christmas week," O'Rourke explained, "Snelling had threatened to put everyone under house arrest until they were found. Fortunately, the Blakes got impatient."

"How did they get caught?"

"Denise faked an appendicitis attack. I think they hoped to create such a commotion that no one would remember the jewels until they'd had a chance to dispose of them somewhere. But Snelling sent me with them and by playing it cagey, I managed to surprise Weldon as he was trying to bury the necklace in a potted plant in the waiting room. No doubt they would have gone back for it in a couple of days."

"Denise wasn't sick at all?"

"No. Just doing a convincing job of acting."

"And where are they now?"

"In a lockup in Bath, awaiting their removal back to London."

"Tell me, how did the Blakes know about the secret passageway?"

"That's the interesting part. Weldon's father had known of it when he was young...and he'd often told Blake stories about it."

"His father?"

"Yes...my cousin Nicholas. I knew there had to be a connection with the family somewhere, but I didn't think about Nick passing his resentment on to the next generation.

"It seems Nick impressed his only son with stories about his bleak childhood and the lack of financial compensation from the Callahans. The two of them dreamed up the robbery scheme, but Nick's health failed and they never put the plans into operation. After Nick's death, Weldon got into a bit of a bind over money, and suddenly all the old resentments just boiled over. He decided to even the score."

"You didn't know Nick had a son?"

"No. When he left, he severed all ties and dropped out of sight. It should have occurred to me, I suppose."

"The name Blake...?"

"Was an assumed one."

"I see. One thing I don't understand is how Nick could have known about the secret passage. How did he happen to be at this..." Kate leaned forward to look O'Rourke in the eyes. "This hotel? It belongs to the Callahans?"

"Well, yes...actually...well, it's one of mine now."

Kate stood up slowly. "*You* own this hotel?"

He nodded.

"Of course! That explains so much!" She began pacing back and forth in front of the fireplace. "Let me guess...everyone else in the place knew about us, didn't they?"

"Us?" he echoed weakly.

"They knew we were divorced—knew you had come here to persuade me to give you another chance! My God, no wonder they applauded your little trick with the mistletoe." She stopped pacing to glare at him. "No wonder I always felt like everyone was watching us. *They were!*"

"Now, Kate, be calm. It wasn't so bad, was it?"

"I was the only person in this whole damned place who didn't know what was going on! I can't believe you would do that to me...oh! I see why there were no rooms available. That was your idea, too, wasn't it?"

"I could hardly get close to you if we had separate—"

"I wondered where Snelling and his people were sleeping if there were no extra rooms. I should have put two and two together...but no, I had to be gullible, as usual."

"Kate, don't get worked up about this," O'Rourke said, getting to his feet. "It hardly matters now, does it?"

"Maybe not to you," she snapped, "but I can see that you've never really stopped lying to me."

Kate was reeling beneath the blow he had dealt her pride. She thought of the things she had forgiven him for, and knew that this last...insult was simply one thing too many. She drew a deep breath. "Our relationship has been nothing but a lie from the beginning."

"That's not true."

"Of course it is. You never told me anything about your family or your past. You failed to mention the type of work you did. You couldn't or wouldn't tell me anything about the robberies, or your efforts to help the police. And you've lied to me since the first day we spent together in this hotel. It would take a lot of nerve for you to ask me to trust you now."

"But the need for secrecy and lies is over, darlin'. We can start fresh, just as we've talked about."

"You know the thing that hurts most of all, O'Rourke? The fact that you let me make a fool of myself trying to save your neck! Ooh, how could I have been so blind? So stupidly noble? I was willing to compromise my professional ethics to...to save a man I was convinced was mentally ill."

"What?" At the look in her eyes, O'Rourke checked his laugh immediately.

"You heard me," she blazed. "I thought you were sick and needed help. I believed the only reason someone would run around taking such reckless chances stealing that horrible necklace was because he was...deranged or something. I was trying to divert attention from you so that I could get you back home and into some kind of professional counseling."

"I knew you were trying to save my hide, Kate, and I loved you for it. But I was caught in the middle. My first inclination was to confess everything. Snelling and Rand would have had my head if I'd done that. You know how it is—when the government is involved, things are done for the good of the masses. The individual's feelings have to take a back seat."

"So you just let them lock me in this room to stew and worry over you?"

"I tried to tell you what was going on...damn it all, Kate, if you had just shut up for ten seconds and let me talk, I could have given you some hint of how matters really stood. I sneaked in here prepared to do that, even though I knew my rear would be in a sling when the others found out. But you were too busy saving me to listen to me."

"Why you pompous jackass!" she exploded. "You always have some handy excuse, don't you? Well, if you think I will stand by and let you make this out to be my fault, you're crazier than I thought!"

O'Rourke ran agitated hands through his hair, leaving it mussed and untidy. "You're not being reasonable."

"No, I'm not, am I? Being the butt of everyone's jokes all week has left me feeling just a bit sensitive...not reasonable at all! In fact, if I had to think of a word to describe how I feel at this moment, it wouldn't be *reasonable*. It would be...*enraged*? *Furious? Irate? Mad enough to do bodily harm?*"

He forced a smile. "I understand your anger...."

"The hell you do!" she exclaimed. "You don't understand a thing about me. If you did, you'd never have allowed something like this to happen."

"Maybe you're right. Maybe I don't understand you. Lady Harwood said you'd be so grateful to learn I wasn't a thief that you'd manage to overlook everything else. But you're not going to let yourself see it that way, are you?"

"Don't you think a liar is as bad as a thief?" she retorted.

"So... that's your last word on the subject? I'm wrong, you're right—end of discussion?"

"You try to simplify everything...."

"Life is too damned complicated as it is, Katie. There's no sense in dreaming up more problems."

"I agree. And because I agree, I'm not sure I want to marry you again."

"What?"

"I need to think. I have to have time to sort things out, to take stock."

"Well, hell," he ground out in disgust. "Why not? Take all the time you need... another ten or twenty years if it'll make you happy."

"Now, O'Rourke," she began, "just because I—"

"Let's forget the whole thing, shall we? Whatever possessed me to think we could ever work things out? God, I probably do need professional help!"

"Where are you going?" she demanded as he turned and started toward the door.

"I don't know. Oh, but don't worry about it—with me out of your way, you'll be free to decide whether or not you want to resume our relationship."

"Now who's being unreasonable?"

"Look, lady, I think that, under the circumstances, I've been about as reasonable as a man could be. I've stated my case, given my testimony and been cross-examined. Now I'm leaving while the jury's still out...."

"Afraid to hear the verdict?"

"Maybe I'm just not sure I'm even interested anymore."

"What's that supposed to mean?"

"I'm tired of arguing," he said quietly. "You know how I feel about you. Now you decide how you feel about me."

"And you? What are you going to do?"

"I don't know . . . but I won't grovel."

"No one has asked you to," she said, but even as he slammed the door on her words, she was wondering if that was true.

Deep down, hadn't she secretly harbored vengeful thoughts of O'Rourke crawling back and begging her forgiveness? It seemed like a perfectly natural human reaction.

But now, suddenly reminded of what a proud man he was, something told her she might have already kept him on his knees too long.

Chapter Seventeen

Kate stared steadily at the figure before her. The woman seemed to have stepped directly from the sixteenth century into the present.

She was wearing a deep rose velvet gown. The flared skirt opened down the front to display a white satin underskirt, held stiffly in place by the bell-shaped Spanish farthingale worn underneath. A heavily jeweled metal girdle circled the woman's narrow waist and fell in front to a sparkling pendant. The gold and rubies in the pendant matched the elaborate ruby necklace that complimented her slender throat bared by the gown's low, square neckline.

Upswept chestnut hair gleamed beneath a tiny jeweled cap, and eyes of darkest midnight blue glowed in the becomingly flushed face. Rose-tinted lips curved upward in an irresistible smile, and Kate found herself smiling back, absurdly pleased with life.

She could hardly believe the reflection in the mirror was her own! It might as easily have been the lady who loved the mysterious highwayman. As she had dressed in the garments delivered to her room for the masquerade ball, she didn't feel that she was donning a costume so much as simply assuming the personality of a woman long dead. Kate Callahan had ceased to exist for the night, and in her place was the image of Lady Aurelia.

Poor Kate, she thought with compassion, she's worn out from all that soul-searching she's been doing for the past twenty-four hours. She deserves a rest.

After one last glance in the mirror, Kate fastened a black velvet mask over her eyes and left the room, hurrying along the hotel corridor. It was late, and most of the other guests were already at the dance. She could hear the music of stringed instruments wafting from the upper story.

The ballroom was a kaleidoscope of color and sound. As Kate paused in the doorway, she was greeted by a masked shepherdess dressed in blue satin.

"You're here at last," Norene cried. "I was beginning to think I was going to have to come down and get you after all."

"I promised you I'd come, didn't I?"

"Well, yes...but I thought you might have changed your mind."

"She was about to launch a major manhunt," said the tall man disguised as Sherlock Holmes. "Or would that be womanhunt?"

Norene giggled cheerfully. "It doesn't matter now—she's here. Come on in, Kate. I think you'll find the person you're looking for over in that far corner."

"Thanks, Norene," Kate murmured, her eyes already searching for O'Rourke. "And thank you again for helping me get into this costume."

"You look beautiful...just like the painting of Lady Aurelia in your locket."

"Need we warn you to beware a certain lusty highwayman?" asked Inspector Snelling, a smile in his voice.

"No, indeed." Kate laughed joyously. "In fact, the way I feel right now, perhaps you'd better warn the highwayman."

"Good luck, Kate," Norene said softly, giving her friend a quick hug. "I'm sure you'll sort everything out with no trouble."

Kate returned the hug, then started wending her way through the crowd toward the back of the room.

As she skirted the refreshment table, Kate spoke to a scowling Jared Harwood, dressed as a magician in black satin. She wondered if he was wishing he could conjure up a spell that would renew Norene's flagging interest in him. Well, she thought with a touch of asperity, he'd had his chance....

"Oh, Kate, we're so glad you're feeling better," exclaimed Mrs. Phillips. Dressed as Queen Victoria, she had her arm through that of Colonel Westcott. The colonel was resplendent as a red-coated Prince Albert.

"How did you recognize me?" Kate asked.

"My dear, no one else could possibly look so much like Lady Aurelia. The gown suits you perfectly."

"Thank you. You look wonderful yourselves. Those costumes are gorgeous."

"Perhaps later you'll join us for some punch and a quiet chat," suggested the colonel.

"Yes, do that," agreed Norene's mother. "And the colonel and I will fill you in on all the excitement you missed by being ill."

"I'd like that. See you later, then."

Kate passed the Rands, dressed as aborigines, as they talked to a man and woman wearing the spangled jumpsuits of trapeze artists. She guessed they were the other couple from Australia, though she couldn't be certain.

It surprised Kate to see some of the most proper guests attired in costumes, thoroughly enjoying themselves at a lighthearted post-holiday bash. The ludicrous sights that met her eyes in all directions added a note of delightful unreality to the evening.

Suddenly, over the heads of the couples dancing past, her gaze met a pair of eyes that, even through a black half mask were incredibly blue.

Kate felt her heart rock dangerously in her chest, then start beating in triple time. Without realizing it, she began walking toward the man who watched her.

He was, beyond all doubt, the most handsome man she had ever seen. He lounged against the wall, arms crossed over his chest, making no effort to come to her. He was taller than any man in the room, broad shouldered and lean hipped. His white lawn shirt was open halfway to his waist, revealing a chest hazed with dark hair; the black trousers he wore clung to his body like a second skin, hinting at the steely musculature beneath, before ending in a pair of knee-high leather boots. There was an aura of danger about the highwayman, an aura enhanced by the mask and the flint-lock pistol tucked into his waistband. A danger that the firmly squared jaw and smoldering blue eyes did nothing to dispel.

Kate drew a deep breath and approached the man. She knew he was not going to make this easy for her.

She stopped directly in front of him.

"O'Rourke?" she half whispered. "I . . . I need to talk to you."

He nodded, and a lock of black hair fell across his forehead. "As you wish."

She gestured to the recessed window seat behind him. "Can we sit here?"

"Of course."

Kate sat down beside him, smoothing her skirts. Impatient with her own nervousness, she forced herself to speak.

"I know you are upset with me, but I hope you will at least listen to what I have to say."

"You know I will," he said quietly.

"Thank you." She glanced up; their eyes met and held for a long moment before she tore her gaze away and fastened it on her hands. She fingered the wedding ring she still wore. "First of all, I'm sorry about the things I said to you yesterday. I've . . . I've had a lot of hours to think about it, and I've come to the conclusion that you did the only thing you could do, under the circumstances. And Lady Harwood was right, I should have been too thankful to be angry."

"But you weren't really treated fairly," he said. "All the secrecy..."

"That wasn't your fault, O'Rourke—nor your idea. You did what you were told to do. You couldn't have pleased everyone, and it was essential that the jewel thief be caught."

"Maybe."

"And, looking back, I see that I should have had more faith in you from the beginning. Had I trusted you in Kansas City, things might have turned out a little differently. As it was, I caused you to have to take the long way around." She raised her eyes to his again, and he could see the shine of tears. "That day at the jail ... my God, why didn't I listen to you? It makes me so ashamed...especially when you were willing to stand by me no matter what."

"I knew you were innocent, Katie. You had no way of knowing I was."

"I should have let you explain. I should have *known* in my heart you weren't capable of something like that. And even if you were, I owed you the chance to defend yourself." She drew a long, shaky breath. "When I came to and found Snelling accusing me of being a thief...when I found I was to be locked up like a common criminal, it gave me a horrible feeling. Now I see how you must have felt."

She laid a hand on his knee and leaned toward him. "I can promise you one thing. My days as a diehard prosecutor are coming to an end. From now on, I intend to exercise a bit more prudence when dealing with people accused of crimes." She saw his half smile and hurried on. "Don't get me wrong. If I think a defendant is guilty, I'll do my level best to convict him, but I'll be more charitable until I'm sure of his guilt."

"That sounds like a fine idea, Counselor."

"How's this for another fine idea? Please accept my apology...and my promise that I'll never doubt you again. And..."

"And?"

"And let's get married."

"I thought the chance to be a rich hotelier would win you over."

"What?" she cried, her voice going shrill. "Why, you!"

His deep laugh rang out and he threw an arm around her, pulling her close against his side. "Good Lord, Kate, I was only joking. You look far too beautiful tonight to be so serious."

Her smile was slow in coming, but lovely once it finally appeared. "I'm sorry. You'll have to give me a little time to adjust to everything that has happened in the last week."

"Agreed."

"How about my proposal? Are you going to accept it?"

"You're damned right I am. And this time, Kate, my girl, I'm not letting you out of our marriage for any reason. You can be as pigheaded and stubborn as you like."

"Pigheaded? Me?"

He chuckled. "Did I forget to mention unreasonable?"

"You did."

"Well, unreasonable then. And ill-tempered..." He turned her toward him, and his eyes moved to her lips, lingering there with a scorching gaze. "God, Kate, but I love you!"

"And I love you—stubbornly, unreasonably, pigheadedly."

"That's all I ask," he murmured, bending his head. His mouth had just closed over hers when a jolly voice boomed out.

"Here now...harrumph! None of that—it'll be giving the rest of us ideas." Lord Harwood was easily recognizable even in his Great White Hunter costume. He stroked his bristling mustache and leered at them. "You'll have everyone in the mood to sneak away from the dance, eh, Carolyne, old girl?"

"Indeed, Cornie. Quite so."

Kate tried gallantly to conceal the look of amazement she was sure was stealing over her features at the sight of Car-

olyne Harwood in a belly dancer's costume. Gauzy char-
treuse draperies fluttered about the woman's ample form,
hinting at more than a small amount of bare skin, and when
she moved, bells at her wrists and ankles jangled noisily.

"Join us in this dance," Lady Harwood suggested. "It's
a medieval ring dance—quite entertaining."

With a wry smile, O'Rourke removed the flintlock pistol
and laid it aside. He then unfolded his rangy frame and took
Kate's hand. "I have a feeling we might as well be good
sports about this."

"Me, too. We can continue our...uh, talk later." Kate's
smile didn't falter as she boldly pressed his hand three times.
I-love-you.

O'Rourke's eyes fairly blazed, but he stepped lightly into
the dance and drew her with him, a gentle hand at her waist.

The steps were simple and easily managed, and Kate
found herself falling into a pleasantly mellow and relaxed
mood. Each time she wove through the other dancers and
came back to O'Rourke's side, he met her with a slow smile
and the flames leaped higher behind the mask.

As the dance came to an end, Kate curtsied low and his
hands cupped her elbows to draw her up and into his embrace. Just then a strolling musician dressed in pink-and-
green-striped satin appeared from the midst of the crowd
and stopped before them.

"Pray, gracious lady and kind sir, wouldst thou permit a
lowly minstrel to honor you with his lute and a humble
song?"

Kate inclined her head. "Certainly," she murmured.

"'Tis a melody composed by our own King Henry VIII,"
said the musician, his nimble fingers coaxing a pleasant
chord from the polished wooden lute he held. "A tune for
lovers..."

Kate felt O'Rourke's arm tighten about her waist and she
leaned close to him.

"*As the holly groweth green,*" sang the musician. "*And
never changeth hue,
So I am, ever hath been,*

Unto my lady true."

The song ended on a soft thrumming note that vibrated through the silent room. Kate clung to O'Rourke's arm, unable to understand her reaction to the simple medieval melody. Everything else swam out of focus, leaving her intent upon the look in O'Rourke's eyes and nothing else.

"Thank you for the song," she murmured faintly, but the musician had already strolled on, disappearing into the milling crowd.

"Kate? Is something wrong?"

She shook her head. "No. . . no, everything is fine."

"You look pale," O'Rourke observed, a worried frown creasing his forehead. "Are you sure you feel all right? Perhaps you should lie down for a while."

Kate smiled inwardly. "Yes, that might be a good idea," she agreed. "The atmosphere in here is a bit stifling."

"Come on then, I'll walk you back to your room."

She laid a hand on his arm. "*Our* room," she corrected. "But it might be better if I go down alone and you follow in a short while. We don't want our absence to be too conspicuous."

O'Rourke's white teeth flashed in a broad smile. "Why, darlin', you've become positively devious."

"Only because I've missed you so," she replied.

"And I've missed you. Hurry along now, and I'll join you as soon as I can."

"Don't keep me waiting. . . ."

Kate stood in the center of the darkened bedroom. She removed her mask and the small jeweled hat she wore, tossing both onto the bed. Then she pulled the pins from her hair to let it tumble around her shoulders. A pleased smile played over her lips as she thought of O'Rourke.

A faint noise caught her attention, and she turned to see the wall sliding open. Standing in the entrance to the secret passageway was O'Rourke, still dressed as the highwayman, but now wearing a long black cloak that swirled about his shoulders. He held out one hand and Kate went to him.

"What are you . . . ?"

He kissed her hand, then turned it over to press another kiss within her palm, and a third to the inside of her wrist. Kate was filled with a rush of heat that left her feeling weak.

"Ah, Lady Aurelia," O'Rourke whispered. "It seems an eternity since last we met."

Kate's laugh was uncertain. "O'Rourke?"

The blue eyes behind the mask moved over her face, as if memorizing it feature by feature. "Come with me."

"But . . ."

"Aurelia, love, please!" His plea was so urgent, so ardent, she could not refuse.

With a vague smile, she thought that it was exactly like O'Rourke to throw himself body and soul into the high-wayman masquerade. Well, just for tonight, what could it hurt if she played along? After all, they'd had enough grim reality lately to last a long, long time.

She stepped into the passageway, and he closed the wall behind them. Surprisingly they were not in total darkness. The pale yellow glow of candlelight spilled forth from one of the small cell-like rooms. O'Rourke led her toward the light.

What had formerly been a cold, dank cubicle of stone had been transformed into a delightful bower. The walls were covered with tapestries, and a feather mattress graced the sagging cot in one corner. On a stand near the bed was a thick wax candle burning steadily, filling the room with warm, clove-scented air.

O'Rourke unfastened the cloak he wore and spread it upon the bed. Then, turning to Kate, he swiftly took her into his arms and lowered his mouth to hers.

A deep stirring of passion within her was ignited by that simple, impatient gesture. It thrilled her to realize he could not wait to hold her, that he was too impetuous to woo her slowly with words of love. The desperation that fed the flames of his desire fired her also. It felt as if they had been apart for aeons instead of mere days.

O'Rourke's mouth romanced her with tender savagery, his hands alternately caressing, then gripping her shoulders, dragging her close against him. His breath came in quick, jagged gasps.

"I desire you, Aurelia," he groaned, "above any wench I've ever known."

Kate's giggle was smothered by his invading kiss. O'Rourke would have made a wonderful actor, she mused, giving herself over to the skilled mastery of his heated mouth.

His lips, firm and commanding, ravaged her senses. They coaxed her own to soften and respond, to part eagerly, to let her very soul express itself in the fiery kisses she gave in return. His tongue, boldly audacious, traced the contours of her mouth, teasing and tantalizing, subjecting her to a sweet torture that left her as impatient as he.

"O'Rourke," she whispered frantically, "please help me get out of this gown. I . . . I want to feel you next to me."

His hands dropped to her tightly corseted waist, and for a long moment he savored the feel of her body beneath his touch. His hands stroked her back, her ribs, the swell of her breasts. And, just as she thought she might swoon from sheer frustration, he began to undo the tiny hooks at the back of the dress. Soon the heavy velvet fell forward and she stepped out of the gown, leaving it to lie on the square of carpet that covered the damp floor. O'Rourke untied the ribbon of her petticoat, and it dropped away to display the ribbed satin farthingale. When it had been dispensed with, she began to struggle with the elaborate metal-and-whalebone corset she was wearing.

"This is a copy of the original thing," she muttered. "I needed help to get it on."

"Here, permit me," he said, gently moving her hands aside. "'Twould not be the first time I have aided you with it." His tone was intimate, his breath warmly teasing against her cheek.

Kate experienced a moment of surprise that he so easily extricated her from the confining corset, to leave her clad only in a pair of very twentieth-century lace bikinis.

She heard his sharply indrawn breath. "Aurelia," he said with a moan, "this garment must be the Devil's own design. Surely 'tis a sin for a mortal woman to wear such a contrivance."

Slowly Kate divested herself of the skimpy panties and stood before him completely nude. His jaw clenched as though he fought for self-control, but as soon as she pressed against him, he abandoned the pretense of gentlemanly restraint.

O'Rourke swept her into his arms, and, after crushing her mouth to his once again in a fevered kiss, he laid her gently upon the bed. Then, with purposeful motions, he began removing his own clothing, starting with the heavy boots. He stripped away his shirt, revealing a gold chain and medallion that nestled against the swirls of dark hair. The candlelight caused it to gleam with burnished brilliance, luring Kate's attention. She raised herself on one elbow to reach out and trace the medallion's carved contours with an inquisitive finger.

"What is this?" she asked, slipping her hand beneath the heavy gold to softly caress his furred flesh. "I don't remember seeing it before."

"'Tis the medallion you yourself gave me, my lady. The one you said would protect me and bring good fortune."

Kate frowned, puzzled. But just as she would have asked more questions, O'Rourke unfastened his black pants and stepped out of them, kicking them aside.

She thought he looked magnificent standing there wearing only the black mask and the gold coin around his neck. The candle glow washed over him, highlighting the virility of his splendid athletic physique.

"Oh, love," Kate heard herself murmur, and her hand lifted to take his and draw him down beside her.

She snuggled deep within the warm haven created by his limbs as he wrapped them about her. Her fingers trailed upward along his throat until they reached the ribbon of the mask he wore. Then, with slow, deliberate movements, she untied it and slipped it aside, dropping it carelessly upon the floor beside the cot.

O'Rourke gazed at her, his blue eyes hazy with passion. When his mouth took her again, the flame spread. It ignited feelings within her that blazed out of control. She gloried in the sensation of her taut breasts against the steely wall of his chest, the seduction of his ardent mouth as he lowered it to tease her hardened nipples. Her hips cradled the thrilling heat of his arrogant maleness, and when his hands slid down to lift them so that he might thrust deeply within the warmth she offered, Kate cried out in wonder.

"My love, my lord," she whispered joyously. "I love you! I love you endlessly."

"And you, my lady," he murmured against her ear, "you have claimed my heart for all eternity."

As they moved together, bodies worshipping each other, they were lost in timeless ecstasy. Love words uttered in soft, low tones drifted upward and were lost in the night—the faint, erotic shadows cast by the candlelight onto faded medieval tapestries danced, then stilled. The silence of four centuries crept back into the room as the pleasantly sated lovers slept.

Kate stirred, turning her cheek into the softness of black velvet. Instinctively her hand reached for O'Rourke . . . but he was not beside her. She sat up and looked about in surprise. How had she gotten back into her own bedchamber?

The room was dim, for the only light was that of the log fire, but she could see her gown neatly folded over the back of a chair . . . and the stone wall was intact, guarding its secret.

She herself was nude, wrapped in the black velvet cloak O'Rourke had worn earlier. She realized she must have fallen asleep after their lovemaking and he had carried her back to the old-fashioned tester bed. But why had he gone?

The door to the hallway burst open, startling her and causing her to pull the cloak more tightly about herself. She looked up to meet O'Rourke's agitated gaze.

"Oh, God, I'm sorry, Katie," he muttered, crossing to her side. "I know I was going to follow you right up... but Snelling and Rand cornered me. There were a few loose ends they needed to tie up concerning the Blakes." Sitting on the edge of the bed, he reached for her hand. "Will you forgive me this one last time? I promise, it won't happen again."

Kate frowned. "What are you talking about?"

"About abandoning you. I hoped you'd understand."

"Well, I don't." She sighed. "You didn't abandon me—far from it, in fact." She raised his hands to her lips and kissed his fingers.

"Now I don't know what you are talking about," he stated.

"Did we or did we not just make mad, passionate... *glorious* love?"

He gave her a half smile, his cheek scored by the elusive dimple. "You were asleep, Kate. It's obvious you've had a very enjoyable dream. I envy you."

"Dream?" she exclaimed. "It most certainly was not a dream! The candlelight, the tapestries... that feather bed! Those things couldn't have been anything but real."

"Tapestries? Feather bed? Darlin', are you feeling all right?"

"I've never felt better," she whispered, flashing him a coy look. "And I owe it all to you." She moved into the circle of his arms, rubbing her palm over the triangle of flesh bared by his open-necked shirt. "Where is your medallion? I hope you haven't lost it."

"Medallion?" He drew back to look at her. "I wasn't wearing a medallion. Kate, are you sure you feel okay?"

"You were wearing a medallion—a gold coin on a chain. And this cloak! O'Rourke, why are you trying to pretend we weren't together just now? Is this some kind of joke?"

"I get it... you're angry because I made you wait and you're trying to frustrate me, right?"

"Who's trying to frustrate whom?" Her navy-blue eyes snapped. "We made love in one of those little cells in the secret passageway. There was—"

He threw back his head and laughed. "Now I know you're teasing me. Why on earth would we have gone into a damp, dark place like that when we could have been perfectly comfortable right here?"

She slipped off the side of the bed, drawing the cloak around her. "It seems I will simply have to show you to make you believe," she said, walking away and leaving him to follow.

When they stepped into the hidden passageway, it was pitch-black. O'Rourke touched her arm. "Wait a second, Kate. Let me get a flashlight...and your slippers. It's freezing in here."

When he returned, he handed her the light, then knelt to slide the slippers onto her chilled feet. Taking his hand, she used the flashlight to find her way into the little cell that had so recently glowed with flickering candlelight.

"I can't believe this," she gasped, shining the beam over the bare stone floor and walls. She whirled to face O'Rourke. "You've got to believe me. There were tapestries on these walls, even a carpet. And the bed..." The beacon of light showed it to be nothing more than a broken-down wooden cot.

"Katie," he said gently, an arm over her shoulders. "It was a dream. It had to be."

The light swept the room once again, and with a cry of discovery, Kate bent to pick up a black half mask lying on the cold floor.

"See? You left your mask."

With a rueful smile, O'Rourke reached into the pocket of his shirt and pulled out an identical mask.

"But...how can that be?" she cried. "We were here—together! You held me and kissed me...."

"Perhaps it was the ghost of the highwayman," he said in an attempt to lighten her mood.

She stared at him oddly for a long moment. "Perhaps it was," she agreed, shaking her head. "All I know is, it wasn't a dream."

"Come on, darlin', you'll catch your death in here. Let's go back to the warm bedroom where I can more fully appreciate your lack of attire. You look very beautiful, you know."

"That's what *he* said," she murmured, allowing him to lead her down the chilly corridor to their room. Even when the wall had closed on the darkened passage, Kate couldn't get the image of that sensual and romantic lovers' tryst out of her mind. Something told her it was burned into her memory for eternity. And she would never believe O'Rourke had not shared the beautiful experience, though in what dimension of time and space she did not know.

O'Rourke stepped up behind her, putting his arms around her waist to pull her back against him.

"If you don't quit staring at that wall, you're going to have me jealous of a man who's been dead for nearly four hundred years." His breath teased her ear.

She turned in his arms. "Believe me," she said with a wide smile. "There was nothing the least bit moldering about this particular fellow."

"For shame, Kate. How can you make jokes when you've just confessed to... adultery?"

"If I was with you in that hidden chamber, it wasn't adultery. And if I was with... someone else, you still don't have a case. Once you told a courtroom I had been bedded—most willingly, I might add—by a highwayman who's just a ghost of his former self, no judge in the world would hear you out."

He chuckled, then bent his head to place a warm and loving kiss upon her mouth. "No doubt you're right, Counselor." The kiss deepened, and Kate stood on tiptoe to return it.

"My, my," she whispered, her lips straying to brush his ear. "This is certainly déjà vu."

He unfastened the cloak she wore and pushed it off her shoulders, letting it drop to the carpet. "Come to bed, Katie, and let me love you," he suggested huskily. "After all, I've got my work cut out for me if you're going to be constantly comparing me to your long-lost lover."

"Yes, you'll have to stay on your toes, won't you?"

"I'd best get started," he growled, his eyes sparkling.

"There's no hurry," she demurred. "We have lots of time—centuries and centuries of it."

But she made no protest when he swung her effortlessly into his arms and carried her away to bed.

Epilogue

Their suitcases had already been loaded into the waiting taxi, but Kate and O'Rourke lingered to say goodbye to their new friends.

Lord and Lady Harwood, he in a military-style jacket and she in a geranium-red pantsuit, issued an invitation for the Callahans to visit them at their estate in Kent before being whisked away by their chauffeur-driven silver Rolls-Royce.

Jared, looking a bit less sullen than he had for quite some time, departed soon afterward, driving his own sports car. He had confided to Kate and O'Rourke that he thought he might have persuaded Norene to come to London for a fortnight so he could show her the city. It was evident he expected to take full advantage of Inspector Snelling's absence.

Mrs. Phillips, following the bevy of bellboys carrying her luggage, stopped to wish them good luck in their forthcoming marriage.

"I shall send you a wedding gift as soon as I get home," she announced.

"That's really not necessary," Kate protested.

"Oh, but I feel I owe you both so much. You helped m' daughter discover what an attractive woman she can be And, I understand I have this naughty man..." she pause for a flirtatious glance at O'Rourke " ...to thank for get ting the colonel and I together. I simply must repay you fo everything."

"So you and Colonel Westcott hit it off?" tease O'Rourke.

Mrs. Phillips tapped his arm coyly. "Whatever are yo suggesting? Oh, I had a pleasant enough time with the co onel, but don't think I'm about to settle for the first ma who shows an interest in me. Goodness, no! Now that I'v discovered how much fun I can have with...ahem, the op posite sex, why I have all sorts of plans. Beginning," sh said with a mischievous wink, "with a singles' cruise to th Bahamas next month. I read about it in one of Norene' magazines."

"It sounds like fun." Kate smiled. "You have a goo time."

"Oh, I shall, never fear. Ta ta, now!"

Mrs. Phillips left the hotel, issuing shrill orders concern ing her suitcases, and Kate and O'Rourke exchanged a amused look.

"There you are," cried Norene, coming down the hall way on Snelling's arm. "I was afraid you'd leave before got a chance to thank you...for everything."

She hugged first Kate, then O'Rourke, blushing at he own temerity.

"We wouldn't have left without saying goodbye to th two of you," O'Rourke assured them. "We wanted to le you know we plan to come back here next summer and wer hoping the four of us could get together again."

"Splendid idea," Snelling stated. "I don't see why w can't, do you, Norrie?"

"No, indeed. I'll be looking forward to it. Do you hav my address, Kate?"

"Yes, and I'll write as soon as we get settled at home. Be sure to let me know if you . . . uh, change your address or anything. I understand you're planning on getting better acquainted with London soon. . . ."

Norene cast a swift glance at Snelling and blushed again. "Jared told you about his invitation, didn't he? Well, I suppose I should explain that, while I intend to accept it, I will be bringing along a cousin of mine. She's an absolute stunner, and I think she and Jared will get along splendidly."

Snelling smiled indulgently, his arm slipping about Norene's shoulders. "I really believe we should be off to the station, my dear. Kate, O'Rourke, have a good trip."

"You, too." Kate replied. "Goodbye now."

"Goodbye," echoed Norene.

"Happy New Year," O'Rourke called after them.

With all the guests gone, the hotel seemed strangely silent. Kate insisted on one last peek into the rooms on the main floor.

"I'm going to miss this old place." She sighed. "I still can't believe we actually own it."

"Believe it, my dear. And next summer I'll show you one or two others you'll like just as well."

"How could I like them as well as Cross Coombe?" she laughed. "After all that's happened to me here?"

"Yes, I guess this hotel will always have a special meaning for us."

"As will Lady Aurelia and her highwayman," Kate innocently observed, opening the locket she wore. "I feel as if I've grown to know them . . . very well."

O'Rourke studied the paintings of the lady in rose velvet and the man wearing a gold medallion around his neck.

"Well, we'll just have to come back often," he teased, "in case their spirits get lonely."

"Hmm, indeed," murmured Kate, snapping the locket shut.

O'Rourke took her hands and pulled her close, gesturing toward the slightly brittle mistletoe hanging overhead. After he had thoroughly kissed her, he said, "And someday we'll celebrate our fiftieth wedding anniversary here."

"Why, that's a wonderful idea. But tell me, Mr. Callahan, on one's fiftieth anniversary, is one too old to steal away to make love in a secret chamber?"

"Not if one remembers to wear one's muffler, Mrs. Callahan."

"Hmm, interesting picture."

He kissed her again. "Well, I suppose we'd better go before our driver gets tired of waiting."

"All right," she agreed. "Oh, by the way—did I think to mention that I'd called the airport and made a slight change in our flight?"

"What kind of change?"

"We're stopping off in Ireland for a few days."

"Ireland?" he cried. After a moment during which he struggled to regain his composure, he added, "For what purpose, may I ask?"

"I would like to meet my in-laws."

"Kate..."

"I want to see if Timothy Callahan is as bad as they say," she stated calmly. "And Lord only knows, your mother must be a remarkable woman."

"I haven't seen my parents for years," he argued.

"Then all the more reason to go. Remember, O'Rourke, you helped me patch up the differences with my family...."

"Well, I wouldn't mind seeing Mum, but you needn't expect me to get chummy with my father."

"Just be civil, that's all I ask. And if he's mellowed any over the years, who knows what might happen?"

"Yes, who knows? Oh, hell, have it your own way," he grumbled, though a smile was tugging at the corners of his mouth. "It might prove interesting to see the old homeplace again. And I would like for you to meet my brothers and sisters."

"So you don't mind my making the flight change?"

"No, I don't mind."

At the front door of the hotel, O'Rourke stepped aside to let Kate pass. As she did so, she murmured, "And on the way to the airport, perhaps you'd like to explain just what you were doing that night I saw you climbing back into our room through an open window?"

O'Rourke grinned. "I was hoping you'd have forgotten about that," he said.

"Well, I haven't."

"Then I suppose I'll just have to confess." He thought of the crumpled bit of red lace still safely hidden in the bottom of his suitcase. Yes, that was one secret he was prepared to divulge. But...

As Kate climbed into the taxi, O'Rourke reached into his coat pocket and pulled out a chain from which dangled a gold medallion.

Should he tell her or not? He knew she was more than a little suspicious, and yet he almost thought she had enjoyed the mystery. Well, far be it from him to spoil it for her—besides, there had been something so *fateful* about last night that he wasn't at all certain some force other than his own wicked sense of humor hadn't been at work.

With a smile, he dropped the medallion back into his pocket. No, he'd keep this secret...but he intended for it to be the last one they would ever have between them.

* * * * *

The tradition continues this month as Silhouette presents its fifth annual Christmas collection

SILHOUETTE
Christmas
STORIES
1990

The romance of Christmas sparkles in four enchanting stories written by some of your favorite Silhouette authors:

Ann Major * SANTA'S SPECIAL MIRACLE
Rita Rainville * LIGHTS OUT!
Lindsay McKenna * ALWAYS AND FOREVER
Kathleen Creighton * THE MYSTERIOUS GIFT

Spend the holidays with Silhouette and discover the special magic of falling in love in this heartwarming Christmas collection.

SILHOUETTE CHRISTMAS STORIES 1990 is available now at your favorite retail outlet, or order your copy by sending your name, address, zip or postal code along with a check or money order for $4.50, plus 75¢ postage and handling, payable to Silhouette Books to:

In the U.S.	In Canada
3010 Walden Ave.,	P.O. Box 609
P.O. Box 1396	Fort Erie, ON
Buffalo, NY 14269-1396	L2A 5X3

Please specify book title with your order.   SX90-1A

ARE YOU A ROMANCE READER WITH OPINIONS?

Openings are currently available for participation in the 1990-1991 Romance Reader Panel. We are looking for new participants from all regions of the country and from all age ranges.

If selected, you will be polled once a month by mail to comment on new books you have recently purchased, and may occasionally be asked for more in-depth comments. Individual responses will remain confidential and all postage will be prepaid.

Regular purchasers of one favorite series, as well as those who sample a variety of lines each month, are needed, so fill out and return this application today for more detailed information.

1. Please indicate the romance series you purchase from regularly at retail outlets.

Harlequin	Silhouette	
1. ☐ Romance	6. ☐ Romance	10. ☐ Bantam Loveswept
2. ☐ Presents	7. ☐ Special Edition	11. ☐ Other _____
3. ☐ American Romance	8. ☐ Intimate Moments	
4. ☐ Temptation	9. ☐ Desire	
5. ☐ Superromance		

2. Number of romance paperbacks you purchase new in an average month:

   12.1 ☐ 1 to 4   .2 ☐ 5 to 10   .3 ☐ 11 to 15   .4 ☐ 16+

3. Do you currently buy romance   13.1 ☐ yes   .2 ☐ no
   series through direct mail?

   If yes, please indicate series: _____
                                            (14,15)   (16,17)

4. Date of birth: _____ / _____ / _____
                  (Month)   (Day)   (Year)
                   18,19   20,21   22,23

5. Please print:
   Name: _____
   Address: _____
   City: _____ State: _____ Zip: _____
   Telephone No. (optional): (_____) _____

MAIL TO: Attention: Romance Reader Panel
         Consumer Opinion Center
         P.O. Box 1395
         Buffalo, NY 14240-9961   ☐☐☐☐☐☐☐☐☐☐☐☐

                                     Office Use Only   SEDK

Take 4 bestselling love stories FREE

Plus get a FREE surprise gift!

PASSPORT TO ROMANCE
SWEEPSTAKES RULES

1. **HOW TO ENTER:** To enter, you must be the age of majority and complete the official entry form, or print your name, address, telephone number and age on a plain piece of paper and mail to: Passport to Romance, P.O. Box 9056, Buffalo, NY 14269-9056. No mechanically reproduced entries accepted.

2. All entries must be received by the CONTEST CLOSING DATE, DECEMBER 31, 1990 TO BE ELIGIBLE.

3. **THE PRIZES:** There will be ten (10) Grand Prizes awarded, each consisting of a choice of a trip for two people from the following list:
   i) London, England (approximate retail value $5,050 U.S.)
   ii) England, Wales and Scotland (approximate retail value $6,400 U.S.)
   iii) Carribean Cruise (approximate retail value $7,300 U.S.)
   iv) Hawaii (approximate retail value $9,550 U.S.)
   v) Greek Island Cruise in the Mediterranean (approximate retail value $12,250 U.S.)
   vi) France (approximate retail value $7,300 U.S.)

4. Any winner may choose to receive any trip or a cash alternative prize of $5,000.00 U.S. in lieu of the trip.

5. **GENERAL RULES:** Odds of winning depend on number of entries received.

6. A random draw will be made by Nielsen Promotion Services, an independent judging organization, on January 29, 1991, in Buffalo, NY, at 11:30 a.m. from all eligible entries received on or before the Contest Closing Date.

7. Any Canadian entrants who are selected must correctly answer a time-limited, mathematical skill-testing question in order to win.

8. Full contest rules may be obtained by sending a stamped, self-addressed envelope to: "Passport to Romance Rules Request", P.O. Box 9998, Saint John, New Brunswick, Canada E2L 4N4.

9. Quebec residents may submit any litigation respecting the conduct and awarding of a prize in this contest to the Régie des loteries et courses du Québec.

10. Payment of taxes other than air and hotel taxes is the sole responsibility of the winner.

11. Void where prohibited by law.

COUPON BOOKLET OFFER TERMS

To receive your Free travel-savings coupon booklets, complete the mail-in Offer Certificate on the preceeding page, including the necessary number of proofs-of-purchase, and mail to: Passport to Romance, P.O. Box 9057, Buffalo, NY 14269-9057. The coupon booklets include savings on travel-related products such as car rentals, hotels, cruises, flowers and restaurants. Some restrictions apply. The offer is available in the United States and Canada. Requests must be postmarked by January 25, 1991. Only proofs-of-purchase from specially marked "Passport to Romance" Harlequin® or Silhouette® books will be accepted. The offer certificate must accompany your request and may not be reproduced in any manner. Offer void where prohibited or restricted by law. LIMIT FOUR COUPON BOOKLETS PER NAME, FAMILY, GROUP, ORGANIZATION OR ADDRESS. Please allow up to 8 weeks after receipt of order for shipment. Enter quickly as quantities are limited. Unfulfilled mail-in offer requests will receive free Harlequin® or Silhouette® books (not previously available in retail stores), in quantities equal to the number of proofs-of-purchase required for Levels One to Four, as applicable.

PR-SWPS

OFFICIAL SWEEPSTAKES
ENTRY FORM

Complete and return this Entry Form immediately—the more Entry Forms you submit, the better your chances of winning!
- Entry Forms must be received by **December 31, 1990**
- A random draw will take place on **January 29, 1991**   3-SSE-3-SW
- Trip must be taken by **December 31, 1991**

YES, I want to win a PASSPORT TO ROMANCE vacation for two! I understand the prize includes round-trip air fare, accommodation and a daily spending allowance.

Name_____

Address_____

City_____ State_____ Zip_____

Telephone Number_____ Age_____

Return entries to: **PASSPORT TO ROMANCE**, P.O. Box 9056, Buffalo, NY 14269-9056

© 1990 Harlequin Enterprises Limited

COUPON BOOKLET/OFFER CERTIFICATE

Item	LEVEL ONE Booklet 1	LEVEL TWO Booklet 1 & 2	LEVEL THREE Booklet 1, 2 & 3	LEVEL FOUR Booklet 1, 2, 3 & 4
Booklet 1 = $100+	$100+	$100+	$100+	$100+
Booklet 2 = $200+		$200+	$200+	$200+
Booklet 3 = $300+			$300+	$300+
Booklet 4 = $400+	_____	_____	_____	$400+
Approximate Total Value of Savings	$100+	$300+	$600+	$1,000+
# of Proofs of Purchase Required	4	6	12	18
Check One	_____	_____	_____	_____

Name_____

Address_____

City_____ State_____ Zip_____

Return Offer Certificates to: **PASSPORT TO ROMANCE**, P.O. Box 9057, Buffalo, NY 14269-9057

Requests must be postmarked by **January 25, 1991**

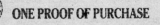

ONE PROOF OF PURCHASE   3-SSE-3

To collect your free coupon booklet you must include the necessary number of proofs-of-purchase with a properly completed Offer Certificate   © 1990 Harlequin Enterprises Limited

---

See previous page for details